A Lone Star Weeps

A Lone Star Weeps

An Inspector Gloria Mystery

JOSEPH GLACKIN

THIRSTY NOIR

© Joseph Glackin 2013

First published in 2013
Thirsty Books
an imprint of
Argyll Publishing
Glendaruel
Argyll PA22 3AE
Scotland
www.argyllpublishing.co.uk

The author has asserted his moral rights.

British Library Cataloguing-in-Publication Data.
A catalogue record for this book is available from the British Library.

ISBN 978 1 908931 38 2 paperback
ISBN 978 1 908931 40 5 e-book

Printing: Bell & Bain Ltd, Glasgow

For Mum

Out there in the dark the stars are your only friends

Prince, aged 13, a former child soldier

1.

UNLIKE most of her colleagues, Gloria Sirleaf had perfected the art of sleeping with her eyes open or, to be more precise, of closing her eyes just enough to give her face a look of intense concentration while she dozed lightly. Some of the people round about her were openly snoring or were slouched so low in the hard wooden chairs they were practically prostrate while the earnest and very sweaty looking British policeman continued to lecture them on police ethics.

It was two months since Liberia's civil war had ended, or at least since Gloria's namesake, Helen Sirleaf, had been elected to the highest office in the land and much applauded as the first woman to do so. Because it was the capital, Monrovia was awash with new appointments, committees and sweeping reforms – but not sweeping the floors, thought Gloria, looking at the carpet of dead and dying cockroaches round her feet.

This partly explained why she was sitting in the suffocating February heat on the fifth floor of the National Police head-quarters in a room whose only clue to its function was the tattered 'Conference Room' sign pasted on the wall. With its missing window panes, broken ceiling tiles and empty light sockets she thought it was a perfect illustration of the current state of her country. Gloria wasn't convinced that the new hope and optimism, along with all that donor money of course, was going to be enough to rebuild Liberia.

Perhaps that's where we come in, she thought – the brave men and women of the National Police. Lord, she really hoped not, remembering how corrupt they had been before the war and how quickly the force had collapsed as the rebels advanced on the city. Most officers had abandoned their uniforms and tried to blend in with the fleeing crowds. It had not been a good time to be an officer of the law. Two of her best friends had been identified as police at a rebel checkpoint in Paynesville and had been tortured and killed. She had seen their heads mounted on poles when she was trying to get through the same checkpoint a few days later. She shuddered. No wonder so many had decided on a safer career after the war. She looked around the room again. Of the thirty or so people only six were experienced pre-war officers, and that included sergeant Borbor the oldest and longest-serving officer on the force. There were only three other women in the room including one she recognised from the Ministry of Justice. The rest were young or middle-aged men who looked either lost or bored as if this wasn't what they had been expecting when they volunteered to join the force. No wonder the British policeman was sweating so much. Shaping this crowd into a modern police force was going to be an uphill task.

Gloria shifted stiffly in the wobbly desk-chair and stretched. Designed for school children, the chairs were cramped and uncomfortable. Added to the heavy heat in the room the discomfort was stretching Gloria's small store of patience to the limit. Had it really always been this hot in Liberia even in February? Could all the shooting, screaming and running of the last ten years perhaps have increased the temperature, she wondered idly?

She had just been appointed as the head of the newly

constituted Family and Child Protection Unit and the announcement had been greeted with a mixture of disbelief and cynicism
by her fellow officers. That didn't bother Gloria. She was excited.
Women and children had always suffered the most in Liberia
and now she had the chance to do something about it. And she
loved a challenge. Proving she was worthy of the rank of
Inspector was something she would relish.

As a young woman of twenty nine she was different from a
lot of her friends. She loved reading, especially detective fiction,
and she enjoyed her own company which, in a country where
few people seemed able to be on their own for more than a few
minutes, made her something of an oddity. She had a fierce
temper, which she managed to keep under control most of the
time, and a sense of humour which often surprised her
colleagues.

Growing up in the rough environment of Westpoint had
been hard enough but the lack of stimulation had been the
hardest thing of all, reducing Gloria to a state of utter boredom.
And it was the boredom which had driven her to study other
people's behaviour. She watched her family, her neighbours and
friends and learnt to listen to the tone of voice rather than the
words being said and to take note of the expression in their
eyes rather than the smile or the frown on their faces. She
discovered she was good at reading people and it was a skill
which had stood her in good stead over the years. By the time a
grown-up noticed her, Gloria had already decided whether they
could be trusted or not.

School was a good example. Gloria had never missed a day
at the JS Kermue Community School although she learnt not to
take everything the teachers said as the absolute truth. It was a
sad fact that many people who were willing to teach in a school
in Westpoint were either woefully under-qualified, barely literate,
or were on the run from something in their past. When a new

teacher arrived it didn't take Gloria long to assess them and work out whether to listen to them, avoid them or just ignore them. In grade five, for example, her teacher had been an overweight lady who made them copy bible verses from the blackboard, sing hymns for hours on end and never turned up on Monday or Friday. Gloria had spent that year teaching herself words from a tattered Webster's dictionary and writing stories which no-one else ever read.

The arrival of a Peace Corps volunteer at the school in grade six had made a huge difference. The standard of teaching had improved a bit but the quality and the availability of books had improved tremendously. Jim, an energetic fifty-year-old, had spotted that Gloria was several rungs above the others but had also understood how that could make life dangerous for her in a community where jealousy was rife. He had always encouraged her but without singling her out.

He kept her supplied with books and information, made sure she had access to news and world affairs and sent her to any workshops, public speaking competitions or other youth events which came up – anything which would stimulate her and expose her to a different world from the noise and smells of Westpoint. Long after Jim had to go back home, his health broken by repeated malaria attacks, Gloria continued to remember him with fondness and respect, and she attributed any success she now had to his belief in her. She still had the pile of books he had left at her house that last day. On top of the books had been a note saying simply 'You can do it Gloria.' And she had.

She had won a scholarship to the prestigious JJ Fellowes School followed by entry into the Police Academy where she had passed with flying colours and graduated just as the war was heading for Monrovia. There was no time for anyone to be jealous of her success. But right now she felt as if she was back at school. It didn't help her temper that the man giving the lecture looked the same age as her fifteen-year-old nephew Abu. She leaned back and stretched again. She knew now why they hadn't been given back their guns. There was a very real danger that if she had one she would have been tempted to end this session right now, whatever the consequences. Even as she had this thought she heard the instructor, whose name she had forgotten again, announce the end of the session and invite them to stand and sing the national anthem.

All hail, Liberia, hail!

All hail, Liberia, hail!

This glorious land of liberty,

Shall long be ours.

Though new her name,

Green be her fame,

And mighty be her powers,

And mighty be her powers.

In joy and gladness,

With our hearts united,

We'll shout the freedom,

Of a race benighted.

Long live Liberia, happy land!

A home of glorious liberty,

By God's command!

A home of glorious liberty,

By God's command!

Apparently singing the national anthem was going to imbue them all with an undying patriotism and a love for peace. Yeah right!

Another reason she hated singing it was that it had become the custom of the group to all look at her when they got to the line 'Though New her Name' in mock recognition of her recent

11

appointment and it had already become a tired joke for her. She wasn't the only new appointment but she was young and she was a woman – and this was Liberia. She managed to ignore the looks and the sniggers and as soon as they had finished singing she left. She really needed to get home.

Her apartment in Mamba Point was empty but there were signs that Abu had come home from school and done his chores. In fact it was particularly tidy which was usually a sign that Abu was going to ask her for something. Well, she thought, it was his birthday in a few days time and his reports from school were really encouraging, despite all the time he spent playing and organising football, so she would be inclined to listen to his requests. Her food was sitting on the stove, just needing to be warmed up – potato greens, one of her favourites.

She kicked off the boots, part of the paramilitary looking uniform which the new government had chosen for them. Unfortunately, a change of uniform was not going to be enough to convince people to trust the police. The residents of Monrovia had long memories and sharp humour and their current nickname for the police was 'Where were you?' It was a not-very-subtle reference to the fact that all the police had disappeared when the fighting had reached Monrovia and it was one nickname Gloria thought particularly unfair. It was not just the street boys and the gronna boys of Waterside who used it either. She remembered the group of women from the 'Battle Axe Ministries' – an appropriate name for a group of ferocious-looking women, she had thought at the time – whose minibus had been stopped for being dangerously overloaded and who, despite their white church dresses and red sashes, had surrounded the unfortunate police shouting 'Where were you? Where were you? Where were you?' The trapped officers had to be rescued by a contingent of West African peacekeeping troops.

She thought back to today's lecture about winning back the

trust of the community through the three 'Ps' of Presence, Politeness and Professionalism. Maybe the money it was costing to get that kind of advice from the British police would have been better spent buying them guns or tazers. At least with tazers they could politely and professionally immobilise the trouble makers who seemed to be everywhere these days.

Only last week the President had left a cabinet meeting and come out onto the steps of the Executive Mansion to confront a mob of angry ex-soldiers who claimed they were owed pensions. She had calmly walked down to the main gates of the Mansion and presented herself to them, with no security guards around her, and asked 'Who wants to kill me then, here I am?' She disarmed them more effectively, Gloria admitted to herself, than even the Navy Seals could have done, and in minutes she had them eating out of her hand. But unfortunately the President couldn't be everywhere and the rest of them had to handle these situations while negotiating with a poker face and an empty hand of cards.

She heard the door open and Abu burst into the room. It was his new thing 'bursting' into a room instead of just walking in, part of his conflicted adolescent 'look at me, leave me alone, give me attention, stop bothering me' thing. Throwing himself onto the couch he immediately started talking about football practice and the game they had coming up in Harbel, out near the airport, and how his team mates were 'not serious' which she knew could mean anything from coming late to practice to not acknowledging Abu's role (a senior one, in his own estimation) in the team.

'It's not easy, Aunt Glo. Half the people did not even turn up for practice or they just come for the last few minutes. This football is a serious business. People have to be serious.'

Gloria nodded. 'So what did you do, fire them?'

Abu laughed. 'Fire them? It's a football team Aunt Glo, we

can't be firing people. No, we just keep talking to them.'

As far as Gloria understood, Abu had started the team and had been both coach and manager for the first few months. She remembered him telling her recently that they had joined a league – she wasn't sure which league and didn't dare ask again – and this had meant drafting in a new coach and a manager. Since then he didn't always feel he was given the respect which was his due. She didn't laugh though, getting the proper respect was a serious business in Liberia. On the other hand, she was hungry and after another ten minutes of football politics she had to interrupt him.

'Yes well, I'm sure it will all work out, Abu. But if you don't go and take bath we'll be eating this food for breakfast.' She ignored his pained expression. 'Otherwise I'll have to tell you all about my day listening to a lecture on good policing.'

The thought of listening to Gloria's description of her day obviously reminded Abu how hungry he was and he sloped – another new characteristic which seemed to be mainly a very noisy and annoying shuffle – off to his room.

She heard the sound of 'African Queen' oozing out of the CD player Abu had bought on the sidewalk. Looted goods were still being sold openly and you could buy anything from fur coats to encyclopaedias. She went out to heat up the food and in the shortest possible time Abu reappeared in shorts and a t-shirt, clean, hungry with all traces of bad humour gone. They sat on her small terrace which gave them a view of the sea, and in the calm, if not cool, of the evening said grace and started eating. It was these moments which reminded her why she loved her country so much. Even a civil war and a fragile peace could not dampen the deep sense of belonging and well-being which Liberia inspired in people, locals and foreigners alike. It was hard to understand why, it just cast a spell on some people and wouldn't let them go.

Her pleasant daydreaming was interrupted by Abu telling her about a body they had seen the police examining on the beach.

'There were three police people there, Aunt Glo, but we saw the body before they chased us. The boy looked small, maybe size like Enoch.' Enoch was her cousin's nine year old son. 'We couldn't see what killed him but it wasn't a bullet, although there was a lot of blood.'

Abu was a very good story teller and loved an audience. He was in his stride now and describing in great detail the condition of the body as far as he and his friends had seen. She hoped the police had managed a similarly detailed description. Her professional and personal curiosity was piqued.

She asked a few questions but Abu had moved on to the topic of his upcoming birthday by now and was, she realised, asking if he could have a party. She knew she had been ambushed but recovered quickly enough not to make any promises until they had discussed it properly (which Abu clearly thought they had), and she had time to think about it (which Abu clearly thought unnecessary).

Gloria couldn't get the picture of the body on the beach out of her mind. Between ritual killings and a civil war, finding bodies on the beach was not exactly an uncommon experience in Liberia. The odd thing was that this was the body of a child and the place it was found was far from the usual haunts of street children. From Abu's description she gathered the body had not been cut up for body parts and if he was the same age as Enoch he was too insignificant for political assassination and even too young for a gang killing. This killing was too random for a society which, even in violence, tended to follow a set pattern.

She called her assistant, Captain Moses Anderson, who answered as always on the first ring with his characteristic 'Boss?'

15

Moses was well suited to working with Gloria in that he was happily married but didn't see that as any reason to spend more time at home than was necessary, an arrangement which, it had to be said, seemed to suit his wife Hawa as well.

'Listen Moses, did you hear about the body of a child found on the beach today?'

Of course he had. Moses had more contacts and better information than the national security service.

'Yes boss. Boy, found on the beach near the American embassy, throat cut, some signs of torture. With a diamond in his hand.'

'A diamond?' she asked.

'Oh yes, in his left hand he had a small diamond.'

Diamonds! Every reference to diamonds she had ever come across in Liberia meant only bad news in one way or another.

'Where's the body now? And who's in charge of the investigation?'

'Well, I told them to take the body to the morgue at Catholic Hospital because I had a feeling you would hear about it and might want to investigate further. He's only a child so I thought it should be referred to us – especially since the CID are not interested.'

Gloria was flattered that Moses believed she had a similar information network to his own and didn't feel it necessary to tell him she had heard about it from her nephew. But they would have to move quickly – no bodies were kept very long least of all that of a street boy murdered on a beach.

'Well done Moses, good decision. Why don't you meet me at the morgue at eight tomorrow morning then?'

'And the training course?' She could hear the reluctance in his voice. He hated the course too but felt he had to mention it.

'Call the office in the morning and tell the trainer *politely* that our *presence* is required on an urgent matter. That's at least two of the three Ps so he should be fine with that'

'Yes boss', she could hear him laughing down the crackly line.

2.

IT WAS ALREADY stiflingly hot when Gloria arrived at Catholic Hospital. The sweating had started as soon as she left the house and by now her uniform shirt was sticking to her back but she had to keep the jacket and cap on while on an investigation. Not that it was really necessary as Bro. Jose, the hospital administrator, knew her well. Spanish, excitable and kind, Bro. Jose was one of those fixtures in Liberia. Although he seldom left the hospital compound, the fact that everyone from government ministers and foreign NGO workers to the street boys and the poor from the slums came here for treatment meant that he was widely known. And because of his kindness he was much loved, and taken advantage of – two things which sadly often went together here.

Gloria started explaining why she was there but Jose interrupted – he was obviously having a difficult morning – to tell her that her 'assiztant' was already in the morgue and he would be grateful if the body could be moved today. She said she would see what she could do and strode off down to the morgue. The corridors, even in this well-run establishment, were full of people lying or sitting outside the doors of the various doctors, guarded by a formidable body of nurses who would have served equally well as the Presidential Guard.

It was just before eight and time for morning devotion and

the head nurse, as eloquent as any Baptist preacher, was exhorting everyone to raise a hand in praise. The moans and the groans died down for a while and then everyone had to join in with 'The Lord has done it again, he healed the sick and he raised the dead.' And they sang with such gusto, the clapping reverberating around the waiting hall, maybe hoping that enthusiastic singing would endear them to God or, more importantly, to the nurses guarding the doors. Gloria kept on walking. Nextdoor at the busy TB clinic a similar scene was being enacted except each one of the hundred or so patients was wearing a handkerchief around their mouths and noses in a nod towards germ prevention, and the nurses were even more burly. It looked like nothing so much as a bandit convention and she thought giddily for a moment about arresting them all for offences against singing and good taste.

By the time she reached the morgue Moses already had the body of the boy out and was examining it closely. Not even the Catholic Hospital had a pathologist – there wasn't one in the entire country at the moment – so they only had their own experience to go on. With a bare nod to each other, and suitably masked, they started their examination. Gloria may not have had Moses' network of contacts but there were some things she certainly knew more about. One look was enough to tell her this was no street boy.

'Look at his feet and hands,' she said, 'they are soft. And no bruises, old wounds or cuts on his body. Did you ever see a street boy who didn't have marks on him?'

Since the war it was hard to find any child without some memento of the conflict on their body. She thought of Abu who had led a relatively sheltered life, if you discounted having to run for his life and being short of food and being beaten up by rebels. He still had marks and bruises that would stay with him for ever.

19

They examined the boy's body inch by inch and could find nothing except the recent cuts and burns which were obviously part of the last hours of his life, and the neat cut across his throat which had finished him. There were no signs of malnutrition, his skin was in good condition, no ringworm or other skin infections which a child living on the street would inevitably have had. His teeth were clean as were his nails and he had a neat haircut. Not only was this not a street boy, this was a seven or eight year old who had never known hardship or violence until the last hours of his life. This was a rare child indeed in today's Liberia.

Neither were there signs that this had been a ritual killing. Although from some of the press you could get the impression that ritual killings happened daily in Monrovia, neither Gloria nor Moses had ever come across it themselves. But everyone in Liberia knew that a ritual killing involved the cutting off or the mutilation of parts of the body since that was how you acquired the power you wanted. This child had been tortured but not mutilated.

They photographed and recorded all they could and then announced that they were finished. The morgue assistant was the quietest man Gloria and Moses had ever come across – all that time spent with the dead did nothing for your conversational skills – but he watched them intently the whole time and coughed loudly when they had finished. If she had been hoping for some words of compassion from him she was soon disappointed.

'That body will have to go today you know. It's not my job to be storing other people's dead bodies unless they are paying for it.' He clearly knew that the police had no budget for morgue services.

'Well, we'll try and do something,' said Gloria.

He made the sucking teeth noise which really annoyed Gloria.

'This one is not a 'trying' business Inspector. If no-one claims the body then it will be disposed of along with all the other unclaimed bodies.'

'All the other ones? How many are there?' Gloria asked.

'It's about ten or twelve a week. Most people can't afford to pay the bills or the funeral expenses so they just leave the bodies here.'

'Great,' muttered Gloria, 'even the dead are abandoned in this town.'

Well, they had all the evidence they were ever going to get from the body, given the lack of any forensic expertise, but it seemed wrong to consign the child to an unknown grave somewhere.

She got her phone out and dialled a number. Her uncle ran a small funeral home on the Boulevard and she quickly got an agreement from him to collect the body and arrange a decent burial for the child that afternoon. Then, more importantly, she vowed to herself that she would find out who the child was and what had happened to him.

'My uncle will call for the body later this morning, we'll bury him this afternoon.' The morgue assistant shrugged and turned away.

'As long as the body is gone before lunch I will be happy.'

Gloria tutted as they were leaving.

'He doesn't seem to care at all, does he? As long as his body count doesn't get too high.'

'Ah, you can't blame him boss. He won't get any thanks and he spends his days with the dead. He must see some terrible sights.'

They had just reached the main doors when she stopped.

'Where's the diamond?'

He opened his hand to show her. 'I thought it better to collect it immediately, just in case. . .'

'Good. Alright,' she said, 'let's get back to the office and see if we can get more information. Start with the photos. Send one down to the Red Cross and those other NGOs that work with children and see if they can tell us anything. Get some of the guys to go around the shelters and the hostels and see if anyone recognises him.'

Moses nodded happily. Now he had permission to shake things up back at the station, he would enjoy getting them to do some real police work.

The journey back to headquarters took twice as long as it should have. The traffic on Tubman Boulevard was even slower than usual and when she got near to the City Hall she saw why. The checkpoint which had been dismantled a few weeks before was now back up and doing a roaring trade. Every taxi, bus and private car – except the many NGO Land Cruisers and official government cars – was being charged to go through the checkpoint. With her head still full of the image of the unknown child Gloria could feel her blood boiling. She stopped the car and walked the several car lengths to the checkpoint. She saw straight away that it was Captain Luseni in charge, his huge belly bursting through the uniform shirt while he demanded money from drivers. If she had a least favourite officer in her unit it was Luseni. Lazy, greedy and totally corrupt, he only survived because his cousin was the Police Director.

'Eh Luseni my man', she said. 'How's the operation going?'

Captain Luseni didn't look pleased to be disturbed on what he considered to be his 'turf' but he stopped and shouted back that it was going fine and the Lady Inspector should just drive through. 'Lady Inspector,' thought Gloria, respect and insolence in one title, Luseni was very good at this!

Gloria smiled back and shouted over, 'Eh Captain, I want to see you, just a minute, I beg you.'

Luseni suspected nothing. Another new so-called superior officer who wanted a cut of his takings, he thought to himself. Well, he would drive a hard bargain. He waddled over, tried to salute and then smirked at Gloria.

'Now Inspector, how can I help you?' The emphasis on the 'help' was too obvious. He really thinks I want a cut of this money he's taking, Gloria said to herself.

'I don't remember authorising this checkpoint Captain.'

Staring back at her he told her that his cousin had approved it. That usually did the trick for these people, thought Luseni. They're here today and then gone, and the last thing they want to do is upset the Director – or his family.

'Really, well I'll just check that with him when I meet him in an hour,' she said. 'In the meantime, if the checkpoint isn't dismantled immediately, and if you and your squad are not in the control room in half an hour for a new assignment, then I will transfer you out to Bomi Hills to help train the new recruits there.'

Her smile hadn't changed but the tone had. Luseni, like many a bully, crumpled almost immediately. Before he could say anything else she held up her hand to stop him.

'Don't make it worse. I will do it.'

The threat of rural Bomi where insecurity was still a huge problem was enough. Luseni said no more. Turning away with a murderous look in his eyes he walked back and gave his men orders to take the checkpoint down and informed them that they had been assigned to a new investigation.

'Oh and Luseni,' Gloria said, 'bring the money here. Let's see what you have.'

Luseni looked even more furious now. So she was going to take everything was she? He showed her a bundle of dirty notes which he said were donations for the police widows' fund.

There may well be a widows' fund but Gloria had never heard of it and was pretty sure no widow had ever benefitted from it.

'Good,' she said. 'Go and give it to Moses, he's our treasurer as I'm sure you know.' As he dragged himself towards the car she shouted after him. 'And what's the balance for?' Luseni turned back trying to look puzzled. 'The balance of the money is in your pocket, I can see it from here. What's that for?'

Luseni tried unsuccessfully to look surprised as he pulled a further bundle from his pocket.

'Tell you what Luseni, you can give that money to those children there and they will help you move all those blocks and pieces of wood off the road.' She called the gang of straggly children over. She recognised some of them. They were far from their usual city centre haunts.

'What y'all doin here? This place is too far from town.'

'Town not good this time ma,' one of them answered. 'Plenty plenty bad people. We live to Twelfth Street now.'

She nodded. 'Ok, that's good. Now, you able to help the Captain clear the road? He will pay you small money when you do it good.'

'Uh huh,' they nodded in unison.

'Right captain, there's your team. Make sure you pay them now or I will hear about it.'

As she walked slowly back to her car, Gloria watched Luseni send one of his officers to give the first bundle of money to Moses, and then share out the rest of it with the children.

Moses was laughing. He had been after Luseni for a long time now and had watched the exchange with delight.

'Take time with that man boss,' was all he said as she drove through the disappearing checkpoint, and he didn't mean the old tyres and bricks which were being carted off to the side of the road by the street boys.

'You don't usually see those kids this far from the town centre or the markets do you?' was her reply. 'They said something about the town being dangerous and full of bad people. It must be really bad if they are scared.'

Assembled in the control room half an hour later, Gloria was face to face with Luseni and his merry men once again but she didn't give him a second thought. She left the explanation of the assignment to Moses and he took a great deal of delight in telling them about their shelter-to-shelter assignment with the photos. Luseni looked stunned, but quite a lot of the others looked pleased and interested, especially the newer recruits. There might be hope of getting a real police force here after all, Gloria thought.

It was only 11.15 but Gloria felt as if she had already done a day's work. When the others had left under the close supervision of Moses she decided she badly needed a cup of coffee. She knew there was little chance of finding one in the building so she decided to combine her search for a stimulating drink with a visit to the place where the body was found. On the way out she caught sight of her boss in the lobby. It was hard to catch his attention given that the lobby, as always, was full of people. There were market women selling snacks and roasted meat, prisoners being brought in, some noisily and others very quietly, and lots and lots of people who looked as if they had just wandered in, which was quite likely in Monrovia, because they had nothing else to do. The description 'milling around' was coined exactly for this place with crowds sitting, chatting and shuffling back and forth.

Her boss spotted her and gave her a formal wave – a cross between a salute and a friendly greeting which was typical of him. He can never decide, she thought, whether he is being too friendly or too authoritarian, and it seems to worry him a lot. The result was always this half-salute, half-greeting and she was never sure whether to respond with a smile or a stand to attention. At this distance, and across a noisy lobby, it didn't matter too much but she squeezed through the crowd until they were within shouting distance – which was practically face to face – and did give him a real salute. Chief Inspector Kamara had a perpetual look of anxiety about him and any uniform, even the smart dress uniform, seemed to hang limply about his shoulders. But none of that had stopped him from navigating his way through the political minefield and rising to his present rank – and she wasn't surprised when he got straight to the point.

'So you're investigating the death of that boy.'

He always knew what was going on – it was the essential survival skill in any government job – and always had an opinion on what should be done. Before she could reply he just nodded as if they had had a lengthy conversation.

'Good, very important. Keep me informed,' he said and walked off towards the lift before swerving back to the stairs – the lift hadn't worked in years – and climbed to his executive offices on the 6th floor.

She shook her head at yet another strange encounter with what passed for authority. Not for this force the regular meetings, updates and detailed departmental planning. His main job was to deal with the relentless attacks on the police from Monrovia's many newspapers and their outrageous accusations. Today's headlines in *The People*, for example, accused the police of selling on over a million US dollars worth of confiscated drugs, and their proof was the police's inability to produce the drugs. The fact that the drugs had never been confiscated and therefore never in their possession – it was well known that the drug trade was protected by one of the new government's most prominent ministers – was irrelevant to newspapers trying to sell copies, or politicians deflecting attention from their activities. While the Chief handled political and media attention he expected his officers to solve crimes, especially high-profile ones, and to be visible on the streets.

She reached her car ignoring the voice calling her name from a first floor window. Even a casual chat could easily turn into a long discussion about something over which she had no control and she didn't have time for that at the moment.

She rolled up the windows, switched on the air conditioning and started to relax as the cold air hit her. She was always slightly worried about theses changes from extreme heat to extreme cold and the stories of people getting ill from their air conditioning but it was good to have on such a hot day, and if she didn't use it she would be worth nothing by early afternoon. She was very proud of her red Polo, the first car she had owned, and was happy to use it for work. The Chief Inspector would have preferred her to use a regulation vehicle but there were two problems with that. Firstly, there was rarely a car available and, secondly, it would have meant parking the Polo in the official car park all day and there was no way Gloria was going to do that. There were more cars stolen from the police car park than anywhere else in town. So she and her car had become a familiar sight around town which she knew might become a problem in the future but suited her fine just now.

The road from police headquarters took her down Bypass and into the area known as Bassa Community. She pulled up near a tiny shack with a lone woman sitting outside. Ma Mary was well known for brewing the best coffee in town, for the few Monrovians who drank coffee and the even fewer Westerners who knew about her. It wasn't good for Ma Mary's business but Gloria was happy to keep it a secret as it meant she never had to wait whenever she needed a cup. Before she had even closed the car door Ma Mary had pulled up a low wooden stool and set in front of her a tin tray with cup and saucer, pot of coffee, powdered milk and sugar. After some brief greetings Ma Mary retired to her seat in front of the coal pot where the ubiquitous toddlers played in the dirt.

Gloria sat back and poured herself a cup of the strong, dark coffee, ignoring the milk and sugar. The smell of it alone was almost enough to revive her and she breathed it in before starting to sip it. Despite the intense heavy heat and the sweat which gathered on her neck and face as soon as she started drinking, Gloria savoured every sip and managed for a few moments to forget her worries and just relax. She had learnt early on that surviving and enjoying life in the chaos that was post-war Monrovia required these little moments of pleasure and the deliberate forgetting of the things that weighed you down. But it didn't last long. She could shelve her worries about Abu and his lack of education, the corruption in the police and the future of the country but the image of that dead child kept coming back to her.

The still, silent form she had seen in the morgue was a reproach to her and all other adults who allowed this kind of thing to happen. How much had he suffered, she wondered. The cuts and burns meant someone had tortured a child who had never known anything but care and love in his life. And what made it worse was that this boy who apparently was brought up somewhere by people who loved him was going to be buried in an anonymous grave this afternoon. To not even have a name, that somehow made the crime so much worse. Even street children and child soldiers had names, mostly ones they had given themselves of course, but this child had none. They would have to call him something at the funeral she realised, but what?

They certainly couldn't use the American 'John Doe' title as Doe had a very particular meaning here, it being the name of the infamous former president who had, in part anyway, caused the civil war. By the time she asked Moses for his opinion she realised that she hadn't had her moment of relaxation after all. The coffee now tasted bitter in her mouth and the sweat was running off her. But it was only right, even after the war and all the killing that followed, that the death of a child should still be an outrage.

As she got up to go, dropping her twenty Liberian dollars on Ma Mary's tray, her phone rang and her uncle's voice came through loud and strong.

'Gloria, I am going to collect the body now. If you are having a funeral this afternoon you will need to get someone to come and say some prayers or something, otherwise we'll just be looking at each other. I do have a reputation to think of.'

Gloria agreed about needing someone to come and conduct the service but her uncle's reputation, she suspected, existed largely in his own head. Otherwise how, in a city where funeral directors were in great demand, could he fit her in today at such short notice?

'I'll get someone,' she told him and cut off the call. Great, she thought, now I have to organise the funeral as well as investigating the murder. At this rate I'll end up digging the grave as well!

When she got to the car she decided she would call Sr. Margaret, an American nun who had been in Liberia for years and ran the only decent training college in the city. Although she still sounded like a New Yorker, Margaret knew Liberia in a way that few outsiders did. In spite of her fierce reputation, and famously forthright manner, she was respected and a little feared by her students, government officials and even the church authorities. She and Gloria had been friends for years, a friendship cemented during one of the rebel invasions when Gloria and her family had taken refuge at the convent. They had spent a lot of time huddled together on the floor while rebels rampaged around the streets outside. Margaret even had them sewing money into the hems of their clothes at one point when they thought the convent was going to be invaded. Gloria remembered and smiled.

She pulled herself out of those memories. It was too easy to get lost down memory lane these days, and there was work to do in the present.

'Hi Margaret, have you got five minutes to talk?'

'If you make it quick, Gloria, I presume you need something urgently as you're calling at lunch time.' Casual chit-chat was never a big part of a phone conversation with Margaret.

Gloria explained very briefly about the murdered child who was going to be buried that afternoon. She didn't go into too many details and finished with an appeal that Margaret would come and 'do something' at the funeral service.

'By doing something I presume you don't mean reciting my favourite poem or singing an Irish love song Gloria?' She didn't give Gloria time to reply, as no reply was necessary. 'Since you don't want to ask one of the priests to go along' – Gloria had already made it clear that, in her opinion, priests required too much advance notice and were usually long-winded, judgmental or just boring – 'I'll get Sr. Anselm to do it instead. I have three classes this afternoon and besides it's not really my forte.'

Gloria thanked her, gave her the time and ended with a promise to call in for supper that week and bring Abu with her.

By the time she had finished making the arrangements Gloria was at the beach. It was deserted at this time of day and she found the spot quickly. She knew where it was because the normally dirty and mess-strewn beach was completely clear where the body had been found. A combination of respect and superstition would keep the locals away from here for a few more days at least, she thought. But it wasn't that helpful. In the bright glare of the afternoon sun the spot was empty, a slight indentation in the sand still visible, or was that just her imagination?

Gloria looked around to where the dirty sand of the beach finished and the massive rock formation surrounding the American embassy began. The closely guarded embassy and the rumours of a strange gang who lived in the rocks were usually enough to keep most people away from here. However, it wasn't a secluded spot and certainly not an ideal place to spend some hours torturing and then murdering a child.

One obvious explanation was that the gang who lived in the rocks was responsible but Gloria doubted it. They were notorious for marauding around the wealthier parts of town stealing from government ministers and Westerners who lived in the high-walled villas and then retreating to the caves in the rocks like old-fashioned robber barons. But they also had something of the Robin Hood about them in that they helped the locals with food and 'work', and there were stories of them helping old people to hospital and even paying for children to go to school. Gloria suspected much of that was just mythology but there were no reports of any calculated violence from them. Still, things happened and gangs could change. They were definitely worth investigating.

The only other structure on the beach, further along in the other direction, was one Gloria was familiar with. The Haven of

Refuge shelter was run by a very dodgy character who called himself Bishop Worthing, although she knew his real name was Andrew Wright. A shelter run by a middle-aged man with only teenage girls in it was clearly wrong. But, as was so often the case in Liberia, setting up something inappropriate was easy, getting permission to investigate and close it was not. That required co-ordination and permission from the Ministry of Justice, the police, the Ministry of Social Welfare and numerous important NGOs. Meanwhile the 'Bishop' continued to run his brothel in full view of the local population and, judging by the number of expensive vehicles parked along the road at night, there was no shortage of customers.

She hesitated but knew she would have to talk to Wright. The impulse to punch him got stronger every time they met but she was well aware that if she did that she would end up as a headline while he would use it to his advantage. She strolled along the beach, surprised at how empty it was. Her car stood alone on the road and the fact that no child had materialised instantly to guarantee to watch it told her that this spot was far from the usual haunts of street children. But then, she reminded herself, the boy had not been a street child. When she got to the shelter a smiling Wright appeared instantly at the door clutching, as always, a large black bible.

'Ah Inspector, good afternoon.'

The dim memory of some character from Charles Dickens floated into her head, distracting her for a moment.

'What a surprise to see you around here. How can I help?'

Gloria suppressed her first answer to that question and instead asked him if he had been around two nights ago.

'Of course,' he replied, 'my girls might need my help at any time.'

Again suppressing thoughts of violence, Gloria was about

to ask him if he had seen or heard anything when a young woman appeared at the door beside Wright. On one side of her head her hair was elaborately, even painfully, braided while on the other it stood up wildly as if some mini tornado had passed down the middle. She was around nineteen or twenty years old, so not one of Wright's younger girls. She already had the hardness around her mouth and in her eyes which showed she had been doing this for a long time. Wright's manner changed as soon as she came to the door, the unctuous tone replaced by the brothel owner's sharp, threatening inflection.

'What are you doin girl, you can't show respect to me and the police officer?'

The 'girl' didn't look at all threatened, Gloria admitted to herself. She looked past Wright and at Gloria.

'You have to find out who killed that pekin, it's not right,' she said.

Ignoring Wright's protests, Gloria pulled the girl out of the shelter and asked her name.

'Benetta,' the girl answered straight away. There was nothing docile or scared about her.

'So Benetta, tell me what you know about the pekin and what happened to him.'

Benetta paused and then, just as Gloria was expecting her to ask for money, she started talking.

'It was very dark that night but I had no-one visiting me. The place is too hot,' she said pointing at the shelter, 'so I went outside to smoke.'

'What time was that?'

'Well it was very dark and there was no moon so I don't know.'

Gloria looked at her. 'Go on.'

'That's it, really. I heard some noise over there.' She gestured towards the rocks. 'There's noise around here every night, but I thought they were church people, you know the ones who roll in the sand, I could hear them praying. Sometimes those people try and 'convert' us you know. Telling us we need to change or we will go to hell.' She rolled her eyes. 'Anyway, I went back inside before they could come over.'

Oh great, thought Gloria, now she could mix religion into the picture, just what she needed.

Benetta had clearly decided that she knew nothing more at this stage and just wandered off with a final 'Find those people' thrown over her shoulder and disappeared into the shack. Gloria went back to her car, avoiding any more contact with Wright. It hadn't been very useful information and had just added another vague lead to the growing list. She called Moses and asked if anyone had recognised the boy but he told her they had drawn a blank everywhere and, in response to his question, she told him they could add religion to the mix of circumstances surrounding his death. She sat in the car for a few moments in the baking heat before reluctantly starting the engine. She had a funeral to attend.

3.

GLORIA had arranged to meet Moses at the funeral home in an hour so she decided to pop home and change before the service. As she was driving up Gurley Street someone waved her down and she recognised the figure of John Kopius from the International Rescue Service. His organisation worked with children who were living on the street and they sat on a few of the same committees. For some reason she couldn't understand, Gloria found herself positioned as the positive face of Liberian policing and consequently she knew all the organisations who worked with children. The drawback was that she was frequently called to advise or contribute to various committees and working groups. John Kopius wasn't too bad. He was a little distant but then she thought that was perhaps just his way of coping with the misery he saw everyday.

'Inspector, have you got a moment?' he said. Since she had pulled over and stopped, she thought it might have been obvious that she was giving him time. 'I hear you are working the case of the boy who was found murdered on the beach.'

It was a statement and not a question so Gloria nodded but he seemed to be waiting for her to say more.

'John, we haven't even identified the child yet. Have you heard anything?'

Kopius either didn't hear or chose not to answer her question.

'But why would anyone do this to a child?'

Gloria was in no mood for this. 'I don't know and I don't care 'why'. I want to find out 'who' and make sure they get what they deserve. So if you know anything or hear anything let me know immediately.'

He was silent for a moment but not in thought, he was staring at her in a way she couldn't explain.

'It's strange', he said, 'that in a town this size where everyone's business is discussed all the time, no-one seems to know anything about him.' And then he straightened up and walked off, leaving her looking at his retreating back.

Now what was that about, thought Gloria. She had heard rumours that Kopius was not coping very well with either his team or with the many demands being made on his organisation. She hoped he wasn't going to have a breakdown.

Forty five minutes later Gloria was at her Uncle's Blessed Assurance funeral home. It was a rambling building badly in need of a coat of paint. Uncle Hilary was standing on the steps waiting for her and formally escorted her inside. The chapel smelt damp but it was clean and he had managed to find a small casket of highly polished wood and put out flowers and lit some candles. Gloria was impressed. Moses was standing in silence with Hawa and Sr. Anselm, any attempt at conversation made impossible by a choir singing 'Lay down my brother' coming through the tinny speakers at full volume.

The speakers suddenly went off leaving a ringing sound in their ears and they looked at Sr. Anselm. She kept it short, a few prayers and a few words and then a moment's silence. The casket was loaded into a van and they drove to the cemetery where the rest of the ceremonies were completed just as the rain started. Sr. Anselm sprinkled some holy water on the casket as it was lowered into the grave and covered over and she finished her prayers with 'in the sure and certain hope of the resurrection' and a mumbled 'Amen'.

Gloria thanked her and then went over to speak to Hawa. Hawa, as always, was beautifully dressed, smart and stylish as befitted an airport official.

'I didn't expect to see you here, Hawa.'

Hawa's eyes were moist. 'Moses told me you were burying him today Gloria. I thought of our own children and how terrible it would be to be abandoned like that. It was the least I could do. Besides,' she smiled briefly, 'it's the only chance we get to meet now, funerals.'

It did feel like that, Gloria admitted. They had been to three funerals in the last month alone.

'I wish we had some of that 'sure and certain hope', Gloria,' Hawa said. 'This peace isn't really what we had expected. I think a lot of people don't expect it to last, it feels so fragile. And these killings don't help either. What kind of future *are* our children going to have?' She took a breath. 'But at least they are alive and healthy, I should be grateful for that.'

Gloria nodded but she was distracted by the sight of a woman across the road who was staring at them.

'But try to come and eat something with us Gloria, and bring Abu as well. We haven't seen him for ages.'

Gloria promised and Hawa walked over to speak to Moses. By now it was raining very heavily so it was hard to see much but the woman across the road appeared to be crying. Gloria made to cross the road to speak to her but, by the time she had negotiated the rubble from broken headstones, the sunken graves and a torrent of water pouring from the broken drains, the woman had gone.

In a few minutes it was only Moses and her left at the cemetery. Two police standing by a half-filled grave. Gloria could feel a tension across her shoulders and in her jaw that she hadn't noticed before but she knew the cause. She was angry, plain and simple. She was very, very angry.

'Come on Moses, this place is a death trap, no pun intended. Let's get back to the office and see if we are winning this one.'

They went in her car as Moses had sent his back to collect the officers who were still out on the street – this was the only way to guarantee they would be at the meeting that afternoon.

'Did you see the woman across the road? I am sure she was crying but she disappeared before I could speak to her. She looked a bit odd to me.'

Moses wasn't interested. 'Ah, this country,' he muttered, 'this war has affected everybody. She is probably missing her family or maybe she was just joining in. You know how we love funerals here.'

Gloria didn't pursue it but something about that woman had suggested a deep personal sorrow. She gave herself a shake, 'a deep personal sorrow', she really was getting fanciful if she saw that in one look. She imagined trying to capture that in her report.

Moving on rapidly she changed tack. 'Abu wants to have a party and I don't know what to do. It's so much money, he is only in 5th grade. . . and I don't like some of his friends.' The last one was hard to admit.

Moses looked at her. 'You don't know most of his friends boss, so how can you like or dislike them. Look, he'll be sixteen, he's been through the war and about as grown-up as he's ever going to be.' This was one of Moses theories about male social development in general. 'Plus the fact, if you don't have one, he'll find some other way to celebrate and then he will have to lie to you as well. Have the party – it will be expensive, embarrassing and no-one will really enjoy it but at least you two will still be talking at the end of it, and he will owe you as well!'

For someone who appeared to have very little to do with his own children's upbringing she was surprised how definite and clear cut Moses' views were. But maybe he was right. Of course she had wanted him to agree with her about it not being necessary – she could even have quoted him to Abu if need be – but what he said made good sense. She would talk to Abu tonight.

'And don't forget boss, at that age he could have been a four star general in the war.'

Gloria shuddered. She had met a lot of those generals, and many of them a lot younger than Abu. She remembered the children at the checkpoints, out of their heads on some concoction of drugs and cane juice, with their angry orders to pass or step to one side. She had been lucky as Hawa had reminded her. At least Abu had survived.

For some reason she had never understood, getting back to police headquarters was always easer than getting out of it. Something to do with traffic flows maybe, she thought as she parked the Polo very precisely, deliberately focusing on the meeting they were going to have. She hoped someone had brought some more definite information.

The still, dead heat in the meeting room was not conducive to analytical thinking. Not that there was much to analyse, the sum total of the information they had collected not amounting to very much. Gloria reported her conversation with Benetta, her brief meeting with John Kopius and her thoughts about the gang in the rocks. Moses summed up what the others had discovered. No-one at the shelters, children or staff, had recognised the child in the photo although a young officer who had gone to the shelter on Benson St. said he had got a funny feeling. When pressed he said he had been surprised to find any children there during the day. Gloria hadn't thought about that but knew that it was a good observation. He added that they were very subdued, just sitting or lying around in the gloom of the old warehouse.

'Who runs that one?' she asked

'It's a fairly new organisation called Lost Child of Liberia.' Gloria winced at the title. Honestly, who did these people think they were, taking children and putting labels on them? What kind of service was that? Plus, she knew many of these children were not really street children. They were not 'lost' for goodness sake, they were hungry and poor. Most of them were either orphans or kids who had left home to look for food and earn some money, often to support younger brothers and sisters. She thought of one of the kids she knew well. He appeared to be as tough as anyone else out there but he went home most nights and gave any money he had earned to his old granny to make sure his younger brother and sister went to school.

But it made the fact that the children were sitting around the shelter during the day, instead of out earning money, even more significant.

'Well spotted,' she told him and the officer grinned.

'But that's not all,' he said. 'Some of those children live around my area and they say a lot of them are scarey, eh afraid.' She insisted they use standard English as much as possible, telling them it made them look and sound more professional. The young policeman – his name turned out to be Paul Doe – said they were talking about children disappearing but they couldn't actually say who, if any, had disappeared. She nodded. Rumours and stories made up three quarters of everyone's life in Monrovia and for these children even more so. But it was definitely worth following up.

The other shelters had not yielded much information so the strands of their investigation as it stood included possible links to the rock gang, an unidentified religious group, diamond smuggling, street children disappearing – they could have come up with that list without even leaving the room she thought. This was all standard stuff.

'Ok, here's the plan,' said Gloria. 'Tomorrow I want a list of all the shelters, drop-in centres, hostels, homes, whatever, which work with street children, child soldiers' – she knew that was still a popular cause among the international community – 'and any others. I want to know who runs them, how many children they have, where they are from and where the children go back to.'

Even Moses was staring at her with his mouth slightly open. It was unlikely that anyone had even half this information. A combination of poorly trained social workers, children who could change their identity at will depending on the circumstances and a lack of co-ordination between relevant Ministries and agencies meant it was really in no-one's best interest to have the information – even if they had the tools and the inclination to collect it. Well, you had to set the bar high, he thought.

'And don't forget the girls – that Haven of Refuge on the beach needs more *investigation*,' Gloria emphasised the word and they knew what she meant. 'As well as our friends at the Monte Carlo training centre on Broad Street and any others you can find.'

Now they really did groan out loud. The girls were notoriously difficult to deal with, tough, mouthy and very aggressive. Well they had to survive somehow and they lived in a very harsh world. But the police were definitely not among their favourite people.

'Captain Luseni,' she continued, 'you can take the girls' shelters. I think it needs your charm. And take Alfred and Alfred with you.' Alfred One was an old dour man with very little to

41

say about anything and Alfred Two was young, good-looking and with just enough charm to make up for his lack of education. It was a winning combination really, she thought, although the look on Luseni's face told a different story.

'Oh and Izena, you join them so we have some gender balance.' And someone who might actually understand them a bit, she thought to herself. Or not. Izena, convent-educated, daughter of the rich Harrison family and with no husband was a bit of a mystery to her. Well a lot of these recruits were, which wasn't surprising considering they had only been together as a unit for less than a month and the mixture of veterans and rookies was hard to deal with.

'Captain Moses will divide the rest of you to cover the boys' places. Right, that's it for the day.'

'For them, I meant Moses,' she called after him pointing at her watch. 'It's only going to four, we can join the end of the training sessions and show willing.'

Half an hour later she was regretting her decision. The room was even hotter than yesterday and the young British policeman – she had finally remembered that his name was Ron Miller – seemed to be talking about the same things as yesterday. Her leaflet told her that today should have been about 'Handling the scene of a crime' which would have been useful if Ron hadn't still been talking about professionalism. Really, she knew professionalism was important but at some stage they had to go out and deal with criminals and solve crimes. This was post-war Liberia not post-prandial Britain. Ron went on for another hour before winding up with the threat that tomorrow would be a catch-up session followed by a presentation by the director of the UN's trafficking unit.

Before she left, though, she thought she would have a word with Mr. Miller to tell him what they were working on at the moment and explain her frequent absences. One-to-one he turned out to be both interesting and interested. Although he was only twenty nine, the same age as her, he had worked as a volunteer in southern Africa when he was a student and, as a police officer, he had worked with police forces in Rwanda, East Timor and Columbia. It only took a few minutes for Gloria to become convinced of his passionate belief in his work and his ability. This was no raw recruit dropped in to tick a few boxes for the international community but an experienced officer who believed in the power of a strong police force to build peace and democracy. They chatted for another ten minutes and Ron told her to focus on her work and forget about the training session.

'Let's be honest Inspector, I am not teaching you anything you don't know already. I know that. The value of you attending these sessions is so that your fellow officers, not all as dedicated as you,' he smiled, 'will take. . .'

'. . . the training seriously.' She finished for him.

'No,' now he laughed, 'not the training but take their role seriously. I read everything I could about Liberia and talked to the few people who had visited or spent time here prior to the war. The police force was obviously suffering from many of the problems common to countries in your situation. Corruption, bad leadership, underfunding. You have a small chance now to build a new force out of the ruins but it means that officers like yourself must be seen to be involved and to be taking it seriously. You can't operate like private investigators with uniforms.'

Now she smiled. That was exactly how she would like to work.

'You need to get involved with the police force.' He stopped abruptly. 'Anyway, that's the end of the sermon but if there is anything I can do to help in any way please let me know. We are all police officers and solving crimes is our priority.'

4.

GLORIA woke up the next morning surprised to find her room was quite cool. She could tell from the silent fan she usually slept under that the electricity had gone off. The mosquito net was still and although it was only beginning to get light, there was a breeze coming in from the ocean. A cool and quiet start to the day was such an unusual thing that she lay for a while luxuriating in it. She knew it wouldn't last. She thought of last night's talk with Abu. After her very generous and reasonable offer to have a party she had been surprised by Abu's casual dismissal of it.

'I don't think a party is a good idea, Aunt Glo. It costs too much, and some of those boys, well you can't trust them.'

How could teenagers so easily wrong-foot you? After agreeing to a party she didn't want in the interests of being a reasonable and understanding aunt, Abu now made it sound as if she had offered something completely unsuitable and, really, she should have known better. Of course it wasn't long before it was followed up by the real request.

'Instead of a party I want to go with the team to Harbel at the weekend for the league. It's really important.'

He had looked very earnest but she knew there had to be a catch. As it turned out there wasn't just one catch, there were several. The 'weekend' actually meant that evening and 'go with' the team meant Gloria was to pay for the 'food, transportation and accommodation' for everyone! Added to this, although she would not admit it, she was very wary about letting him go off for the weekend, even to Harbel which was just up the road. Abu hadn't been anywhere on his own since the end of the fighting and she worried about what could happen – bad roads, bad drivers, bad people – and that was before she did one of her serious mental lists. She said none of this to Abu though, just told him to get her the costs. If he was organising it at least he could cost it out properly. Since his school was closing early she told him to meet her at her office at midday.

Having run through everything again, Gloria got out of bed, squashed a cockroach which had dared enter her room, and got ready for work. Abu's extreme cheerfulness at breakfast was almost as irritating as his usual morning silences but seeing him happy, school uniform neat and tidy, and babbling on about the class elections they were having that day she felt that strange surge of affection for this boy who was as close to her as any child of her own would have been. If Abu was to be believed he was running for class president by popular acclaim and Gloria had to listen to various versions of his speech which all seemed to involve quite extravagant promises about the changes he would make in the running of the school. Luckily the babble didn't require any response from her so she carried on drinking her coffee and let it all wash over her. And ten minutes later, with a casual 'See you' he was out the door.

The office was the usual buzz of activity. She couldn't decide whether this was the regular Friday morning excitement – as if the police closed for the weekend – or a real sense of purpose among her team. They were all in one of the headquarters' many meeting rooms when she got in at eight and she quickly reviewed what they had decided yesterday. There were no questions, except Izena asking when the ladies bathroom was going to be fixed. Gloria looked blank. She hadn't even known there was a ladies bathroom. She looked at Moses who shrugged. As no-one else knew the answer to this they moved on quickly. The groups who had been allocated tasks yesterday and this morning moved out sharply and the remainder which consisted of Moses, Gloria and the three newest recruits – or should that be conscripts? – looked at each other.

These three were part of the integration plan concocted by the UN, the government and several influential donors. Part of the strategy was their brilliant plan to absorb some of the combatants who had been fighting with various factions during the war into the new police, army and civil service. An expert from Colombia had shared that country's experience of reintegration and recommended this move, among others.

Everyone thought it was a great idea – except the combatants themselves who didn't appreciate the discipline and poor pay, their erstwhile colleagues who had suffered at their hands in the war, and the civilian population who could not understand why rebels were being rewarded instead of being put in prison.

It certainly hadn't improved their already delicate relations with the general public. Despite their uniforms and low-cut hair, the new recruits still somehow had an air of being rebels, a certain menace they gave off by the way they walked or slouched or looked at you. Gloria, who wasn't convinced they were over eighteen – one of them looked even younger than Abu – had tried her very best to get them transferred to another division. She had suggested that the Traffic department might be more suitable than the Family and Child Protection Unit but had been told that Traffic was a high profile division. She knew what they meant. Most Liberians fought, bribed, attacked and generally came into contact with the Traffic police on a daily basis while few had ever heard of the Family and Child Protection Unit.

But Gloria couldn't help remarking that the 'skills' these boys had learnt during the war – humiliation, torture, harassment and abuse – would be more suitable in the Traffic division. The Chief's attempt to justify his decision was made harder by the story in that morning's Journal about an American woman who had been stopped by the police on Broad Street and accused of driving though a red light. When she pointed out that the traffic lights had been out of use for over ten years – they were only empty fittings – the police responded by telling her that if they had been working they would have been on red and therefore she had committed an offence. With that kind of logic these people should be lawyers, she had told him – another world where reality could always be bent to fit the situation.

The fact was that she had three recruits she was supposed to train but without actually letting them get too near the public. The three of them had been with different factions during the war and didn't trust each other anymore than they trusted her. Ambrose, who had been forcibly recruited from the junior seminary during the war, was obviously intelligent but very angry with everyone. Lamine was a country boy who had been taken from his village, given a gun and a licence to kill and was still bewildered by everything. Lastly, there was Christian, what a prize he was. He had managed to let everyone know his war name, General Mother Blessing, and still boasted, albeit quietly, about how he had led the attack on the city of Kakata. To say he wasn't completely rehabilitated was the biggest understatement and Gloria had no idea what to do with him.

'Okay you three,' she said, 'this is what we're doing today. Ambrose, you will stay here to answer the phone, if it ever rings, and compile the information we have received so far.' She pointed to a large board in the corner. 'I want everything up on that board by the time we come back this afternoon.'

He didn't look delighted but on the other hand he hadn't 'tied his face' so at least he wasn't sulking.

'Christian, you and Lamine will come with me.' She turned to Moses. 'I thought I would pay a visit to that gang in the rocks. I want to find out if they know anything.'

Moses looked doubtful. 'Ok, but take time boss, it could be dangerous.' Moses was always warning her but before she could answer he continued. 'You remember they don't wear any clothes, don't you?'

She recalled the raid they had staged a month ago searching for a missing child and finding that this gang of men discarded all clothing when they were in their den as a sign of – actually, she couldn't remember what it was a sign of, but it hadn't been a pretty sight.

'Right, well I'm sure these two will cope with it fine. You need to take that diamond and get it valued. If it is real there is a bigger question about why the people who killed him put it there in the first place, and why they didn't take it with them.'

Moses nodded. 'I'll take it down to Hassan at the Lebanese jewellery shop.'

She added, 'I'm surprised no-one has asked about it or tried to get if off us.'

Evidence and confiscated property was a great source of income for some of her superior officers.

'I'm not,' said Moses, 'they are all afraid. Even greed takes second place to a stone found in the hand of a tortured child.'

Gloria agreed. However bad the corruption and breakdown in society Liberians still loved their children, and despite all the death many of them had seen in the war, a single act of torture and murder like this was automatically linked to real evil, organised evil, the kind of evil which could track you down if you strayed onto its radar.

'While you're out,' she said, 'why not see if you can get any more information from John Kopius.'

She thought about their brief meeting and it struck her again that there had been more said in the few words exchanged than she realised, only she didn't know what the 'more' was. Things she was expected to have picked up on but hadn't. When he talked about how strange it was that no-one had heard anything, was he hinting at a cover-up? Well she was clever but maybe Moses' more straightforward approach to people would get them better information.

She really wanted to stop at Ma Mary's but there was no chance of that with these two in her car. She tried to get them talking but Lamine still answered 'Who me?' to every question even when she was looking right into his face, as if perpetually surprised or terrified. Christian feigned complete indifference and kept on checking his mobile phone as if expecting a call.

'Look guys', Gloria said, 'we are just going to talk to these people. As far as we know they are not connected to this murder but they might be able to give us some information. Leave the questions to me, your job is to look around, see if there's any other information you can pick up. Police work is not all about asking questions.'

The blank looks confirmed her suspicions that they didn't really understand that.

She parked the car and they walked across the sand to the rocky outcrop. The rocks were huge pieces of stone, jagged and wet with spray. From this angle the outcrop looked very steep and seemed to stretch far into the distance. They headed upwards and Lamine and Christian had soon left her behind. It was hard work and the higher they went the more difficult it became. Gloria paused and looked down. Far below, the sea was crashing into the shore. She shivered, one slip and she would be finished. A body dropped from here would be washed away very quickly or battered beyond recognition. The other two had almost reached a ridge and she hurried after them determined they shouldn't think she was not as strong as they were. She had worked up a good sweat and had given up on holding on to her dignity by the time she reached them. Her shirt was sticking to her back, her shoes were already turning white from the sea water and her knees felt shaky. Lamine and Christian hadn't altered their stride and had made it up over the rocks without breaking a sweat or offering any comment.

She caught up with them at what she thought was the top. They were standing talking to two very large men who, she could see now, were obviously guarding the entrance to the gang's headquarters. She didn't remember it like this. On last month's raid they had gone in through a space in the rocks further down and found a few narrow caves and a group of five or six young men in what they thought was the main gang headquarters. This was very different. The space they were at now was much higher up and would be impossible to find if you didn't know it existed.

'How did you know it was here,' she hissed into Christian's ear.

He looked puzzled. 'I don't know, it's just where it should be.'

It's just where it should be, great, she thought. Now it turns out he's got instinct!

She pushed past them and found herself looking up into the faces of the two very tall guards. She felt at a disadvantage standing lower than them with the sun blinding her and the sweat dripping off her. Before she could say anything one of them said to follow but they would have to be blindfolded. As if in anticipation of her protest they made it clear that they would go nowhere if they didn't agree to the blindfold.

'The place is hidden ma,' the speaking one said, 'it's not for you to know. But our boss wants to help. We are not happy what they did to the boy, it was not correct.'

As she wondered again at Liberian understatement, she concluded that blindfolds were the only way they would get access. And having risked her life – she had perhaps rather over dramatised the climb in her head – she decided to go along with their games. After all what could they do to her? As soon as she had that thought a whole list of things they could do to her came into her head. She shook it away. At this stage if there was even somewhere to sit down she would be grateful.

'Alright,' she said, 'but one of these officers will stay here.' She indicated to Lamine, who looked relieved. 'And if anything happens he will go for help.'

Speaking Guard shrugged and produced some strips of cloth. She and Christian were duly blindfolded and then, with Christian supporting her elbow, as if she was one of the blind beggars at Center Street's Park N Shop supermarket, they inched their way forward. She sensed they were climbing higher, the breeze was strong and the taste of the sea was in her mouth. It seemed to take hours of shuffling before she felt they were going down hill again and the noise of the waves crashing on the rocks died away. She felt the shade as soon as they entered it. It was cool in here and when she put out her hand she could feel the rough stone of the cave wall.

As Speaking Guard took the cloth off her eyes she saw they were in a large cave which was furnished as an office, with a desk, chair and, bizarrely, in-and-out trays. Behind the desk was a man she estimated to be in his late forties. She was relieved to see he had on shorts and a t-shirt and he started speaking immediately.

'So you need information Inspector.'

No accent, perfect English. The man sounded like her old professor at JJ Fellowes.

'I need to know what happened to the child. Do you know anything?'

'Do you mean did we kill him?'

'I don't think so, not your style from what we know.'

'Yes Inspector, but from what you know you thought we were a gang of five or six rogues, living up here naked among the rocks.'

'True,' she had to give him that one. 'Although that's how you were the last time we called. So did you kill him then?'

'No we didn't but we would like you to catch whoever did. And the child's name was Aloysius, by the way.'

So, some information at last. The Boss, as she thought of him, then told her what happened. Late that night one of the guards had reported movement on the beach. It was rare but not entirely unknown for lovers or others to wander on to the beach but the guards said there were at least four people carrying a bundle which they eventually realised was a person from the squirming and the muffled cries.

'They reported back to me,' the Boss said, 'and we came to investigate. You must understand Inspector that we do not usually interfere with what goes on out there, we are not the police but the murder of a child is different. Unfortunately, by the time we realised it was a child they had down there it was too late. If our guards had reported earlier we might have stopped them but by the time we got down the boy was very still and we thought, correctly, he was dead. The strange thing was the people who did it were still standing around instead of trying to bury the body or get away. That's when we heard his name, when they were praying for him.'

'Praying for him? After they had just tortured and killed him?

Are you sure?' Gloria shook her head. The details of this case were getting stranger and stranger.

'Yes, they stood around and then the tall one prayed for 'the soul of your child Aloysius' and the others said 'Amen' and then they just walked away'

This was so unexpected that Gloria didn't know what to say for a while. 'Were these people Liberians or what?'

'Well accents can be deceptive Inspector, don't you think? But the one who said the prayer didn't sound African or Western. He talked in a way I haven't heard before'

It had been dark that night so they couldn't describe the people and hadn't seen their vehicles or which direction they had gone, and that was the extent of their information.

As the Boss was talking the cave began to fill up until there were close on twenty men crowding around, listening to the conversation. Gloria looked around at them. There was no-one younger than seventeen or eighteen and they were all dressed, and all had bandanas around their faces.

'You look surprised Inspector. What were you expecting? Ali Baba and the Forty Thieves?'

Gloria laughed. 'Well to be honest I thought it would be stranger than this.'

'We have no children and no women here and no-one is forced to stay. The only condition is secrecy. If you leave, and most leave eventually, you must be sure to say nothing of our way of life here.'

Gloria opened her mouth but the Boss put up his hand. 'No questions Inspector. I just wanted you to be sure we were not murderers. Now the blindfolds on please and the guards will take you out.'

Lamine was waiting and looked relieved when he saw them. Gloria took off her blindfold and looked back but there was no discernible path or route. When they reached the car there was another silence until she asked them what they thought of the experience. Both Lamine and Christian had spent years with warlords and their crazy commanders so they didn't find the set up of the gang at all strange. That was a worry to Gloria. If that kind of behaviour was going to be accepted as 'normal' then they were in for a fun ride in Liberia in the future!

Lamine volunteered that the guard who had stayed with him was not even Liberian.

'That man, tha so so Nigerian and a real soldier'

'Did he tell you that?' asked Gloria.

'He didn't need to ma.'

'Inspector' she corrected him.

'Inspector. The way he were talking and the way he carry the gun, I tell you tha Nigerian soldier there. Probably one of the ECOMOG people who didn't go home.'

Gloria thought that was probably true, or at least possible. The ECOMOG, the West African peacekeeping soldiers, the majority of whom had been Nigerian, had been a mixed blessing for the country. Although they had stopped the fighting and prevented some of the worst abuses, they had also looted every conceivable item of any worth from the country and shipped it back home (hence the Monrovian interpretation of their acronym ECOMOG as Every Commodity or Movable Object Gone) But they had also been mired in politics and corruption and there were a significant number who had decided to stay when their tour of duty was finished and had 'disappeared' into the populace. She hadn't thought of them joining, or organising gangs, but anything was possible.

'What about you Christian? Any thoughts you want to share with us?' Said without much hope she was again surprised when he answered.

'The boss man you spoke to, I know him. He is Francis Bryant, used to teach literature at Lincoln Memorial School, Buchanan.'

Gloria was taken aback yet again at both the information and the fact that Christian had taken the trouble to form a whole sentence.

'You know him?'

'He is a very smart man. Don't overlook him because you see him sitting in the rocks. You need to take time with him. . .'

'Right,' she interrupted before Christian could complete his warning. 'Good work, you guys. You did just as I asked you. I've got no time to be investigating that gang until we find this killer but I need one of you to get a bit closer to them. They might be a lot more important that I first thought. I don't want to overlook them.'

Lamine jumped in almost before she could finish. 'I will do it ma. . . eh Inspector. I can get close to them.'

'Good. Let's get back to the office first and see what the others have found.'

There was no-one else around when they got back and she realised it was only just after eleven. She added Aloysius's name to the board and the information about the odd burial ceremony and the accents of the people but didn't put in anything about the gang. You could never be entirely sure who would see and use information on the board and it sounded as if Bryant might be someone to keep an eye on.

Ambrose had posted everything they knew so far – which wasn't a great deal – but when he saw the name he commented, 'Could be Catholic.'

Although a Catholic herself Gloria didn't get the connection. Names in Liberia, as far as she knew, were just a personal choice – or invention – unrelated to anything else.

'What do you mean?'

Ambrose looked a bit surprised as if he wasn't used to being listened to and went on.

'Well I know Aloysius is not a common name and there is one small church in Bomi called St. Aloysius which they almost completed just as the war was starting to reach them about eight years ago.' As if caught out by his own enthusiasm, he shrugged and turned away.

'Wait, this is good stuff, Ambrose,' said Gloria. 'So he could be from there, born around the time the church was completed and given that name. That would make him about eight years old and what, a Gola?'

Ambrose just nodded. He was from the Gola tribe himself but thoughts of his home county and his previous life made him angry and depressed. And, thought Gloria, it was a well known diamond area as well as the route in and out of Sierra Leone. They could actually be on the trail of the killer now.

She told Ambrose to add the information to the board, tentatively – Ambrose understood words like that which was nice – and then Gloria went back to her own office which she hadn't seen for days.

5.

NOTHING had changed in Gloria's office. Piles of paper, lots of dust, some shaky furniture and an ancient computer which didn't work.

It wasn't long before a loud 'boc boc' announced Abu's arrival, with one of his friends. They were clearly very excited and were almost dancing around the office and talking at the same time.

'All right, give me your list, come on don't waste time. And Morris,' this to Abu's friend – or was that 'bro' as she'd heard them call each other – 'you go and get us some soft drinks please.'

She handed him twenty dollars. She needed a drink but she also needed to talk to Abu alone and highlight all the possible dangers he needed to watch out for in Harbel. As it turned out she didn't say any of those things. They went through the list Abu had brought: costs of minibus hire, gas for the minibus, food for the weekend and money for accommodation. She drew the line at the item marked 'stipend'. She didn't mind funding the trip but she wasn't paying the players as well! They were getting a weekend away for free. She was pretty sure some of the people going were not even football players but she let it go. It was a huge amount in Liberian dollars but very reasonable when translated into US dollars which she still did out of habit even though she was paid in her own currency.

Before Morris came back she gave Abu the money and a brief, casual warning to take care. Then he and Morris spent twenty minutes telling her about the class elections and Abu's winning speech which had included references to freedom, friendship – and his Aunt Gloria's high rank in the police!

Gloria stopped them there before she heard too much – you really could hear too much. She reminded them to be back in town on Sunday before dark and took their nods as agreement.

She guessed from the noise coming from the office next door that some of the team were back and reckoned it was time to divide up the rest of the work that was coming their way. She had so many cases on it was becoming difficult to prioritise.

One of her many roles involved being part of the team investigating a fire which had broken out at the Executive Mansion on the day of the President's inauguration. Although no-one had been hurt, in Monrovia's paranoid atmosphere speculation about plots and coups had run high. Unfortunately their investigations were turning up nothing more sinister than faulty wiring but they would have to keep the investigation going a few more days anyway to mark its seriousness.

The other two serious complaints they had at the moment involved accusations against a member of an international NGO and a government minister. It was obvious to her from the evidence in the first case that the accusations against the Minister of Mining and Minerals were nonsense. The man had not even been in the country when the alleged assault had taken place. But the opposition were using it to attack the government and once again a 'thorough' investigation had to be seen to be taking place. The second case was more serious, a report of NGO staff involved in inappropriate behaviour, but paradoxically she was under pressure not to investigate this one too thoroughly in case it jeopardised the donor funds they needed so badly! Carrying out an investigation would be so much easier than having to navigate the politics that surrounded everything.

At the team meeting it became clear that the amount of information they had collected after a day's work was meagre and most of it had come from her trip to the rock gang. The children's shelters and the other centres had promised to come up with lists of users.

'But I wouldn't hold my breath waiting for them ma'am.' Paul looked very disapproving. 'Some of these places obviously have no records at all or they just have piles and piles of paper everywhere. They say their numbers are down but they have no baseline figures so I don't know what they mean by that.'

The girls' centres were the usual chaos and judging by Luseni's face they were still not very friendly towards the police. Even the Alfreds looked a bit shaken.

'Those girls are crazy ma'am. One of them picked up a pair of tailoring scissors about this long.' Young Alfred extended his arms. 'And tried to stab the Captain, almost got him.'

'She was going to stab you for asking questions, Captain? That is serious. Do you want to make a complaint?' Gloria looked at Luseni who was trying to hide a tear in the sleeve of his jacket.

'That's the strange thing ma'am' – she realised that Alfred was mocking the Captain now – 'she tried to stab him before he even started with the questions.'

Luseni looked embarrassed and muttered something about the girl mistaking him for someone else. Yes, he was sure he did not want to lodge a complaint against her.

Izena just raised one eyebrow but said nothing and Gloria made a mental note to have a word with her afterwards. She might know what Captain Luseni was really up to.

Moses reported that John Kopius had apparently gone to Sierra Leone to meet with some donors.

Gloria brought everyone up to date with the latest information, that they now had a name and the possible Bomi lead.
She then instructed Luseni to take his men and follow up on
the accusations against the NGO worker – his political
connections and his complete lack of sensitivity might be the
right combination to deal with this one. She and Moses would
go to the Executive Mansion in the afternoon to try and persuade
everyone the faulty wires were getting all the attention they
deserved.

She talked through with Moses her idea of assigning Lamine
to keep an eye on the rock gang and then sent him off. She
wasn't sure that Lamine undertood he wasn't going 'under-
cover', as the gang already knew him, but she had the feeling
they wouldn't treat him badly.

The rest of the afternoon was spent at the Executive Mansion
with Moses and the Chief Inspector who had decided it would
be good for him to be seen giving the case his personal attention.
Gloria had been to the Mansion twice before, both times in
connection with the fire and each visit confirmed that the original
shoddy workmanship, coupled with the years of neglect during
the war, had made the fire a question of 'when' and not 'if'. She
had suggested this to the Chief but he hadn't responded –
weighing up the politics against the facts probably. They were
met at the entrance by the Chief of Protocol, a fussy young
woman called Matilda Wesley who seemed to be under the
impression they were coming for an audience with the President.
It took several minutes before she understood they were just
coming to look again at the fire on the fifth floor and didn't
have to bother the President at all.

'I'll show you up then but I'll have the security officer stay
while you carry out your investigations.'

Gloria couldn't be bothered pointing out the anomaly of
security officers checking on the police while they checked out

a potential arson attack on the President. It was just easier to get on and get out.

The lift was working again and although it creaked as if on its last legs, it got them to the fifth floor without incident. The fifth floor of the Executive Mansion, she knew from her previous visits, had been designed as the living quarters of the President. It had last been decorated under the Doe regime. Who had decided that burnt orange, together with worn green carpets and faded yellow wall hangings, was a good colour scheme? There were still one or two pieces of the heavy plush, gilt furniture which had filled most rooms in the Mansion but much of it had been damaged or stolen in the war and replaced by very utilitarian chairs and tables. Whatever the government revenue was being spent on it certainly wasn't going on lavish re-decoration schemes at the Mansion. She could appreciate that was a good thing when the government had so little money but thought it must be quite depressing for a Head of State to live and work in such shabby conditions.

She left Moses talking with the security guards and went with the Chief Inspector to the sitting room where the fire had started. It was a room with a striking view of the ocean and a wide terrace which would be a lovely cool place to sit in the evening. She wondered if President Doe had sat on this very terrace as the rebels advanced on the capital. Maybe the view had helped him blot out the panic in the dying city below him: people streaming out of town, willing to brave the terror of the rebel checkpoints or take a chance in overcrowded boats, in order to avoid the inevitable slaughter; children and old people abandoned at the side of roads, too weak or sick to carry on; his death squads roaming the streets in a last savage attack on a terrified population. If he had known what his own fate would be – capture, torture and death – perhaps he would have accepted the American offer of safe passage. Maybe the war would have been over sooner, the killing less, the peace easier. But he didn't, she thought, and here we are today examining the wiring.

'Enjoying the view Gloria?' Kamara interrupted her thoughts.

'Got a bit lost there, sir. Too many memories.'

Kamara nodded as if he knew what she had been thinking. 'And too many ghosts. If I was the President I would have let the whole place burn down and started fresh with something new and clean.'

They had walked over to the side of the room where the fire had started.

'Well she did have the whole place exorcised before her inauguration, sir.' The re-dedication ceremony had been shown on television.

Kamara looked at her and smiled. 'All the praying and chanting didn't stop the war. Gloria. I don't believe it would do much to clear out the kind of bad spirits that must be hanging around here.' He shrugged and pointed at the offending wall. 'Anyway let's deal with what we've got here.'

The blackened wall was just as it had been after the fire, the wires showing and part of the ceiling having collapsed. The experts who had looked at it, and that included the engineers from the American embassy, had concluded that years of neglect during the war had been the main cause of the wires shorting which had started the fire. The ceiling tiles and the old drapes had fed it quickly into a blaze which had in turn provided the dramatic back drop to the President's inauguration. All the reports had been written, the recommendations, including the rewiring of the whole building had been presented to the Cabinet but nothing had been done.

'We have done everything we can do, sir, and it all points to an accident. Why can't they just get on and do the repairs.'

'It's not that easy, Gloria. If the Cabinet moves too quickly there will be accusations of a cover-up so they have to go through this whole rigmarole of re-checking the damaged wall, discussing it over and over as well as investigating non-existent leads to possible plots.' He rolled his eyes. 'I think they have almost exhausted all the options though, so I believe we will be able to finally wind up the investigation soon.'

On the way back out she briefed the Chief about developments with Aloysius. She was quite surprised at his interest and his animation.

'To be honest, Gloria, I did wonder if you were going to get anywhere with it. This is good news. You know the newspapers are going to be filled with stories of witchcraft and 'heart men', we need to get the real story out as soon as possible – and find the people responsible, no matter how rich or how well connected they are. This could mark the real change for us as a force, and especially show people how your new unit will be operating.'

Such passion, she thought cynically. Chief Inspector Kamara was something of an enigma. He had been an unexceptional Director of the Police Academy when she was doing her training, rarely seen by the recruits apart from graduations. When the war started he had been in America attending a conference but to everyone's surprise he had come back to Monrovia in time for the death throes of Doe's regime. She wasn't sure how he had survived the madness that followed but he re-appeared in Monrovia when the peacekeeping force had established the uneasy peace. He had set up a private security firm, Prime Guards Security Services, which had made him a lot of money and raised his profile. He had surprised a lot of people again when he had accepted the invitation to re-join the police when they were re-formed and now gave the appearance of being fully committed to developing a professional service. Gloria hadn't made her mind up yet. High ranking jobs had a way of eroding people's better intentions in her experience.

The rest of the day, being a Friday, kind of fizzled out. By the time they got back to headquarters most people had found excuses to be out finishing some enquiry and 'just going home from there.' Moses, of course, showed no inclination to go anywhere. Since Abu would have gone by now Gloria didn't feel any need to rush home either and she suddenly felt they were making some progress. They had a name, a link with a diamond area and perhaps even a particular community. It was a huge leap in just a few days.

Moses informed her that Hassan had been very impressed with the diamond.

'He says it was expertly cut, that it's probably not from Liberia and that it is definitely worth a lot of money.'

And the murderers had left it behind. The circumstances around this killing were extraordinary but they just couldn't interpret them yet. They needed more information.

'Where's the diamond now then?'

'Oh I left it with Hassan, thought it would be safer'

Gloria nodded. That was the reality, a very expensive diamond was safer with a Lebanese businessman with an unknown past than in the national police headquarters.

At the end of the day even the heat and dust of the office acquired a kind of soothing quality which she found relaxing. With the office empty she tried to separate the facts from the emotional and political boiling pot. What did they really know?

'Let's go through it again Moses. We have an eight-year old boy called Aloysius, clearly from a good family, possibly from the Bomi Hills area. He is taken to a lonely beach at night where he is tortured and killed by people, at least one of whom is not

Liberian. Left on display after they have prayed for him, he is found with an expensive foreign diamond in his hand.' She paused, giving him a chance to comment but he just nodded. 'None of it makes any obvious sense but the fact that these people were not afraid, that they took their time to kill the child and then left him on open display, along with a very expensive diamond, suggests we are dealing with something bigger and more organised here. Since all of this was done in the open it says to me they were sending a message to someone.'

It reminded her of the brazen display of power they had seen during the war from all the participants, whether children with guns or the lunatics aspiring to be president. Only this looked more calculating, not fuelled by drugs or rage but by a cold, hard sense of purpose.

'We still need to find out more about Aloysius,' Gloria said, 'surely there must be a family looking for him and it could be a family in Bomi. We should go tomorrow, it's Saturday so we'll have a chance of meeting people. What do you think?'

Moses agreed instantly, which made her feel a bit guilty thinking of his children, but it was a passing guilt. Moses' relationship with his family was not really her concern. So, Gloria would try and find out where the St. Aloysius church was and they could go and talk to a few people. It was a few years since she had been to Bomi and she wondered what it would be like.

'Moses, can you find out who is in charge up there. We might need to check in with whoever it is.'

'Bomi is a mess boss. The police there are either raw recruits or ex-rebel commanders. They run it like their own personal territory, like they did in the war. It might be better to avoid them if we can.'

'Yes I'd heard that too, you're probably right. We can play it by ear, no uniforms and we can go in my Polo instead of an official car.' Moses did not look delighted at the thought but he said nothing. 'Right Moses, off home and say hello to your children and to Hawa. I'll pick you up from your house at nine.'

'No don't worry, I'll walk down to your place. Hawa is working tomorrow anyway and the old ma is taking the children to town to buy their shoes and then to the beach.'

Obviously neither of those things filled Moses with much enthusiasm.

6.

SATURDAY dawned hot and still, the milky clouds obscuring the sun but intensifying the heat. It was the kind of Saturday that, for some reason, always took Gloria back to her childhood in Westpoint. The dull boredom of washing clothes in basins of water hauled from the well, while all around people squabbled and shouted. Her mother always busy at the coal pot preparing food and getting ready to press clothes with that charcoal iron she hated. Getting ready for Sunday – which is what it had mainly been about – had been a struggle for most of the day. Everything had to be cleaned, the house and yard swept and washed, food bought and prepared and then later trying to use the spiteful iron which was either not hot enough to press the clothes or spitting red hot sparks, singeing everything.

But it had almost been worth it to enjoy the freedom of the late afternoon when they could go to the video club and watch some movie, or the football, or go down to the water and paddle about or even go out in a canoe into the bright sparkling water. Saturday evenings had usually been spent sitting on the porch around the light of a single bulb or the flaring heat of the kerosene lanterns while her uncles and aunts told stories about the family or the neighbourhood or argued about money and property. So much had happened in the intervening years she sometimes wondered if she perhaps exaggerated or even made up these memories but when she asked her uncles they assured her they were true.

Saturdays were different now. Having someone to wash clothes, clean the house and prepare the food was great but she did sometimes miss having to do these things for herself and worried that Abu was missing out on more than just the discipline of having to work. But when she thought about it his Saturdays were not much different. He worked in the morning and played football and watched videos in the afternoon and evening. She decided she should focus her worry on finding a killer.

At exactly eight-thirty she heard Moses' 'boc boc' before he walked in. He knew there would be just enough time to drink some of her coffee. It was Kenyan and one of her favourites. Now she remembered why Moses had volunteered to walk down and meet her here. Not to escape the family but so he could enjoy a cup. She liked having someone else who shared her enjoyment of good coffee and handed him the 'Queen Elizabeth II Silver Jubilee' mug, which Abu had given her at Christmas, filled with the precious liquid. They sat in silence looking at the flat sea and the crowds of teenagers who had been on the beach since the early morning practising football. There must be at least twelve different teams down there, she thought. For a few moments without saying anything she and Moses enjoyed the scene and the atmosphere and reminded themselves why, despite everything, they wouldn't want to live anywhere else in the world.

In the next half hour they set off and managed to get through Bushrod Island, which was even more crowded than usual with the Saturday market, and were on the road out of town. It was about an hour's drive to Bomi now that the checkpoints had gone and the road was clear. During the war getting to Bomi had been a long and dangerous journey but not this morning. The Bomi Highway, which ran all the way into Sierra Leone, was a wide tarmac strip framed on both sides with tall trees making it a lovely shady road. They passed a few minibuses packed with people and loaded high with baskets of fruit heading to market. There were also the inevitable taxis broken down at the side of the road. One was surrounded by resigned-looking people spread out on lappas and blankets quietly eating bananas and roasted corn. The other was a buzz of activity as people helped the driver to change the wheel, cursed him for not maintaining the car and tried to negotiate a reduction in the fare due to the delay.

'Abu and I spent a month in there at the start of the war, St. Gabriel's church,' Gloria pointed to a small compound on the left as they sped past. 'There were hundreds of us.' She shuddered.

'Did you get up as far as Bomi?'

'No, from there we went to Clay Ashland and ended up in Guinea. That was truly terrible. Where did you go?'

'We squeezed onto the Bulk Challenge.' They looked at each other and laughed.

'I think I would still choose Guinea over that boat, Moses, if we ever have to run again. Or I might just sit where I am and take my chances. What a nightmare.'

The villages and small towns they passed through were very quiet with only a few old people sitting in the shade of their porches or spreading out peppers from their gardens to dry in the sun. The road was punctuated with numerous bridges and these were the liveliest places on the journey with crowds of women washing clothes in the streams below and children playing in the water. Everyone stopped to wave and shout at them seemingly full of high spirits.

Within the hour they were on the outskirts of Bomi's

administrative and social centre, the city of Tubmanburg. There was no waving here and Gloria was glad she couldn't hear what people were shouting. The ravages of the war were more apparent, both in the number of burnt-out or looted buildings they could see and in the large numbers of young people who were sitting on either side of the road, talking or just lounging around. Not for Tubmanburg the early morning football practice, she thought. They probably didn't have any footballs, or any motivation. Many of these would have been the same fighters who terrorised the town during the war and who now found themselves stranded among people who, by turn, hated or feared them.

This whole area had been occupied by various rebel groups and a largely rural way of life, ruled by ancient customs, had been decimated. Children had been abducted and forced to fight, sometimes to destroy their own villages. Traditional sacred places had been looted, the masks and fetishes sold as souvenirs in Monrovia, and centuries of respect for elders and tribal traditions had vanished in a few short years. 'They have torn out our heart' was a common phrase among many of the older people and in this place she had a sense of what they meant. It was definitely not the cheeriest place to spend a Saturday morning.

She was about to say this to Moses when he started on one of his favourite topics.

'So where are all the NGOs and what happened to all the millions of dollars we heard about? I don't see much rehabilitation going on here. Monrovia is full of those land cruisers and NGO people and here it looks as if nothing has changed or developed at all. It's like the Wild West and no-one's doing anything about it.'

Gloria groaned out loud. 'Alright, Moses. enough. Save the politics for later. Just keep your eyes open. My Polo is the only decent car on the road and there are a lot of people staring at it.'

They saw a sign for Tubmanburg police station but when they followed it they came to a building consisting of four burnt walls with a piece of blue tarpaulin stretched between them. Three young men in jeans and bandanas were slouched outside on an old bedspring. One was frowning, one was glaring and the third was sleeping. In her head Gloria immediately named them Sullen, Scary and Stoned.

'Are they the police or the criminals do you think?' she whispered to Moses.

Moses gave them a disgusted look. 'Probably both boss. Let's not bother stopping.'

Gloria agreed and they went back to the main road and followed the signs for the Catholic mission instead. Ambrose hadn't been able to tell her anything about the location of St. Aloysius church but advised that they call in at St. Dominic's, the main mission church. They parked outside the rough-looking mission house next to the church but got no answer to their knocks. It not only looked empty, it looked abandoned.

'Does anyone actually live here?' asked Moses looking at the dirty windows and the dusty porch.'

'I think they spend all their money on helping people.' Gloria pointed to the long lines of stick-thin people standing outside what had been St. Dominic's High School. 'They're still in emergency mode out here. They've got starving people, rebel commanders in town and no schools open. It's like the war never finished.'

A quick inspection of the church revealed a group of people sitting with bibles on their knees listening to a tall man explain something in what sounded like Gola, one of the local languages. As soon as he saw the visitors he stopped and asked if he could help.

'We are looking for St.Aloysius church,' Gloria said. 'Just the directions to get there. Oh, and a look at your baptismal registers, if you still have them.'

The tall man turned out to be the catechist and when he heard who they were he took them into the house and brought out the registers, which had survived the war by being first buried in a hole at the back of the house along with the church silver, which was actually mostly tin, and then taken to Monrovia for safe keeping. Gloria told him they were looking for an Aloysius baptised seven or eight years ago and sure enough after a ten minute search among the hundreds of names – they did seem to baptise a lot of people here – they found an Aloysius Cooper, son of John and Fatima Cooper.

Even Moses looked a bit excited and they asked where the family were now. The catechist made a face Gloria couldn't interpret and then said he had no idea.

'The war disrupted everything here, Inspector, and to be honest it sometimes feels as if the war is still on. Fr. Garman' – his tone and the slight curling of his lips told her that he did not approve of Fr. Garman – 'baptised hundreds of people. Most of them stopped coming to church when the food stopped or they moved out of the area. I have only been here for two years' – he made it sound like a prison sentence – 'so I don't know the family you are looking for.'

'What about your group there, would they know anything?'

He looked at the small group of people with contempt. 'They know nothing, they were baptised years ago and still have no idea what being a member of this church means.'

Eventually he gave them directions to Gbaybo community where, as far as he could tell, the church of St.Aloysius had been built but warned them not to expect too much. Fr. Garman – again that tone of voice – had built hundreds of little chapels, many of them had never been completed and most of them were not in use any more. He had never visited that one himself.

'Someone's happy in their work,' remarked Moses as they drove away.

'Those poor people, imagine being frowned on by him.'

'I would say 'poor Fr. Garman', whoever he is. If he ever puts a foot wrong that cat. . .'

'Catechist.'

'That catechist will have him strung up.' He tried to imitate the catechist's nasal tone. 'I myself have never visited that one.' They laughed, relieved to be away from the oppressive atmosphere of the mission.

They followed his directions and drove out of town. Within twenty minutes they were turning off the road past the deserted sugar cane factory and onto a narrow track which took them over a precarious three-plank bridge and past a handwritten sign pinned to a tree which said 'Gbaybo community.' Around a bend they could see a clearing straight ahead and suddenly they were in a wide open space surrounded by. . . nothing. Closer inspection revealed the remains of buildings around the clearing, but all completely overgrown. No-one lived here now and it looked as if there had been no-one here for a long time.

It had clearly been a modest-sized community and moderately thriving. There was a rusty 'Pharmacy' sign and a track leading to a group of burnt-out school buildings behind the village. Now there was nothing. At the far end of the village some of the bigger houses, maybe the chief's house, had some walls standing and the ubiquitous blue tarpaulin indicated that someone still lived here. They approached quietly listening for any sounds and they could hear the mutter of conversation and some music playing. Gloria looked through the space where the window had been and in the dim bluish light she saw some figures sitting on the floor. There were five teenagers sitting or sprawled out on the broken cement. An old cassette player that looked as if it may have belonged to the original inhabitants of the house, was playing some song she remembered from her childhood. 'Green Revolution' – the name of the song popped into her head. And the name of the singer followed, Francis Varney Kanneh. This was real old-time Liberian music. Where was Kanneh now she wondered? If alive, did he know his music lived on in a remote part of Bomi County?

The teenagers looked neither surprised nor interested in either the music or these strangers who had turned up. The smell of marijuana was thick in the air. Gloria could feel it catching at the back of her throat, and it was obviously part of the reason why the boys were just vacantly staring up at them. Two of them had the familiar rebel matted dreadlocks and they were dressed in filthy t-shirts and shorts. They didn't look more than fourteen or fifteen years old. It was obvious they were some of the flotsam left washed-up after being disarmed or demobilised, or having just slipped away. Who knows why they were living here? Maybe they didn't want all the rigours of settling back into society or maybe they were scared of local people or their fellow former fighters. Moses asked for their names but there was no answer so he switched the tape player off and repeated the question in a loud voice. That got their attention and the one lying nearest the tape player grinned and said he was General Executive Killer. The others laughed but before they could say anything Moses butted in loudly.

'Right that's it. On your feet all of you. Now.' He was growling now and even Gloria thought he looked quite ferocious. 'I want your real names, don't you guys know the war is over? You should stop this nonsense before it gets you into more trouble.'

The boys stood up awkwardly, half to attention, half slouching. They turned out to be two Samuels, a Togba, a Tamba and a Varney. They had found the place a few weeks before having passed through the bush to escape the official demobilisation sites. They had no answers to any of Moses questions about the community or who had lived there. When they arrived the village was empty.

'All the scary old people run away-o, no-one can stop us.' The others giggled at Samuel, alias General Executive Killer. 'We chakla the whole area during the war, it will stay long before these people come back here.'

Gloria could see Moses clench his fists but she knew he wouldn't do anything stupid. Whether they knew it or not these children were victims almost as much as the people they had terrorised. She took out the photo of Aloysius but although they were interested in looking at the dead body they had no idea who he was.

'I'm telling you old ma this whole place is fini, no children here, no women here, no nobody.'

They didn't even know what the place was called, never mind the name of some anonymous dead child. Gloria knew it had been a long shot to come here but she still felt disappointed. She was sure this was Aloysius's village, a place where he had been happy, and now it was just another forgotten corner.

In a sudden mood swing the same Samuel volunteered to show them around. Further on from the Chief's house he led them to a small building that had obviously been the church. Part of the roof and the walls were still intact and although the rough cement floor had sprouted weeds it was still by far the most complete building in the village.

'Why don't you stay in here?' Gloria asked him. 'This place will keep the rain out and the sun off you better than that old tarpaulin.'

Samuel just pointed to a large wooden cross hanging by a few nails to the far wall and a pile of old hymn books in a corner. They were reminders of what it had been and that was enough to scare off these tough teenagers.

Apart from that there was nothing much else to see and if the boys were telling the truth, there were no original villagers they could ask. Gloria thumbed the picture of the child she carried in her pocket and felt a little foolish. What had they expected to find after eight years of war and destruction? But she also felt another wave of emotion hit her, realising that this was where Aloysius had grown up. He was a real person whose life had been taken away from him.

She wrote out her details for Samuel but saw the paper fall out of his pocket as he turned to walk back to the house.

'Should we call in on the police and ask them to keep an eye open for us?'

Moses shrugged. 'I don't think anyone is coming back here boss. There is nothing left. And the only thing the police would do is come and harass those boys. I think it's better to leave them in peace.'

'Even General Executive Killer?'

'Yes, even the General.' Moses gave one of his sighs. 'Poor kids haven't got a chance.'

Gloria started the car before Moses could get back onto the subject of the failings of the international community. They were quiet for the first half of the journey back.

'It's easy to forget how a lot of those communities have been uprooted or spoiled boss, isn't it?' Moses said, breaking the silence. 'I mean in Monrovia we just moved back to our old house, fixed it up and got on with life again. I don't know what they are going to do up here and it must be the same in Lofa, Nimba and all those areas.'

Gloria thought about it. 'Well for a start half the people from up country are still living in Monrovia, aren't they. We've got an over-crowded capital and an empty interior. What a mess.'

'And ideal conditions for a murderer, whole communities displaced, families killed, people forgotten or missing. Lord knows what's going on out there that we don't even know about.'

'But we do know about this one Moses, and now we have his name and his family's name as well. So today has actually been quite successful.'

She dropped Moses home and then, deciding she couldn't stand going back to an empty apartment, she thought she would call in on her mother. It had been a long time since she had been to visit and she could spare an hour. In the end she spent the rest of Saturday with her mother and various other members of the family. They still lived in and around the home she grew up in at Westpoint and although it was just down the hill from her apartment it was a different world.

It was a world she always enjoyed visiting, safe in the knowledge she would never have to live there again. She liked the fact that although she was in the police and now lived in the good part of town, she could still count herself and be accepted as part of the Westpoint community. Westpoint had an image and a mythology all of its own, part warm-hearted, lively sprawling slum, part dangerous 'don't go alone' territory. But if you were born there you belonged there and no matter how far away you moved Westpoint would always extend to you its strong, slightly grimy, embrace.

On a steamy Saturday afternoon it was a relief to squeeze onto the tiny porch along with numerous family, neighbours and friends to eat jollof rice and share the Club beers she had brought along. Nobody asked about her work. That way they could ignore the fact she worked for the police, which was still a source of some embarrassment to the family, and instead she could just fade into the background and soak up the stories, the jokes and the news from the week.

It sounded as if it had been a good news week in Westpoint. One of the neighbours had accused her chicken of stealing five hundred Liberian dollars and had it arrested. It was now in custody. In a statement to the police, she said she saw the chicken going out the door with the bundle of money under its wing, her aunt was telling everyone, and although they were all laughing she would have bet half of them were only laughing because the chicken had got caught and not at the notion of there being such a thing as a thief chicken.

One of the neighbours asked Gloria when she was going to get married. She thought it was a bit rich considering no-one else, not even her own parents or the neighbour who asked the question, were married. But she gave her stock reply. 'When I meet the right man. Weddings are dangerous, you know.' The neighbour agreed and, as if on cue, launched into a long story about her niece's wedding being cancelled because the caterer had run off with the money and the bride's sister. There was a moment of silent head-shaking then before her cousin said something about a shelter for street children collapsing two nights previously.

Westpoint was a narrow strip of land jutting into the water and erosion was a daily reality. Apparently the encroaching water had undermined the foundations of the building and the children had got out just in time. Gloria only knew of one organisation working in Westpoint, the St. Luke's shelter, and she had some good contacts there. She was sure she would have heard if it had collapsed.

Her cousin Flomo, a big brawny lad of twenty or so, told her this shelter had only opened a month ago to cater to the children who slept on the beach.

'It was soon after one of your people beat that boy to death on the beach.'

By 'one of your people' Flomo meant the police but it was true unfortunately. The children worked with the fishermen by day or night, hauling in the nets and collecting the fish, and spent the rest of the time in the video clubs and the market.

'The police used to harass those pekins at night on the beach and take their small money off them. The new shelter opened soon after that boy died.'

'Yes, that was bad,' agreed Gloria.

'Well it collapsed a few days ago. People are laughing because they say those crazy pekins destroyed the place themselves, they knocked their own house down.' Flomo found this very funny and had to stop talking.

'What do you mean?' Gloria asked.

'The room next to the shelter was a bakery and they would fix the bread at night. Can you imagine those gronna boys lying in the dark smelling the bread next door? They even started calling the place the 'Smell No Taste Center'. One night they tried to dig under the wall to get at the bread and the whole thing fell down.'

Gloria shuddered at the thought of a bakery stuck between Westpoint's dirty beach on one side and a mob of street children on the other.

'What happened to the children?'

'Oh they moved them somewhere else.' Flomo clearly wasn't too interested in those details and Gloria did not like not knowing. She would have to do some investigation here. Who were these people anyway? She wondered if any of her team had been to visit them to ask about Aloysius.

Flomo walked with her back along the road to her car. It was dark and quiet beyond the houses but another good thing about being a resident, or former resident, was that no-one would dare touch you or your car no matter how long you left it and everyone knew the red Polo was Gloria's.

'Look Flomo, find out everything you can about that shelter and the people who run it and let me know, eh.'

'Sure, no problem, Gloria.' Flomo was out of work at the

moment, in fact he had been out of work since leaving school, but he was a great source of local information. 'I'll ask around tomorrow and let you know.'

Reluctantly she invited him to come by the apartment tomorrow night. He and Abu were close but she knew Flomo had his eye on the spare bed in Abu's room and she had steadfastly resisted taking in any more of her family – something she was frequently criticised for. The fact that she and Abu alone shared a two bed apartment really annoyed a lot of her extended family.

'You are too kwi now Gloria, too white. It's not correct.' She heard this every time she refused the offer of some distant relative to come and cook for her or wash her clothes. But Gloria shrugged off accusations that she had become too western in her ways. If her family had their way they would have had every second cousin and brother's niece living with her, cluttering up the apartment and expecting to be sent to school or set up in business. Yes, family was great but here they really needed to be kept in their place – which as far as Gloria was concerned was about two miles from her apartment.

When she reached home she closed the front door behind her and took a deep breath, relishing again the cool breeze, the space and the quiet. She enjoyed it even more after the noise and heat of a family gathering. The bar down the hill was doing good business, mostly the ex-pats out frantically determined to have a good time, convinced they deserved it after all their labours of the week. Even from this distance she could hear the music of the latest Western boy band pouring out – no Francis Varney Kanneh for them – and the loud laughter of Monrovia's new aristocracy. Crowds of young, self confident foreigners who controlled money and exerted an influence they would never have been allowed in their own countries. It was they who decided where the clinics would be opened or whether the people of this place or that place needed a new road. It was they who introduced the new language you had to speak in order to get a good job or support for your project, obscure things like 'log frames' and 'periodic stability indicator tests.' And it was they who left after a few months or a few years for a new and more interesting assignment in someone else's civil war or famine.

She pulled herself up mentally. 'Whoa, some of these are good people,' she thought. She knew many of them and appreciated that a lot of them put themselves in danger to help others but the memory of Tubmanburg, and all those young people abandoned there, riled her immensely. Especially since the NGOs were claiming the demobilization exercise had been a great success. But apart from that she remembered the description the rock gang had given her of a tall individual with a strange accent. Could one of these agency workers be involved in the death of Aloysius? They were not all angels sent to help and, if they were so minded, were ideally placed for dodgy dealings of all kinds. Access to government, routes in and out the country, money and influence.

No, she didn't really think that was likely but her thoughts continued to wander back and forth around the fragments of this murder jigsaw. Here she was on day three, or was it four, and not much further forward. She had inspected some wiring at the Mansion, talked to a gang who lived in caves under the American Embassy and spent half a day in a ruined community in the company of a disgruntled catechist and a few teenage rebels. It didn't really add up to very much. She knew if she continued thinking like this she would not get any sleep so she pushed those thoughts away and reminded herself that at least they now knew the boy's name and where he came from. That was a start. And with that scrap of positivity she went off to sleep.

Sunday passed quickly. Flomo dropped by and filled her in on what he knew about the shelter and the people running it which wasn't much. It was run by volunteers from abroad and they were never seen in the community. That was as much as he knew.

By late afternoon they were waiting for Abu to return and fill the place with his stories of triumph or noble defeat. But it was after eight before she heard him clatter up the stairs and burst in. He was positively glowing with success.

'It was great, Aunt Glo, we won all our games. I scored three times and I was Man of the Match.' He showed her a tiny trophy.

'So, no accidents then?'

'Accidents?' The thought of accidents had obviously not occurred to him. 'No, it was fine, the bus broke down coming back, that's all.' And, most importantly, he had obviously been restored to his former position of respect.

'It was the best birthday ever,' he remembered to add, and then he and Flomo got lost in a description of games played, goals scored and future plans for the team.

It was after ten when she suggested it might be time for Flomo to go home. Yes, she assured him, as a police officer she was sure it would be safe for him to make his way back to Westpoint at that time of night, and she pointed out the many food stalls and small shops, the video clubs and the bars which were still doing a roaring trade up and down the road. Far from being a lonely walk home, as he described it, he would have to elbow his way through the crowds!

With Flomo, and his technical audience, gone, Abu seemed to deflate about three sizes. Two nights with no sleep and some tough games began to take their toll and finally, conceding defeat, he went off to bed. Gloria saw him hesitate at the door to his room and in anticipation of his question quickly shouted after him, 'Yes, you are going to school tomorrow.'

Abu grinned. 'What a detective you are, Aunt Glo. But really, I am too tired now.'

'If you're ever going to finish high school before your thirtieth birthday,' she told him, 'you'll need to speed up, so go and sleep.'

He didn't argue anymore and instead stumbled off only to reappear a few seconds later. She thought he was coming with a new argument as to why he needed to stay home from school but before she could speak he produced a large pineapple from behind his back.

'A gift from Harbel, Aunt Glo.'

Over a breakfast of fresh pineapple the next morning Abu was on another tack altogether. Out of the blue, he asked her if she had heard about the 'heart men' who were now active in Harbel. 'Heart men' were a long established part of Liberian society and still managed to instil terror wherever the subject came up. The kidnapping of children and the extraction of their organs for various rituals was not something she would normally have cared to discuss at breakfast but she was curious what the connection was.

Abu was in full swing. 'They found two bodies, Aunt Glo, right on the edge of the rubber plantation. They had been missing for a day and a night and when they found the bodies, their throats had been cut.' He made a cutting gesture with his hand. 'But the surprising thing is they hadn't been cut open, no organs had been taken.' He shrugged. 'Maybe someone saw them and they ran away, I don't know. But we were scared. The people told us we shouldn't even sit on the porch at night so we stayed inside.' He groaned. 'The heat was too bad. Nobody slept.'

She stopped him there as she realised this story could go on a long time and also because the obvious connections to

Aloysius were making her excited that it might be a lead, and terrified at the thought that Abu had been so close to it again. She packed him off to school and then sat down to finish her coffee. More gruesome murders and the geographical spread was widening from Bomi all the way to Harbel. This didn't feel good at all, especially not on a Monday morning.

7.

GLORIA knew if she went to the office she would get caught up in the usual Monday madness. There would be the weekend's activities to catch up on, office politics, promotions and demotions, and the tedious planning process for the week which effectively reduced their work time by several hours. She called Moses, explained what Abu had told her and said he should organise the team for the day. She would collect young Paul Doe and take him with her out to Harbel. Moses clearly would have preferred to go with her but understood that wasn't possible. He agreed to send Paul and promised to catch up with her in the evening.

By the time she managed to collect Paul it was already nine-thirty, the traffic on Tubman Boulevard was at a standstill and the road was shimmering in the sun. Even with the air conditioning on the glare and the heat seemed to seep into the car. Paul was fiddling with the radio and was pleased with himself when he found a music station. He turned up the volume and then relaxed back in the seat.

Gloria looked over at him. 'Hey this isn't a school outing. While I'm driving you can read through those papers.' She pointed to the pile of papers she had managed to collect on Harbel. 'And also the newspaper cuttings about the activities of the so-called heart men.'

Once they were past Twelfth Street the traffic eased up and with only a slight decrease in speed at Red Light, where the market seemed to be winning the battle for control of the road, they were soon on the Robertsfield highway. It seemed cooler, whether it was the wide road or the glimpses of the sea to their right she didn't know but it was much less stressful.

Paul had been steadily reading through the newspaper cuttings and the other information she had given him. She was surprised to hear him laughing.

'What's so funny about heart men?'

'It's this,' he pointed at the paper he was reading, 'it's mine.'

Gloria shook her head.

'I wrote this paper when I was at university, I was really interested in heart men.'

Gloria knew that Paul had attended university – he made a point of telling everyone at every opportunity – but not that he might be the nearest thing to an expert they had. She was pleased then when he observed that the pattern of killings associated with heart men was completely different to these murders. This confirmed her belief that this was no upsurge in ritual murder but either a random killing or somehow directly linked to the killing on the beach.

Harbel soon came into view but on the outskirts of the town they came up against a homemade checkpoint, a long rope stretched across the road. These kind of 'gates', as they were known, were not unusual but nowadays they were generally manned by groups of children trying to earn some money by repairing the road – repairs they often dug up again in between cars. The group on this one though looked like a throwback to the war, teenagers with bandanas on their heads and serious attitude. She was relieved to see they didn't have any guns, at least not on display, but the threatening behaviour was very familiar and she could see two cutlasses on the grass by the side of the road. As they slowed down to avoid driving into the rope, Paul wound down the window and started talking to them quickly and aggressively, his genial persona completely transformed.

'Hey pekin, wha happen here. Tha your checkpoint is embarrassing us, move it.'

His Liberian English was rapid and he sounded very angry. The reaction was instant. Their heads went down, their attitude disappeared and instead of bold young fighters they were just ragged teenagers. The smallest one unhooked one end of the rope, dropped it and Gloria drove through. She gave them a wave but their eyes were on the ground. When she looked at Paul he was laughing, good humour restored.

'Well, commander, you showed them who the boss was. That's not your old unit is it?'

He just laughed and explained he had been in Harbel with his family during the war and that he had got to know the fighters and their commanders very well. She could believe that. It was a feature of the war that, in amongst the harassment, stealing and senseless killing, fighters and locals often developed a kind of uneasy truce. It was much harder for the boys to behave too outrageously towards people they knew and spoke to every day.

Their commanders knew this of course and they worked really hard at alienating them from their families and communities by feeding them drugs, encouraging terrible acts of violence. At the same time they were cultivating a huge sense of guilt and shame among the boys so that they felt they would never be able to go back home to their families. But in Liberia cutting off all personal contact was impossible and many of the fighters, after their initial attacks on a town or village, developed a relationship with the locals where they were sometimes the conquerors and at other times young boys not daring to disobey their elders.

Paul confirmed that the boys were the ragged end of the group of fighters who had overrun the area and harassed the local population for years.

'I'm surprised they dare to carry on like that still. Why do the locals not deal with them?' It had happened in other places. She told Paul about the boys they had met on Saturday.

'They're still bluffing about what they did in the war but actually living in an isolated uninhabited village. But these are right on the road using their same old tactics.'

'Ah, but these boys,' Paul reminded her, 'had been, or still are, nobody's completely sure, members of the IFLL.' Yes indeed, Gloria did remember. The Independent Fighters for the Liberty of Liberia had been one of the most infamous factions during the war. They had acquired a reputation for violence even among the other factions, partly because their leader, Prince Julu, had specialised in the taking and training of very young children. The Small Soldier Units (SSU) had spread fear wherever they went and after the war officially ended they were the most difficult to rehabilitate. In fact she knew that a number of organisations had unofficially given up on them, claiming the specialist support needed to work with these very damaged children, and the community support to integrate them, was just not available. Officially, the reports would tell you that the rehabilitation process had been largely successful but everyone knew that most of these children had been more or less 'bribed' with money, a mattress and some rice to disappear back home. Now they were beginning to see the results, the drift back to the towns of untamed and alienated teenagers.

It wasn't made any easier by the fact that Prince Julu had managed to rehabilitate his own image and transform himself into a respectable politician. His appointment as the new Minister of Defence a few months ago initially caused an uproar but, as no-one wanted to actually put themselves in the spotlight by criticising him, the attacks on his appointment had all been from anonymous sources which weakened their credibility. It wasn't long, even for Liberia's famously short collective memory, before his appointment was being hailed as a brilliant tactical move to preserve unity in the country. He was now talked about as the 'strong man' or the 'real soldier' the country needed to renew and unite the armed forces and defend their borders.

That would explain why the boys were still allowed, or at least tolerated, to operate their makeshift checkpoints. As long as they didn't resort to violence she presumed. It didn't explain completely why Paul was so swiftly able to disarm them but she stored that away as another insight into her new team, along with his revelation that he had a special interest in heart men.

They decided to start the visit by going to the local police and talking to the officers who were leading the investigation into the recent murders. The Harbel police station was in surprisingly good condition. It was a small neat brick building with flowers growing in tidy beds outside and wooden seats under a cool porch. It was so unlike any other police station she had come across that both she and Paul stared at it for a few seconds.

'Built by the company,' Paul said to her.

She knew, of course, that the rubber plantation here in Harbel which once laid claim to producing the highest quality rubber and latex in the world, had been responsible for Harbel's infrastructure, but seeing the smart police station directly linked to big business made her very uneasy. How much freedom of operation would these police have? Or were they just here to keep the local population in order so that production was not disrupted?

Inside the station the officer behind the desk seemed to be expecting them and greeted them as if they were visiting dignitaries. This was so different from the normal Liberian reaction to visiting officialdom, which might range from indifference to complete insolence, that Gloria began to suspect her visit, even at such short notice, was going to be very carefully managed.

They were taken through to the back office where the two officers who had carried out the investigation on the children were sitting waiting. Again the welcome they were given and the accompanying courtesies were so different from the normal that Gloria began to feel they were in some kind of rehearsed drama where everyone knew their lines and their role, everyone except her and Paul.

'Inspector Gloria,' the first officer launched into immediately, 'we are very happy to have you visit with us today and thank you for showing an interest in these terrible murders. We really appreciate any help you can give us.'

Gloria blinked again. She really would have been much more comfortable with the hostility she had expected, as the city police interfering in the business of their country cousins. That or complete indifference but not this courteous pulling of chairs and placing of files and reports in front of them. When they brought in the coffee, which she was really in need of, she knew this was a set-up. She had never been offered coffee before, never. Not only was the visit arranged but they had obviously researched her in detail, right down to her preferred choice of beverage.

While all this activity was going on the same officer, who hadn't actually introduced himself, continued talking.

'Someone came to my house early in the morning. It was one of the rubber tappers who was on his way to work. He said he had been hurrying on the road when he saw something in the ditch and when he went over he saw the two bodies. We' – he pointed at the officer next to him – 'went straight there and just as he had said there were two bodies together in a ditch at the side of the road. Both had had their throats cut and there were some signs they had been tortured. It didn't take us long to identify them because family and neighbours had been out looking for them the previous day. They were neighbours apparently but not particularly close friends and they had gone missing the night before. They had both been sent down to the shop for bread and cigarettes between seven and eight o'clock and hadn't come back. The families had started looking for them a couple of hours later after they were convinced they hadn't just run off to play. The search had been called off late that night and the families claimed to have spent the night praying and worrying. Apparently they hadn't thought of reporting it to us' – few people reported things to the police, the police in the Liberian mind were there to solve crimes not to help in preventing them or to co-ordinate search parties for missing children – 'and now the whole area is afraid.'

The officer then spread some glossy photos on the desk in front of him, as if in conclusion, and sat back.

Gloria listened closely without a word and realised the recital, for that's how it sounded, had finished for the time being. She looked at the pictures in front of her and frowned. They were the colour originals of the photos which had appeared in the newspaper and for Gloria that was a serious breach of procedure.

'So what do you know about these boys and their families?'

There was a pause and the second officer shrugged and mumbled something vague about them being ordinary people, 'nothing special' was the phrase she thought she heard.

'You say they were neighbours, so had they lived in that community a long time?'

'No they were people who came here during the war and just stayed,' the first officer said. 'They live in some old rubber tappers' houses at the far end of the plantation. Why? Do you think there's some connection between these two boys and your body on the beach?'

Gloria made a non-committal motion with her head and asked them if there was any chance they could see the crime scene and bodies. Both officers jumped up as if on cue and started to the door.

'You can just follow us and we'll go straight to the hospital.'

With that they were out the door. Despite all the apparent co-operation Gloria knew they were being told nothing they couldn't read in any newspaper, or pick up from the local gossip.

Paul was quiet when they got into the car. 'Don't bother speeding behind them ma' he said to her. 'I know where the hospital is. And those two are treating us as if we know nothing.'

'Oh, you noticed as well,' Gloria said, 'but why go through the motions, why not just refuse to meet us or even tell us we have no jurisdiction here?'

'Oh that's easy,' Paul chimed in, 'the one doing all the talking is the new commander here although he didn't bother telling us that. He is Sampson Moore. He was Prince Julu's second in command here during the war. He has been told he needs to be 'exemplary' in his behaviour now, so that's why he's being so co-operative, but he also knows his first loyalty is to Julu – and Julu's being paid by the rubber company, everybody knows that. He has to treat you properly but at the same time he's telling us nothing that might upset his boss.'

And by 'boss' Gloria knew that Paul didn't mean the Director of Police in Monrovia.

She nodded, impressed again by Paul's knowledge and insight. She did wonder though exactly what he had been doing during the war here. It didn't sound as if it had been the typical displaced person's experience.

She drove deliberately slowly so that the officers who had sped off had to slow down so as not to lose them. Gloria sped up a little and then slowed down again, setting the pace even from the back. Liberia was all about power, everyone wanted it and everyone exercised it in some way or other. Her little game with the car was just that, letting them know she was not dependent on them for directions and in a wider sense for solving the killings. Let them continue with the drama they had rehearsed, she was going to change the script.

They arrived at the hospital at the same time as the officers. Sampson Moore and his colleague gave no sign they had even noticed what was going on.

'It's this way,' Moore said very politely and held open the door for her.

Harbel hospital reminded her of the police station. It was a low, brick building with verandas and flowers in front. It was conspicuously clean, no dust or dead cockroaches, no missing panes of glass or broken ceiling tiles. There were even curtains at the windows and nurses in smart uniforms. She had no idea how good the medical services were here but she suspected they were on a par with the décor.

The morgue was very small but as there were no fees to pay there were very few bodies left unclaimed. The two bodies had been brought out in preparation for them and the officers waited outside. It didn't take long for Gloria to see these were just two ordinary kids. Although older than Aloysius they looked younger, smaller and less well fed. Their bodies had all the scrapes and cuts of children who grow up in a rural community and except for the burn marks on their hands and the line of dried blood where their throats had been cut they didn't look anything like Aloysius.

'Was there anything in their hands when they were found?' She felt silly asking the attendant the question.

'Their hands no, but they each had one of these in their mouths.'

And he showed them what at first looked like the little diamond they had found in Aloysius's hand but which, on closer inspection, turned out to be just a glass bead. She rubbed the bead and then held it up to the window where it caught the light.

'Did you show these to the officers?'

'Of course, madam, but they said it wasn't important and to throw them away.'

'But you didn't throw them away. Why did you keep them?'

'It's part of my job to keep all the evidence even if the police are not interested. These beads were put in the children's mouths, that has to mean something.' His facial expression hadn't changed but she got the message. The local police, despite the nice uniforms and neat police station, were not to be trusted.

'Good job. Can I take one with me?'

'Of course, madam, they should be police property, not mine.'

She put them in her pocket while Paul took photos of the bodies and then they left.

'So what do you think, Paul?' They were standing in the corridor while doctors and nurses moved around them with quiet efficiency. Gloria found it a little unnerving.

'Well ma'am we have Aloysius who is from a good family, as far as we can tell. He is tortured and killed but the killers say some prayers for him and leave him with a very expensive diamond. These two children are from poor families. They are also tortured and killed but their bodies are just abandoned in a ditch and instead of a diamond they have a glass bead put in their mouths.'

'Good summary, but what does it mean?'

'Well ma'am,' he looked a bit nervous but rushed on, 'my opinion would be that the murders were committed by the same people but these ones are like a cheap imitation of Aloysius's killing. Maybe the killers are mocking us or they are sending a message to someone else.'

'Good thinking. But it leaves us with more questions. If they are mocking us then we need to know why. If they are sending a message then what is the message and who is it intended for.'

'Eh?' Paul was frowning. 'But what kind of people kill children just to send a message? That is really horrible.'

Gloria agreed. It felt like a different kind of violence to what they were used to. This violence was cool and efficient – a bit like this hospital, she thought and shivered.

'Come on, let's get out of here.'

As they left she could see that Paul was upset and she began to warm to him. He had proved to be very helpful on this trip so far and was obviously someone with good observation and reasoning skills as well as quite a lot of life experience. Actually, she thought to herself, he is exactly the kind of person international NGOs were looking for. She wondered why he had chosen the police as a career. Gloria really believed that being in the police was a good place to start to make things better in society, or at least to stop it getting worse. Despite Liberia's obvious failings and massive problems, she still believed it had a good future. It was a bit like her family – loud, often unreasonable and insensitive, but she still loved them. Maybe Paul was similarly optimistic. She didn't know but she would certainly keep an eye on him.

Their colleagues were waiting for them on the veranda.

'I hope it hasn't been a waste of time' Sampson said, although his tone said otherwise.

'No, it's been really helpful,' replied Gloria. 'I think we have learnt a lot. At least we can be pretty sure it's not heart men, so we can cross that off the list.' She paused and took in his expression. 'It was probably some locals, or maybe someone killed them for the bread or cigarettes, some people are that desperate now. Like those ex-fighters we saw on that checkpoint on the way in, Paul. No money, no future, frustrated and angry. It could happen so easily.'

For the first time that day she saw Sampson's mask slide a little. He stiffened. Whether it was the reference to his former young comrades or the fact that she had seen they were still operating illegal checkpoints on his territory she wasn't sure. But the point was made.

'I'll just take a look at their homes,' Gloria said. 'and then we'll be on our way. Don't worry' – she had caught Sampson's expression – 'Paul here knows the area well so we'll manage on our own.'

Sampson gave Paul a look. 'Maybe he knew the area well but places can change very quickly. You know the proverb Inspector, He who brings in damp firewood must prepare for sand flies. If his information is not accurate you might end up with nothing but sand flies and sand flies can be. . .'

'Irritating, I know.'

'I was going to say dangerous, Inspector. Sand flies can even kill you if there are enough of them. You take care now.'

He gave a salute and walked back to his car where she saw him say something to the other officer who laughed.

Gloria and Paul got into the car and watched as Sampson and his sidekick waved casually and drove away still laughing.

Gloria looked at him. 'Is that even a real proverb? Damp firewood and sand flies?'

'Probably something he heard on the radio. You know people send proverbs into the BBC World Service and they read one out every day but I'm sure half of them are just people having a laugh.'

'And could sand flies kill you? I mean really, could they kill you?'

'I suppose anything could kill you ma'am, if there was enough of it.'

They both laughed. Death by sand flies was a threat they hadn't heard of before now. But something was clear, Sampson and his officers had either carried out a very shoddy investigation or were covering something up and Gloria was reluctant to leave until they had something more than a glass bead to take back with them.

8.

HER PHONE rang as they left the officers behind so she pulled over. It was Moses reporting in, and probably checking she was alright, she thought.

'We tracked down Richard Bennett, ma'am, the British guy who runs the Lost Child of Liberia project.' She could hear Moses had taken a dislike to him. 'Mr. Bennett told us he had never been anywhere in Africa up until last year when he visited a number of poor countries to find somewhere to spend his money. He decided we needed it more than our neighbours so he breezed in with a bag of money, recruited some people and set up his Lost Child project for street children.'

Moses wasn't a big fan of the British at the best of times. He said their politeness and constant smiling was just a mask for their sense of superiority. That wasn't Gloria's experience but it sounded as if Richard Bennett had managed to confirm all of Moses' prejudices.

'How old is he?' she asked him, picturing some retired colonel type.

'Oh I don't know, he talks as if he's about fifty but I think he's only thirty or so.'

Great, she thought, one of the new breed.

'And we've also found another guy who runs some of these shelters. He's called Marcus Drake. His outfit is KVG Inc. It turns out he has been out of the country for the last few weeks and has just got back.'

Gloria remembered Flomo telling her that KVG was the name on the shelter which had been washed away in Westpoint, so that was one of Marcus Drake's.

She told him to get any information he could from them particularly about children disappearing from their shelters.

'Let them know we are not impressed with their record keeping and will go to the Ministry of Social Welfare to follow up if they don't improve.'

She briefed him very quickly on their reception by the local police and their initial findings on the two children, especially the glass beads, but left out the other details Paul had given her on the situation. Sometimes paranoia was a useful tool and she felt it would be better to give him all the details face to face. She did ask him however to set up a meeting with Prince Julu for the next day if possible and, ignoring his groans, told him they would be back in town by early afternoon.

Keeping someone informed about your movements was a habit they had all picked up when the police had been re-formed. In those early days going into any neighbourhood had been a completely unknown quantity. With large numbers of demobilised fighters everywhere, and arms and ammunition sloshing about, any minor dispute could turn into a firefight. It was a habit which had stuck, not so much for security, although there were still a lot of guns around, but because it gave them a sense of being part of a team, of looking out for each other.

'We need to talk to more people,' she said to Paul

'Who?'

'I don't know yet. This is Harbel, you tell me. Who else should we talk to that won't just give us some prearranged speech and then send us home?'

There was silence and then Paul said, 'Well I was surprised

you hadn't asked to see the Commissioner. If anyone should know of anything suspicious going on it should be him. His house is very close to the squatter area where those boys were from so we could call in there.'

Gloria wasn't too hopeful. The Commissioner was even more of a political appointment than the police and she could not imagine him (she was sure it would be a 'him') giving them much useful information. On the other hand she had no intention of driving back to town after being here for only an hour. 'Fine, we'll go there after we've seen the families.'

They drove down further quiet roads, with the rubber plantation on both sides and the occasional glimpse of a little church on a hill, or the noise of a school breaking through the undergrowth. At the central market it was busy but also somehow subdued. There was noise and there were people but it didn't seem to have the same bustle and vigour that Monrovia's markets had. Was it her imagination or did all of this have the feeling of a film set, with all the main characters fluent in their script and all the other people just extras placed there to give some background to the story. She glanced back as they drove through, half expecting to see the market being dismantled or the people wandering off to their real lives, but of course it wasn't like that. She shrugged off these fanciful thoughts and focussed on the road ahead.

A little way out of the town Paul directed her down a track to a group of cottages which looked quite rustic until they got up close and could see the holes in the roofs and cracks in the brick walls. In fact the houses were almost derelict. One good rainy season downpour would probably finish them off altogether. The people standing and sitting outside looked in no better shape than the buildings. Thin, ragged and bowed over, they looked exactly what they were, more debris of the war, washed-up in a strange place with no work, no support and no hope. And now their children had been killed and no-one was taking it seriously.

'Take time with them, Paul. Remember they are victims here, not suspects.' Paul nodded and got out, taking Gloria's words as his cue to lead on the questioning.

Gloria watched as Paul established who the spokespeople were going to be so he could start asking his questions. Unfortunately there were only old people and children in the group and as the old people did not speak English Paul found himself talking with a very shy seven-year-old girl who answered every question with a whispered yes or no. No wonder Sampson and his crew could carry out such a shoddy investigation, these families literally had no voice. After ten minutes Paul looked over at her and she shrugged. They got up to go and the little girl followed them to the car. Gloria found some candy in her pocket and offered it to her.

'Are you a police lady?' Gloria barely heard the whispered question. She crouched down so she was at the same level as the child. She knew she wasn't being fanciful when she saw the fear and the responsibility in the child's eyes. 'Yes, my name is Gloria. What's your name?'

'My name is Famata,' she paused and looked directly at Gloria. 'Auntie, we all scarey for the bad people to come back, the people what kill my brother.'

Gloria took Famata's hand and looked around at the bewildered group of adults and children. 'Don't worry, I will make sure nothing bad happens here again and I promise we will find those bad people and punish them severely.' Her heart sinking even as she made the promise, she asked Famata to translate what she had said for the others. They started clapping.

As they drove out onto the road again they saw the large sign pointing to the Commissioner's Residence.

'It's worth a try,' she said to Paul, but without much

conviction. If the police had prepared for their visit with such attention it was unlikely the Commissioner was going to tell them anything radically different.

'Well, after your promise ma'am, I think we have to talk to him. How are you going to keep those people safe?'

'I don't know yet but those are exactly the people we should be helping.'

As they drove into the residence they couldn't help but notice how grand it was. The house wasn't huge but it was built to impress. Yes, it truly was a 'residence'. Two storeys painted white with a red-tiled roof, it reminded her of the pictures of plantation houses from North Carolina. An interesting design for the Commissioner of an area that included the largest foreign-owned rubber plantation in the country. Since they were not expected, as far as she knew, she decided the best approach was to go straight in before the Commissioner could put a story together. She knocked the front door while opening it and going in. A long dim hallway stretched through the middle of the house with a staircase to the right. It was empty and the rooms on both sides appeared to be empty, in fact the whole house felt empty. Having burst in they now felt unsure what to do next. No-one appeared and no alarms went off. The heavy silence was finally broken by a deep voice from the end of the corridor enquiring if there was some way he could help them. The voice belonged to the Commissioner himself who was standing in the shadows at the end. In response to Gloria's introduction, a tall thin man walked slowly down the long corridor towards them. He ushered them into a small room with drapes pulled against the afternoon sun. In the gloomy light and stifling heat Gloria began to outline their story but only got as far as their arrival in Harbel before John Banks, as he introduced himself, interrupted.

'This is a very sad story, Inspector. The world is truly a wicked place but I'm sure the police will deal with it properly.' He started to get up but stopped when Gloria jumped in.

'It's a sad story, Commissioner, but it's also a criminal story and I'm afraid I don't share your confidence in your police.' She outlined the shoddy investigation, the photos of the dead children which had been leaked to a newspaper, the terrified families of the victims and the general lack of professionalism. 'It is not acceptable.'

'Well that may be your opinion but this is Harbel, Inspector, well out of your territory so I think you need to leave this to your colleagues.' John Banks was looking very uneasy. Paul had never actually seen anyone squirm in a chair before but that was exactly what he was doing.

'Let me put you right on a few things, Commissioner,' Gloria was in full swing now, 'I am in charge of the *National* Family and Child Protection Unit which means I am responsible for investigating anything that happens to children so I will not be leaving this to anyone else.' Gloria didn't bother mentioning that the exact jurisdiction of her unit was still a hot topic of debate between the senate and the senior police management. 'And another thing, the families of the children who were murdered live right behind your house. They are very afraid that something is going to happen to them but I have promised them that they will be safe. Do you hear me Commissioner? I have promised them, and I am leaving that responsibility with you. If anything happens to them, anything at all, I will be back for you.'

Paul fully expected Banks to start blasting at his boss but he made no response. They sat in silence for a few moments and then Banks stood up as the signal for them to leave.

Gloria did not move but was a little thrown by his lack of reaction. He was like a lost soul. She hoped they weren't going to get outside and meet the real John Banks and find they had been talking to a ghost. She tried a different approach.

'Can you tell us anything about those murders Commissioner?'

'Bad people' was his only comment which was no more useful than seven-year-old Famata's answers. After another half hour of the same vague responses Gloria had enough. This shadowy house and shadowy man, both seemed full of sadness. She couldn't see how he was running anything here. They got up to go and on the way out she looked around the room. Her eyes had adjusted to the gloom and she could see it was full of photos and mementos. On the cupboard by the door were all kinds of frames with pictures of groups and individuals, on picnics and at football matches and solemn family meals. She lifted a large frame with a smiling baby in it to make one last attempt at conversation with Banks but she hadn't reckoned on the poor quality furniture. As she lifted the frame the cupboard rocked and she stuck out her hands to save the other pictures knocking one down the back in the process. Banks was now quite animated, urging them to leave but Gloria picked up the frame which had dropped and studied it. It was a simple wooden affair with a faded colour photograph in it. A large group of children were crowded together on a beach but her eye was drawn to the front of the group where, lying stretched out in the sand with a cheeky grin in his face, was Aloysius.

She stopped dead and looked again. It was faded but still clear enough and Banks himself was in the middle of the group, looking strong and laughing.

'That's the boy,' she said excitedly to him, 'that's Aloysius, the boy we have been telling you about.'

For the first time since they had entered the house Banks seemed to come to his senses and she felt he was really in the room with them.

'No, that's my son, that's Benjamin.'

Gloria looked again at the photo. The boy in the picture was wearing a baseball cap so there was a slight shadow on his face but she would have sworn it was him.

'Is Benjamin around, sir?' she asked.

The answer came immediately and unlike his previous half-finished responses to her enquiries this was fully formed and complete.

'Benjamin is with his aunt in Kakata. He is spending the holidays with her.'

Gloria persevered. 'Have you heard from him recently, sir? And what holidays? The holidays finished two weeks ago, all the schools are open.'

He paused, but just for a second, before replying that Benjamin had been sick and was recovering with his aunt and would be back the next week. He didn't seem to be the slightest bit worried that a body bearing a strong resemblance to his son had been found. His 'resigned' air had come back but he was sticking to his story with complete conviction.

'Come on, Inspector,' – it was the first time he had really addressed her – 'how many children of that age look the same or very similar. I am appalled that a boy the same age as my son has been killed like this but it will probably be better not to start looking at every child and seeing your victim.'

Gloria looked at the photo again, but there was a shadow of doubt there now. Was it Aloysius? And Banks seemed so sure his son was safe, telling them he had spoken to him on the phone and that he would be back next week so they could come and check. Maybe she was mistaken after all. Why would a father lie about something like that? She wanted to pursue it but didn't know how.

'Look Inspector, if you are still not sure next week then please come back and meet Benjamin.'

Still somewhat reluctant, Gloria could think of no way to

take the conversation any further so nodded to Paul who had been staring straight ahead as if embarrassed, and they left the house.

'Well, I hope I didn't make it difficult for you,' she launched straight in, the full frustration of the last few days finally hitting her. 'Don't tell me, you know Banks as well and now I've insulted him and all the other men who run this place and you won't be able to come back and do whatever it is you do here, since you seem to be so well known or well informed. I don't care, I have spent the last few days meeting people and going places where everyone talks and nobody tells me what they really know and I am tired of it.'

'He's lying.'

It took her a moment before she understood what Paul had said.

'What?'

'I said he's lying. You really think I care about any of these people here and their secrets and their deals? They are all lying, but him worst of all.'

Gloria decided that the best thing to do would be to drive so she started up the car and as they headed out she asked him to explain.

'I haven't been a policeman for very long but one of the reasons I decided to take this badly-paid, under-appreciated job was because of what happened to me and my family in the two years we lived here as refugees. . . refugees!' He was talking louder now. 'Refugees in our own country, in a place barely twenty miles from where our family home was, where my mother was a member of the church guild and my father had a successful garage. We sat here under the mercy of these people, being polite to boys with no education and lots of attitude, ingratiating ourselves with those commanders who swaggered around taking *anything* they wanted. . .'

He tailed off. Gloria was surprised, partly because she had never heard anyone actually use the word ingratiating before, and partly because Paul seemed like one of the ones who had survived the war by his wits and with his sense of himself intact. Obviously not so.

'Well we've all got our war stories, Paul. I still don't see how that led you to think of joining the police?'

'If I learnt one thing in those two years it was that there have to be rules and there have to be people to make sure we keep the rules. I will never again live in that situation – where my freedom and my life depend on the whim of some ignorant country boy with a gun.'

'Well, it's a good reason although I would never say 'never'. This is Liberia and we all had to do things to survive – and I don't hear anyone else talking about those things in the office, do you?' It was the unspoken agreement in most places that apart from the occasional reference or joke the war was not spoken about.

'Anyway,' Paul went on, 'that guy is lying and that makes him worse than all the others. They are thugs and criminals, I don't care how fancy their uniforms are, but he is someone's father and he's lying about that.'

'So you think that was Aloysius in the photo'

'Of course it was him.'

Gloria couldn't decide whether to feel proud she had noticed the picture in the dark room or embarrassed she had let herself be convinced by Banks.

'But why would he lie about it, his own son, lying dead on a beach?'

'Whatever he said to us he knows that's his son and he knows that he's dead. Look at the house, silent and dark. And where are all the other children and his wife? Whatever is causing him to lie, it must be something more than money or to keep his job. What could be serious enough to make him sacrifice his son?'

'Maybe his other children and his wife,' said Gloria. 'We need to get back to town anyway. It will give me some time to try and think this through.'

Their return was delayed a little as Paul persuaded her to stop at his mother's house on the way out. Although she was impatient to get on the road she felt she couldn't ignore his mother, especially after what Paul had shared. He explained that his father had died at the start of the war – shot by a neighbour who owed him money – and his mother, reduced from the vigorous, strong woman she was before the war, couldn't face moving back and starting again in the ruins of their old home. She decided to stay on in Harbel with her married daughter. It was familiar and she felt safe.

As it turned out, Paul's sister lived in one of the company houses, small but a decent enough place. Although she greeted Paul quietly it was clear his mother was truly delighted to see him. She was only in her fifties but the war had taken its toll on her, making her look much older. But she seemed healthy enough and bustled about making them comfortable and insisting they eat the food she had prepared. It was fried fish served with boiled cassava and Gloria found her mouth watering at the smell. The tensions and frustrations of the day had knotted her stomach. Although she was no further forward, and in fact their investigation seemed to be growing darker and darker, she felt herself relax as they sat outside in the late afternoon heat and ate the delicious food. Paul must have told his mother about her love for coffee because she was given a strong smooth coffee in a very dainty cup and saucer. It was delicious and, ignoring Paul's comments about the madness of drinking hot drinks in the heat, she sipped it. It was a smooth taste with just a hint of bitterness but she didn't recognise it. Rwandan maybe?

'Rwandan coffee out here,' Paul's mother laughed, 'it's actually Liberian coffee, Inspector. Grown and prepared here.

Gloria had heard of Liberian coffee of course but, as far as she knew, she had never tasted it before. It was lovely. This surprise discovery delighted her, both that it was Liberian and that she would be able to buy it much more easily now. Although she thought 'smooth with a hint of bitterness' was the exact opposite of Liberia, it was still a good drink.

Despite Paul's passionate speech in the car, in true Liberian fashion, the strong feelings seemed to have passed or been put back in their place. The three of them chatted about everything and nothing. The cost of rice in Harbel, the new owners of the plantation (were they Malaysian or Chinese, no-one was sure), an upcoming wedding of one of Paul's cousins – all harmless family gossip and as far from politics, security and the 'old days' as they could get.

The half-hour stop stretched to an hour but finally after many thanks and promises to come back and visit they were able to leave. There was no checkpoint on the road now and she wondered if the boys had gone home for the day or if Sampson Moore had paid them a visit.

'So what did we accomplish today,' she asked Paul before he could get to the radio.

He thought for a moment. 'Well you have let those people know we are watching them and that will hopefully protect the families, that's one good thing. Although we haven't got lots of facts we know there is something wrong. There is a cover up among the police, or Banks is afraid of something. It's not a lot but it has given us some new leads, I think.'

Gloria agreed. There was something very wrong about that situation.

She dropped Paul off at 12th Street telling him to complete his report on the day's events and have it on her desk for tomorrow. He didn't say anything but as she turned the car she heard him tell his friends at a nearby bar that he wouldn't be joining them tonight and laughed at the shouts of 'The old ma on your back-o' that followed him up the street. Yes, the old ma was on their backs, she thought and that's where she would be staying for the foreseeable future.

9.

BACK AT POLICE headquarters the office was empty except for Moses who, as usual, looked as fresh as if he had just woken up. She didn't know how he managed that but she envied him, especially at moments like this when she felt like a wet cloth.

They sat in the conference room with the windows open to catch any breeze there might be. She told Moses all the events of the day, with all the frustrations but leaving out Paul's personal story in the car on the way home. She knew for certain that was not meant to be shared with anyone else and didn't want Paul to regret talking to her. But the more she discussed with Moses what had happened that day the more confused she felt. If this had been a crossword she would still be on clue one down, she thought to herself.

'It feels as if we are getting tiny snippets of information which are useful but we're not really moving on much, or at least not very quickly.'

'Sounds to me as if we are actually getting somewhere boss. We know the child's name and now we have a very definite link with the Commissioner of Harbel and our police colleagues there. Of course there are lots of questions but that means we are making progress.'

Gloria wasn't convinced. 'It's the speed Moses, or the lack of it. At this rate we will still be asking questions this time next year. And I am worried we are only asking the questions the killer wants us to ask.' She looked at Moses' half smile. 'No, it's more than just a feeling Moses. I think this killer is calculating and very sure of himself. We are being manipulated here and I don't like that.'

'Prince Julu.' Moses pronounced it as if it was an answer to a question he'd been asked. Gloria shook her head and waited for him to go on. 'Well you say 'he' and I think you are right. His name keeps coming up. We know he's capable of killing, he's still got interests in Harbel and he's powerful enough to push us around. He'd make a very good criminal mastermind.'

'He is the obvious one. It doesn't give us any reason though, I mean if he's after money then why draw attention to himself. If he's after power I don't see how killing children helps him.'

'Yeah, well maybe he's after both, they usually go together.'

Gloria yawned. 'Ok Moses, enough. I need some sleep if I am ever going to make any sense of this. Let's leave it here for tonight.'

They agreed to meet in the morning at her place and go straight to Julu's office. It was well known he prided himself on being at his desk early, demonstrating some of that army discipline he was famous for, but that after ten he was very difficult to find. In interviews he claimed that he spent a lot of time at the military bases and training camps. He said it was important he was involved in the army re-structuring. A lot of people thought it was more likely he was just ensuring his popularity with the army stayed strong. After all, the army was his power base, the constant unspoken threat he brought to all his negotiations. He really needed to keep them loyal to him.

On the way back home she had three calls. Ron was asking if they could meet up as he was interested in giving any help he could, Luseni needed to brief her urgently, apparently, and finally Sr. Margaret was reminding her that she and Abu were expected at supper that night. She could not remember when that arrangement had been made but there was no point in arguing about it. When she got into the apartment she could hear music from Abu's room so at least she wouldn't have to go and drag him off the practice ground to accompany her to the convent, which may have been difficult. When she called him to come out and told him what they were doing he only put up a token resistance and went off to change. The thought of good food and then all that attention from the nuns was too big an attraction even for a cool teenager like him.

By seven they were at the convent just in time to be greeted by the sisters coming from their prayers. The number of sisters varied every time she visited. There was always one or two of them off at a meeting somewhere in the region and one or two others visiting from other places. No wonder they were always better informed than either her government or the UN. If you wanted to know where the next big conflict was going to break out, or who was going to fall from power, you only had to ask the nuns of Sacred Heart Convent. Sr. Margaret as always was in front and talking. This evening she was wearing what looked like a pair of pyjamas in some very bright African cloth while the others were dressed variously in shorts and t-shirts, loose shapeless dresses made also of African material and a few of the older ones in veils and crosses. She would never have said it out loud but they could really do with a communal make-over, Gloria thought.

Sr. Angie, a middle aged American, had already cornered Abu to find out what the youth were up to these days. She worked with the girls in a number of schools, trying to combat the teenage pregnancy phenomenon which had reached epidemic levels since the war, and she was always looking for more information about what the boys were up to.

'Come on Aboo,' she drawled, 'sit over here.' She patted

the chair beside her. Abu, although a good looking teenager, was extremely shy around girls and did not yet even have a serious girlfriend as far as Gloria knew. However he loved an audience and was happy enough to pass on his opinions at great length in response to Sr. Angie's barrage of questions about what teenagers were thinking and what the pressures and influences on them were. Their flow was interrupted however by Sr. Tony. Tony was short, stocky and opinionated.

'It's all about sex,' she shouted across the room interrupting Angie's flow.

Tony ran a clinic in Westpoint and knew more about sex and talked more about it than anyone else Gloria knew.

'All this prevention stuff is a waste of time,' Sr. Tony said. 'We keep talking at them when what they need is some help to keep safe. They don't live in convents, Angie. They live in those houses full of people crammed together and, if they're lucky, they go to school where there's even more pressure on them to have sex. We need to get real.'

This was clearly a discussion they had had many times and Angie was ready to get back with her arguments when thankfully the conversation was cut short by Sr. Ethelreda, the only Liberian sister in the community. Ethelreda didn't hold with all this talking.

'Y'all mun come eat now my sisters, leave your plenty talking.' Ethelreda went very Liberian in her speech when she wanted to make a point and the others knew it. The table was heaving with food and after a short blessing they all tucked in. Gloria realised from her previous visits that eating was a serious business in the convent and the first moments were a blur of dishes being passed around and expressions of satisfaction at Ethelreda's new rice and vegetables recipe.

The conversation ranged around a variety of topics although, in deference to Abu, clerical gossip, which in Gloria's experience was by far the most interesting, was kept to a minimum. When Abu blurted out that he had found a body on the beach though, the conversation quickly came round to Gloria's present investigation. Aloysius's story, which they had already heard from Sr. Anselm, elicited the usual tuts and outraged clucks around the table but when she told them about her trips to Bomi and Harbel she really caught the sisters' interest. Tony knew for a fact that street children had been disappearing from Westpoint.

'Those children know they can come to the clinic for free but in the last couple of months the numbers have dropped. And as for that Marcus Drake' – she made a face that would have scared stronger people than Gloria – 'he is a real piece of work. I was going to that shelter every week. Those kids were all hungry and scared – no matter what I said they wouldn't talk to me but my nurse said she heard them speaking Kpelle and Gio and she said a lot of them didn't even speak English. I asked Drake one day where the kids came from and the next thing is he tells me my services are not needed any longer!' Tony was not used to being told that obviously.

'He can't stand the sight of me,' she said, 'I'm sure it's some religious thing, you know, Catholics being in league with the devil or something.'

'Maybe he's afraid you're going to steal them away from his church,' Gloria threw in.

'Well that's the strange thing,' Tony went on, 'he is obviously part of some church or other – the title KVG gives it away – but there is nothing religious about the place. It's not there out of tolerance or respect for those kids, it's as if they are not worthy somehow. I saw his face one day when the children were praying and he had such a look of contempt. But more important than that, I asked him about the children who would be there one week and then disappear. He told me they were free to come and go and that was not his business.'

Gloria confirmed that they were asking all the agencies about children disappearing. 'Actually they all say the same thing, they're not really sure but they don't think so. Record-keeping is not a strong point, you know.'

'I'd keep looking, Gloria, if I was you. I don't know the other agencies but Marcus Drake needs investigating even if he's not involved in this crime. Some of these NGO people need to know they can't just come here and do anything they like.' This was one of Tony's recurring themes.

'Unlike us religious people, eh sister?' Gloria sensed Ethelreda's comment was the signal for the start of another well-worn and passionate argument and thought that it was a good time to go.

Abu talked all the way home and his grumbles about having to listen to all the 'old ma's' talking couldn't disguise the fact that he had thoroughly enjoyed the attention and having his opinions taken seriously – because obviously Gloria didn't treat him as an adult. He had only quietened down when Sr. Angie, mistaking his enthusiastic answers for interest in her work, had invited him to join her youth group. The only group Abu was interested in was his football team and the thought of 'sitting around talking about Jesus', as he described it, was not his thing at all.

'But Aunt Glo, what about all these missing pekins, aint that your business?'

Gloria acknowledged it was her business and told him he shouldn't go around talking about finding dead bodies or anything else. She would find out who was responsible but it didn't look good if people thought she was discussing police business at home.

At eight the next morning she and Moses presented themselves – yes, that's what it felt like – at the temporary Ministry of Defence building on Benson Street. The guards on duty were in very smart uniforms and escorted them quickly upstairs to the fourth floor and pointed them towards the Minister's executive secretary. The secretary was a huge woman in a flowing dress of vivid purple and gold with a matching head tie and very conscious of her own importance and authority. She hardly glanced up before telling them imperiously to take a seat and then proceeded to bury her head in her desk and, unless she was psychic, made no attempt to let the minister know they were there. After ten minutes, although she knew it was a losing battle and after Moses had made it clear he wasn't going anywhere near the secretary, Gloria approached the desk and waited for the woman to look up from the bible she was reading. Before she could start what Gloria was sure was going to be a blistering verbal assault, the door behind the secretary's desk opened and out came Prince Julu himself. The secretary's mouth closed without any of the words coming out and Gloria and Moses were ushered into the office.

For a man with a fearsome reputation Prince Julu was unremarkable in appearance to the point where he might be completely overlooked, until he started to speak. His voice was very deep and rumbled out of his mouth slowly but very smoothly. His tone, however, was cold and dismissive.

'So what do you want to see me for? You're not going to lecture me on the behaviour of my' – she noticed the 'my' – 'soldiers are you? You do realise the peace we are enjoying is only possible because of what my' – there it was again – 'men are doing?'

Even though she could sense Moses silently urging her to be calm, Gloria had had enough of being talked to as if she was simply a well-meaning amateur by one set of men after another.

'Is it your men manning the checkpoint on the road into Harbel then? Are they keeping the peace for the neighbours there? And what about the children who have been killed, perhaps they were dangerous spies or traitors and needed to be taught a lesson? So no, Minister, I haven't come to talk to you about your soldiers' behaviour, not today anyway. But I am investigating a murder and I will keep on investigating it until I find out who did the killing and who is covering it up.'

She paused, expecting a tirade but there was only silence for at least a full minute, which is a long time when you are sitting across from someone with the reputation of Prince Julu. When he looked at her his voice had dropped even further so it sounded more than ever like a growl but the coldness had gone from it. Prince Julu sounded worried!

'Inspector' – now he was using her title and it sounded as if he was treating her as an equal – 'I have heard about the murders and I can assure you I am as shocked as you are. With all our faults in Liberia' – which Gloria thought was a generous description of a brutal civil war – 'at least we used to have the reputation that we loved our children. But these killings, so cold and calculating! This is really not good. However I can give you some advice if you like. Don't use these as a test case to prove the effectiveness of your new unit. Go after someone else, there are plenty of other bad things happening to children in this country. Things you might actually be able to do something about.'

Gloria could clearly hear the warning but strangely it sounded as if there was a note of real concern in his voice, as if he was anxious for her. She could feel herself relaxing just a little when his next words threw her completely.

'How's that nephew of yours, Abu isn't it?'

She froze. It was exactly the same feeling when the rebels had come to her house at the start of the war and they had hidden in the roof. That feeling of absolute cold dread, of paralysis, as they listened to them ransacking the house, was exactly what she was experiencing now.

But Julu hadn't finished. 'We are looking for new recruits you know. We need a new army and so many of these boys are too old for school now, wouldn't you say? It wouldn't surprise me if your nephew just disappeared one day and offered his services. Now that he's sixteen he can do that. You might not see him again. . . for a very long time, if ever. Even the training can be dangerous unfortunately. Anything can happen.'

Before she could speak Moses had stood up and was leaning across the Minister's desk. She thought he was actually going to fight him but he stayed calm enough to reply. 'Whoever you are hiding sir, we will find them. You and your damn gangsters are not running this country now, even if you have 'honourable' in front of your name and work from a big office. We know you are nothing but a rebel and sooner or later everyone else will see it as well. And let me tell you. If Abu 'disappears' every officer in the police force from here to Zwedru will be looking for him and we will start the search right here.' He jabbed the desk. 'So you better take time yourself.'

He turned to her and took her by the arm.

'Let's go boss.'

Julu continued sitting in silence. He was expressionless but, ignoring Moses, he looked straight at her.

'Inspector, you have good friends and colleagues but that is not always enough here. Think about what I have said.'

They walked in silence to the car, the guards in their strangely formal uniforms now looking sinister. Once in the car, Moses banged the steering wheel, 'Ay bah, ay bah. . .' She had never heard him use that common expression before. 'He threatened us, he threatened us right to our faces.'

'Well actually he threatened Abu and me, I think, Moses.'

'You know what I mean. The message was clear, stop investigating or something bad is going to happen. So what are we going to do?'

'Well clearly we are not going to stop investigating. We must be getting closer, and it's his boys who are involved, maybe even him. It must be the diamonds. But why are they killing children? Everyone is already scared of them. And what are we going to do about Abu? That wasn't an empty threat.'

By this time Moses was already halfway up Benson Street. He seemed to be back to his usual relaxed self, back in control, but Gloria knew he was thinking back to what had just happened. Speaking to any 'big man' in this town the way Moses had was very dangerous but to a former-rebel-turned-Minister it was almost suicidal. She suspected he might be regretting it and felt she ought to say something but Moses beat her to it.

'I should have beat him,' he said. 'I should have flogged him good and proper right there in his own office. How do they still get away with all this?'

So he wasn't regretting in the way she had thought.

'Moses, thank you. I won't lie to you, I was frozen. All my words just stuck in my mouth and I was afraid. It all happened so fast I didn't know what to do. All I could think of was Abu. If anything happened to him. . .'

'I know,' Moses interrupted her, clearly deciding there had been enough emotion for one day. 'What you need is a coffee.'

She saw they had pulled into Ma Mary's place and the smell of the roasting coffee beans hit her as soon as she opened the door. She appreciated this almost as much as Moses' defence of her in Julu's office. The presence of Ma Mary forced them to talk about other things and after a few sips of her coffee Gloria asked Ma Mary where the coffee came from.

'Tha coffee from right here, it's the only thing they not able to steal from us – no Nigerian, no NGO people and no rebel.'

Ma Mary had the general public's low opinion of rebels, foreigners and other West Africans. There was no new Liberia for them, only a small chance to claim back some of the old Liberia, at least enough to make life bearable.

With her strength restored Gloria thought it better to go before Ma Mary got into her full swing. She had only two 'settings' – silence or full flow talking – and Gloria sensed today was a 'full flow' day. That could be interesting but they didn't have the time for it.

Back in the office there was a message for her to go and see Chief Inspector Kamara at once which didn't sound as if it was going to be good news. Leaving Moses to rally the troops she went up to the twelfth floor. It was a different world on the top floor, clean, quiet and air conditioned. Her boss was looking particularly uncomfortable as she walked in. There were two other people in the room, sitting with that casual authority that Westerners seemed to have.

'Inspector, come in and meet these people. This is Matthew Pendle and his assistant.' Apparently the assistant was too lowly to have a name and right from the start it was obvious Matthew Pendle was the star of this show. 'Mr. Pendle is a journalist with one of UK's biggest newspapers and he's here. . .'

'I'm here,' he said, interrupting, 'to do a piece on how women, in particular, are working to transform Liberia after the war. The Chief Inspector has very kindly agreed that I follow you around for a while and use you as an example of the new Liberia.'

Gloria had met a lot of journalists during and after the war and she could read them like a book. This guy was not the type who did the heart-warming stories about women police officers in the new Liberia. This was the kind who sold graphic descriptions of misery, violence and death thinly disguised as political comment or social analysis. In his prose, whichever newspaper he was writing for, Liberians could only be helpless victims, psychopathic killers or corrupt officials.

She looked at him. 'Very impressive Mr Pendle but tell me, what's the real story you're looking for? Surely you people are not still writing stories about child soldiers eating their victims' hearts or Oxford-educated warlords responsible for wholesale massacre?'

Pendle didn't miss a beat. 'Well only if it happens in another country, we have done those stories from every angle here. No, now we are looking to the future and informing our readers how their taxes are being spent to develop democracy and freedom in Africa.'

He was lying and he didn't care that she knew it. She would have to watch herself around Mr. Pendle. What a pain that was going to be. With the niceties over the Chief Inspector asked Pendle and his assistant to take a seat outside.

'Inspector, I have just had the Minister of Defence on the phone' – Gloria was impressed he had a working phone in his office – 'and he is advising very strongly that you close the file on the boy on the beach and the other two children. Put them down to random killings or 'heart men' or whatever you like. He says there is no point in carrying on with the investigation.'

Gloria slumped in the chair, tired with the politics of it all. 'So that's it, is it, the soldiers shout and we jump? Will we have to run our entire workload past him in the future and let him decide what should be investigated?'

The Chief paused a moment and then continued, 'I am just telling you what he said to me. There is no way he, or even I, could order you to close an investigation without very good reasons. I certainly don't have any, and if he had then he kept them to himself.'

When she looked up he went on. 'So carry on investigating until you get to the bottom of it, keep me informed and I will back you all the way. But' – she knew what was coming – 'watch yourself. These are powerful people.' She nodded and told him what Julu had said about Abu, and what Moses had said in reply.

'Understandable but foolish. You will have to talk to Abu and explain to him what the dangers are and tell Moses to warn his family too. I knew this unit would be controversial but I didn't expect it to stir up so much trouble and so soon. Anyway you know the procedure. Keep your phone charged and on. Don't go anywhere alone and always let someone here know your movements.'

Gloria was touched by his support but really couldn't handle any more emotion today. 'Better be careful, sir, we're in danger of turning into a real police force at this rate.'

'Right, back to work Inspector. And try and show your face at the training sometime. If you don't get the certificate next week you'll have to do the whole course again when it's repeated in three months time.'

Ouch. She cringed at the thought. As she was leaving she collected Pendle and informed him he could accompany her today. She would be down on the fifth floor attending a training conducted by one of his countrymen.

'I'm sure your readers will be delighted to see how their taxes are being spent training us.'

10.

THREE DEATHS, threats of violence against her family and a host of suspects and here she was back in this very hot room where it looked as if nothing had changed since she was last here. In fact she suspected old Borbor, fast asleep in the corner, might not have left at all. He was the oldest surviving member of the old police force and very proud of the fact although that was just about his only claim to fame. Although he represented everything she hated about the way the police had been run before the war, the corruption, harassment of street children and prostitutes and the acceptance of the 'culture of impunity' as the ex-pats described it, it was hard to dislike Borbor personally. Lazy, venal and corrupt he was, but he was also kind and soft-hearted when circumstances allowed. He was so well known that he had been allowed to continue directing traffic on Broad Street all through the war, tolerated by all sides in the conflict. He had become something of a local celebrity and featured in any number of international magazines and news-papers as either an illustration of the madness of the war – his picture side-by-side with those of the rebel soldiers in wedding dresses and dressing gowns – or as an example of the strength of the human spirit, the lone police officer carrying out his duties in the midst of chaos and violence.

The truth was Borbor had been too lazy to run away and discovered that going out in his uniform – or a version of his uniform – he had taken to wearing white gloves and very fancy epaulettes which were never part of the standard issue – between the fighting had given him some status with the various factions. It was not without its dangers though and Gloria had to concede that surviving the random violence which was always a major feature of the war had been nothing short of a miracle. Although the new authorities had told him to get rid of the epaulettes they couldn't actually get rid of Borbor, who was still a recognised face internationally, so they had sent him for re-training in the hope, she suspected, that he would retire of his own accord. One look at him snoring in the corner, in perfect contentment, told Gloria that Borbor was going to ride out the restructuring with the same style he had ridden out the war.

She had sent young Alfred round to Abu's school to tell him to come straight home when school finished. Alfred, who practiced with Abu's team and played sometimes, had been very worried when Gloria explained the threats and had wanted to wait for him and make sure he got home. Gloria was pretty sure Julu was not going to try anything on the same day he had made the threats and besides Abu would have enjoyed having a personal body guard way too much. No, she had said, let him come home and I will talk to him tonight.

Her only satisfaction was the sight of Pendle sweating and fidgeting in the heat. Well, he was the one who wanted to know how British tax money was being spent, and here they were. The session she had joined in was actually quite interesting though. Ron was asked a question about how to handle former child soldiers who were causing havoc in the schools and in their communities. Random violence, petty thieving and harassment had all become more common. He explained the facts of an infamous story from the UK where the children responsible for killing two younger children had divided public opinion and many people felt with hindsight that the due process of law had been abandoned to satisfy the public's need for revenge. The children had been tried as adults, their privacy had not been respected and they had been given a very severe sentence.

Ron explained that, no matter how heinous their past crimes and how terrible their behaviour was now, the police duty was to protect these children from mob justice and to make sure they were treated as children, not as adults, when they were brought to book for some offence. The new juvenile justice legislation, he indicated Gloria on the back row, which the Family and Child Protection Unit was helping to develop, and would have a key responsibility in implementing, should be a big help to them in ensuring that children were dealt with appropriately.

Although no-one in the room looked particularly enthused by his presentation his last words really struck her. 'Remember these are the future leaders you are dealing with whose experience of the last twelve or so years has been violence and betrayal. Your task is not just to punish them but to help create an equitable society where they will have a chance to develop their talents and play their part in society.'

At this stage Pendle decided he could take no more and, whispering loudly in her ear that he would see her tomorrow to discuss his programme in more detail, he left the room. Gloria stayed where she was and endured the singing of the national anthem and the thunderous roar of 'Though new her name' one more time. She wanted to have a word with Ron. Partly, she wanted to make sure he knew she was attending the sessions so she would not have to repeat it all again, and partly because she realised he was an experienced policeman very committed to his work. She needed his advice.

Ron was obviously delighted when she asked if they could talk and even more so when she suggested they do so in a local bar where they could have a cold beer. She suspected that Ron was spending a lot of time on his own in the hotel when he wasn't doing the training. The NGO community were not the most welcoming, from what her friends in various agencies had told her. The 'in' crowd among them, so-called experts in health, nutrition, disaster management and any other problem you cared to mention, took themselves very seriously and were not keen to mix with the likes of Ron Miller and others who came in for a few weeks or months.

Her friend Annie, who worked for the charity Global Vision, had told her over lunch a few weeks ago that she often attended meetings where a roomful of people, some of them young enough to be her children and some who had only been in the country a matter of months, made crucial decisions about where money was to be spent.

'At most of those meetings I am the only Liberian in the room, Gloria, and I'm only there to take notes and serve coffee. Honestly, I sit there listening to people who know almost nothing about our country deciding that we need clinics here or there or we need a strategy on this or that.' But clearly she didn't always just serve coffee and take notes.

'Last week, for example, I had to point out that distributing seeds now was a complete waste of time and money as the rains would start soon but they said that distributing seeds was part of this month's action plan so it had to be done.' She and Annie had laughed. 'Then they discussed their measles vaccination campaign. I couldn't stop myself, Gloria. I butted in and asked if they had not heard that the UN had conducted a hugely expensive vaccination campaign last year. They hadn't. Again I said if they were still going to go ahead with it they should at least wait until the dry season otherwise they would not be able to reach three quarters of the country as most of the roads will turn to mud. Their answer?' She and Annie had recited together. 'But it's in the plan so we have to do it.' They had laughed again but it was frustrating. It was such a waste, spending money on services that were not needed, delivered by agencies which did not understand Liberia and couldn't even talk to each other, never mind ask ordinary Liberians what they needed. And, Gloria thought to herself, they think we are the ones who need help.

Ron, on the other hand, was different. He was approachable, friendly and, well, quite humble. He always asked for people's opinions, he listened and took note of what people said and, what especially endeared him to his police audience, he didn't take himself too seriously. It got Gloria thinking rather guiltily to herself that she may have been a bit rash in her judgements. They agreed to meet at seven in a local bar. Gloria didn't want to be too far from Abu while they had Julu's threats hanging over them.

The office was full when she popped in for an update. They had all heard about the threats against Abu and they were all taking it very seriously. Izena had suggested they provide twenty four hour protection for Abu which made everyone, even Luseni, laugh out loud. 'Eh girl, this is Liberia, not New York. It doesn't work like that. But maybe we can put him on our Witness Protection Scheme,' which provoked even louder laughter. A few weeks earlier a local newspaper had printed the names and photos of all the people who had been promised anonymity and protection if they gave evidence in secret at the Truth and Reconciliation Committee. Three had fled the country and one had been found dead at his house. Since then the press had re-named it the Witness Detection Scheme and corruption at the Ministry of Justice and the National Police had been blamed. A new song mocking the police motto 'To Serve and Protect' was now doing the rounds. 'To Swerve and Collect' accused the police of avoiding their duty and just harassing people for money as in the old days.

'Are we here to serve you?

No, only to swerve you.

We're supposed to protect

But we only collect.'

Not the cleverest lyrics in the world but a great tune which meant everyone was singing it!

'Anyway,' Gloria went on, 'I will warn Abu to stay alert and that's all we can do at the moment. What about the rest of you, any news?'

There wasn't much to report. Izena was meeting with the heads of the various agencies which worked with street children later in the week to bring them up to date with what was happening and see if they had any further information. Lamine was still with the Rock gang and Moses told Christian to go and bring him back the next day before he ended up joining them. Ambrose was trying to do some research on KVG but as the only decent internet connection was in the NGO community he was having to beg various friends who worked there to give him some time on their computers. Gloria told him what Sr. Tony had told her about Marcus Drake but said for the time being they should focus on Prince Julu and his 'boys'.

'Paul, we need to find out more of what's going on in Harbel,' said Gloria. 'I want you and young Alfred to go and spend a few days up there and just get as much information as you can about the Commissioner and his family, the fighters who are still active there and generally what kind of activities are going on. Keep a low profile but if anyone asks – specifically Sampson Moore obviously – just tell him you are following up on the murder of the two boys with a view to closing the case.' She barely paused.

'Come in tomorrow and Moses will make sure you have transport' – that will be money for a taxi, she thought – 'and some communication support' – credit for their mobile phones – 'and remember to check on the families of those murdered children to make sure they are safe.'

Paul and Alfred looked delighted at the prospect of spending a few days out of Monrovia but Gloria wasn't worried. They would enjoy themselves but they would also do the job, she was sure of that.

As the meeting dispersed she told Moses she was meeting Ron for a drink and, unsurprisingly, he jumped at the invitation to join them so they arranged to meet at seven at Mickey's bar.

It was only five when she got home to find Abu slumped on the chairs in the living room with some books lying unread on his knee. He jumped up as soon as she came in.

'Aunt Glo, I can't do this. Alfred says I can't go for practice, that I should just be going to school and then straight back here. I will go crazy. In fact I think I might be going crazy already.'

Gloria came and sat next to him. He was growing up fast and he was going to be tall – he was already tall in fact, and strong. But oh he loved a drama and she couldn't take any chances.

'I know it's tough Abu but Julu is a dangerous man and it would be too easy for him to use you to get at me. I don't think you're going crazy yet though. Sitting still is not a sign of craziness you know. You never know, you might even improve your grades.'

'What, you're going to lock me up and then expect me to improve my grades as well? Look Aunt Glo, please, I will take time, I promise. I will come straight home after practice, I will be with the boys and I won't go anywhere else. But I can't miss practice. In fact Morris and Leo can stay here, no-one would try anything then for sure.'

Gloria realised she was losing this battle. In truth she knew he was serious about the football, it was his passion and if he couldn't play he might actually go crazy, or send her crazy. And she knew Morris and Leo well. They had been together for most of the war. Morris was very easy going and popular, always ready with a joke. Leo was quieter but very smart and a natural leader. They had been friends for years and due to the circumstances of the war they were all very able to look after themselves – she knew they could cook, wash their clothes and clean. So that would be no problem. It might be worth giving up some of her space if it meant Abu could get on with his life and she could worry about him less.

'All right, Morris and Leo can stay for a while. Do I need to contact their people to explain the situation?' She realised she didn't know much about their families despite knowing them for so long. But Abu was already jumping up.

'No worries, their people will be ok. They will be happy for them to come here.'

'Well it still means you have to be aware of what's going on, I mean it. And you go for practice and then straight back here and the three of you study and then sleep.'

Abu was nodding but she could tell his mind was somewhere else.

'And not tonight. You can call and tell them, if they have phones.'

He looked at her pityingly, of course they had phones, everybody had a phone. But he agreed.

'Now, I'm going out for a few hours but just down the road to Mickey's so you stay in and study and keep the door locked, but there's no way anyone is going to do anything tonight.'

'So I could have gone to practice then,' he said following her logic, 'and we could have started all the security tomorrow.' The hard-done-by teenager was back!

She heard the beat of 'To swerve and collect' coming from his room as she was leaving but let him have his moment of rebellion and went out locking the door behind her.

Ron was already sitting at a table outside when she arrived. Mickey's wasn't exactly a place for fine dining or a quiet drink.

It was cold beer, roasted meat and very loud music but it was ideal for a discreet conversation. Moses was already getting them beers and Gloria and Ron swapped general conversation. She apologised for being late and explained her latest sparring round with Abu.

'He's smart and helpful and logical – and then acts like a child demanding attention.'

Ron laughed. 'Well some of us never develop further than that no matter how old we get. I have two children but they are still small.' He took out his wallet and showed her a photo. Two smiling blond-haired children were sitting on the grass in a sunny garden twisting flowers into the hair of a woman lying in front of them laughing.

'Is that your wife?'

'Yes, that's Laura. That was just before I came away.' He stared at it again before putting it away. 'Sorry, I have to stop pulling that picture out at every opportunity.'

'You must miss them.'

'I do but Laura understands this work is something I have to do. She is really supportive. But it's hard missing the children growing up. After this trip though I will be at home for the rest of this year. I am starting a course so I am looking forward to that.'

Moses came back with the beers and talk turned again to the facts of the case. Recounting the details of the deaths after seeing Ron's picture of his children somehow made it all the more poignant, and Gloria made no attempt to hide her frustration. Ron listened as best as he could over the music, nodding and slowly sipping his beer. Then they went quiet. Gloria realised she was expecting Ron to give some wise answer, maybe even to magically tell them who was responsible and why. Annoyed with herself for thinking like that she started talking again going over and over the details of what Prince Julu had said, the fighters in Harbel on the checkpoint and his obvious control of the area. To her surprise, Ron seemed to want to discuss something quite different. He made it clear that, threatening as Julu had been, there were things that puzzled him, especially the diamond. No rebel or common thief would leave a valuable diamond behind, no matter what point they wanted to make.

'In fact no-one would leave a diamond behind. Most people in this town survive on less than a dollar a day. A bag of rice costs more than a teacher earns in a month, if they even get paid that is. One diamond would represent a staggering amount of money.'

Ron nodded at Moses. These are criminals. They are about making money not giving it away in some grand gesture. And the group on the beach, the only sighting of the murderers, certainly didn't sound like former rebels. The accents, the standing around and the praying. All of that sounded like something quite different. Ron wasn't sure what, but he certainly didn't have the answers.

'The key is Aloysius himself, I think you'd agree?' he said to them. They did agree and said so. 'The other children, as you said, were really just an imitation. Poorer kids, replicas of the well-brought-up Aloysius with replicas of the diamond on them. That is way too twisted and thought out for any of Prince Julu's lot. You need to pursue it further. Go back to the father and find out what is really going on with him, check for the other children and his wife.'

Gloria thought about it. It made sense although it didn't make any sense at all.

Ron was animated now, the slightly apologetic trainer replaced by an enthusiast. 'A few years ago we received information that a gang were going to steal the Koh-I-Noor diamond. It is part of the British crown jewels and we were allowed to see it as part of the security arrangements. They told us it was a very rare diamond and of the highest quality. It just looked white to me and really quite ordinary. I was fascinated how something so ordinary could be the focus of so much attention so I did some research. Diamonds are not like other precious stones. The word itself comes from a Greek word 'adamas' which means 'invincible'. Not only are they the ultimate symbol of power but there are still people who believe they have supernatural powers and also, in the case of the Koh-I-Noor, put a curse on the owner.'

Ron's narrative style was much more engaging than his training style and both Gloria and Moses listened intently. For Gloria diamonds had always been associated with the war, a 'resource' to fight over so that rich women in the West could wear them. She knew nothing of this background and while she couldn't see any connection between that and the crime they were investigating, it was an interesting story.

'The way the diamond was used and placed in the hand of an 'innocent' and the way they treated the body with prayers says to me it was more like a sacrifice of some kind, the deliberate giving up of what is pure and valuable for some higher purpose.'

Ron stopped and looked a bit embarrassed. 'Sorry guys, I don't know where that last part came from, I hadn't given it much thought until you started telling me the details. And to be honest I don't really know what I meant by that. But it seems to me that this is about more than a gang of thugs running some kind of smuggling racket. Do you have any resources you could draft in? Maybe you need to think about getting other departments involved.'

Moses was very quick to respond. 'It sounds to me as if you're giving us the same warning as Julu Ron. Get off the case, it's too big for you, you'll never solve this. What is it about this particular murder that's got everyone on our backs?'

'No Moses, it's not like that. I am only hearing the details from you now. I wasn't saying stop investigating, I'm saying that there might be a lot more involved here than the murder of some children.' He stuttered. 'Sorry, that came out wrong. The murder of children, nothing could be worse than that. I meant the case itself might be about more than the murders. And to solve the murders you will have to understand the bigger picture. Now I certainly don't understand the bigger picture but the 'strange accents' and the respectful care of the body of a child they have just tortured and killed is not, as you say, typical of Liberia. So there must be something bigger at play.'

Gloria was finding it hard to concentrate now. She really was a morning person and by this time of an evening – and not forgetting the beer – she found it hard to focus on what Ron was saying. Her attention wandered away from the table to others who were in the bar. Mickey's was a favourite haunt of the international community as well as politicians and business-men. Across the small courtyard tonight, for example, she recognised a minor official from the Ministry of Education sitting with a woman who was definitely not his wife, deep in conversation. Beside them were the members of Monrovia's newest musical sensation, Bad Boyz Beat, surrounded by a crowd of adoring girls. In the far corner she saw three people, heads close together, talking intently. Even in the dim light Gloria recognised them, John Kopius, Marcus Drake and that Pendle guy. Now what on earth were they talking about? She supposed it was natural for Kopius and Drake to know each other but Pendle?

Ron and Moses were still in discussion and they nodded absently when she got up. 'I'm just going to have a word with some people, I'll be back.' She pushed her way through the now crowded dance floor. The three men didn't notice her until she was standing right at their table.

'Well Mr. Pendle, I wouldn't believe anything these guys tell you, if it's a story you're looking for you'd be better to stick to the police.'

Pendle and Kopius looked up at the sound of her voice. Kopius smiled thinly and nodded.

'Actually he's telling us about his plans for a documentary about your work.'

So, thought Gloria, a lie straight away. They really must have something they want to cover up.

'As long as his documentary doesn't interfere with my work I'll be satisfied. What about you John, I thought you had travelled? We wanted to have a word with you, and Marcus.' She stretched out her hand. 'We haven't actually met Mr Drake but I recognised you from your photo.'

Marcus Drake had looked up from a pile of papers in front of him but didn't smile or offer her a hand in return.

'We are just having a quiet drink Inspector. On our own.'

Before Gloria could reply she heard her phone ringing and excused herself. It was Abu's name flashing on the screen. She pressed answer and heard Abu's voice immediately, but sounding much younger and very scared. 'Aunt Glo, please come back, there's people at the door, they're trying to break in and the power has gone off, please come back.'

In the background she could hear the noise of smashing and banging.

'Abu, go into my room, get in the cupboard.'

It wouldn't hide him but might give her a few minutes to get back. She was already heading for the exit, gesturing to Moses who sensed her urgency across the courtyard and was right beside her by the time she got out the gate. She just said 'Its Abu' and then they were both running in the dark up towards the apartments which they could see were in complete darkness. Gloria was sweating before they had gone a hundred yards but she could only think of Abu, hiding in the dark. 'Come on,' she said, more to herself than to Moses who was already passing her. It was only five minutes to the apartments but the dark and her anxiety combined to make it feel much longer, like those dreams where you are trying with all your energy but your legs are like lead weights.

They reached the apartment entrance where there was huge confusion. There were lots of people milling around in the dark, laughing, asking questions and shouting to each other. Gloria shouted at them to get out of the way while Moses pushed his way through. Up the stairs there were groups of people on every landing, it was impossible to tell who they all were. Torches, lighters, cell phones were all being used to give people their bearings and added to the confusion.

When they reached her landing she could see, even in the uncertain light that her door had been forced open. Slower now, her instincts kicking in, she pushed the door open. The apartment was silent and dark. She heard Moses hiss something behind her and knew he was warning her, as if she needed that right now. But she went in slowly all the same. She could feel she was walking on broken glass, then bumped into an overturned table, her own house felt so unfamiliar. She headed straight to her room and went in just as the power came back on, momentarily blinding her. The room was a mess. Every drawer was open with clothes, books and pictures scattered everywhere. Gloria, with Moses right behind her, went straight to the cupboard but one glance was enough to show her it was empty. All the clothes were out and on the floor.

'He's not here Moses, I told him to hide in there, but it's empty.'

Moses and Ron – she hadn't known Ron was with them – turned around and started for the other rooms. The apartment wasn't that big and a few minutes' search told them Abu was gone. Moses sat her down and told her they had to go down to the station and start the hunt right away. They should go to Julu's house and office, they should send men up to the barracks, and they should do it now, before the shock set in, before the trail got cold. She knew all that but felt paralysed until the cold seething anger descended on her. If she found Prince Julu tonight she would likely kill him herself.

She stood up, brushed Moses off and was heading for the door when she heard the tiny scrape of the screen door which led out to the balcony. She was across the room and pulling the door open, even as she could feel it being pushed from the other side and found herself uttering those instant heartfelt prayers. 'Let it be Abu, please let it be Abu.' And it was Abu. A bruise on his cheek and a torn t-shirt but it was him. She pulled him towards her, hugged him tightly, relief rushing through her, scared to speak in case she started crying and couldn't stop. And just held him. He must have been scared because he hugged her back for a few seconds and then, seeing Moses and Ron and the rest of the crowd who had gathered, he pulled back.

'Eh Aunt Glo, I am ok. They couldn't get me. I was too smart for them.'

She held him at arms length and touched the bruise on his cheek.

'Did they hit you?'

'No, Aunt Glo, I was too quick for them.' Shaking her hands off him Abu launched into his story.

'They were banging on the door and I could hear it was going to open. I pushed the chairs and the cupboard up against it but the power went off and they started banging even more. When the cupboard fell in it caught me here,' he pointed to the bruise, 'and tore my shirt but that was all. I went on to the porch and closed the door before they got in. I could hear them going through the rooms but you got back before they came out here. Although, I was ready if they tried to get me. . .' He demonstrated some kind of karate move and Moses roared laughing, breaking the tension. Abu was playing to his audience now, which was a good sign, but Gloria didn't hear any of it, hopefully she would get the real version later. For now all she could think was how close she had been to losing him, these people killed children without a second thought. Abu could have been the next victim.

'What are we into Moses?' she asked him as they left Abu with his admirers. 'Really, what is going on?'

'Whatever it is we are making some people very angry, so we must be on the right path. We can talk more about that in the morning. Where are you staying tonight?' He had started picking up bits of broken glass and china.

'Where am I staying? I'm staying here of course. This is my apartment. It won't take long to clear up.'

Moses knew that arguing with her was a waste of time and the easiest thing would be to start the clear up, get the crowd out of the way and make sure Abu was ok.

'Here's one casualty boss.' He held up the pieces of her Queen Elizabeth II Silver Jubilee mug. 'Ah well, some things won't be missed.'

Gloria smiled. 'Just make sure Abu doesn't see it, it was a gift from him.'

Gloria's neighbour, Dr. Bartu, had already examined Abu's bruises and pronounced his injuries 'superficial', which didn't please Abu very much.

'It's a medical term Abu,' said Gloria, 'it just means you don't have to go to hospital. Why don't you call your friends and see if they can come over now, they can take taxi and I will give them the fare when they get here.' That worked fine in restoring his good humour.

Ron and Moses finished the job of setting the furniture back up. They got rid of most of the broken glass while keeping an eye on the crowd who had materialised, making sure nothing went missing in the melee. In a matter of half-an-hour the place was patched up including a new lock on the door courtesy of another neighbour, Rohit, who ran a large hardware store on Bushrod Island.

Gloria spent the time putting some order back in her bedroom. That she had to do herself, to make sure it was done properly and also to give her back some control.

By the time she had finished, Moses had come back with some beers and both Morris and Leo, summoned by Abu, had turned up with their school uniforms, which meant they were moving in now as well. In addition to the neighbours some of her family had miraculously found out what had happened and come to find out the details. The noise and the joking were just what they needed. Abu's heroic performance had grown to epic proportions by the time he had told his story for a fourth time but the rush of adrenaline made him oblivious to the good natured teasing that greeted his story as he launched into it again for the sake of some newcomers. It was after two when people started to leave. Abu and his friends had retreated to his room with every intention of discussing the day's drama but judging by the silence they had all fallen asleep. It was only when Gloria got up from the chair to say goodbye to Ron that she saw Moses settling down on the couch.

'What are you doing?'

Moses didn't even look up, just went on shaking out the sheet he had found from somewhere.

'I'm not arguing or even discussing this boss. I'm staying tonight, and yes Hawa knows and has no problem about it so why don't we just leave any more discussions until tomorrow.'

By the time he had finished talking he was starting to take off his trousers so Gloria beat a retreat to her room. They certainly would discuss this in the morning. But before she could think any more about it she was fast asleep.

11.

AT 7:22 precisely that morning her mobile started ringing and it went on and on until she was forced to roll over and pick it up. It was the Chief Inspector.

'Gloria, you need to get down here now. I'm at the Mamba Point hotel. And find Moses, I can't get him.' Gloria didn't bother explaining that Moses was only a few feet from her. Really, that's how rumours started.

She didn't ask Chief Inspector Kamara why. He rarely phoned and hardly ever called her by her first name so he must be really stressed. She was up and dressed in minutes, calling to Moses to get ready. They were both heading for the door, hardly a word said, when Gloria remembered the events of last night and that she now had Abu and his two friends in her house. In the cool light of morning it occurred to her they were potentially at risk from another attack. Why had inviting more teenagers over to her house seemed like such a good idea last night? They were still sleeping and she didn't have the time or the inclination to try and get them out to school but was worried about leaving them in the house on their own. Caught in her indecision she noticed Moses at the front door talking to someone and then coming over to her with Rohit, her neighbour, in tow.

'Inspector ma'am,' Rohit was always formal but always friendly. 'I wanted to let you know I am working at my house today.'

His apartment was directly below Gloria's.

'I have some of my workers over here today working in my house and doing some repairs on the building. So please don't worry about Abu, no-one will get up the stairs without a good fight.'

Gloria had seen Rohit's workers on a few other occasions when they had done some work in the building. They all looked like professional wrestlers. His concern and kindness hit her like a blow and for one terrible moment she thought she might cry. She held herself together and just smiled at him which was as much emotion as Rohit could cope with too.

'Thank you Rohit, that is really good. I will try and not be too late.'

'Don't worry about that, they will be here until late, there's a lot of work to be done.'

Gloria knew there wasn't a lot of work. He was just providing a free security service for her and Abu.

She and Moses were in their cars and down the hill to Mamba Point hotel in minutes. It was only as they got to the hotel it dawned on them that the one person they both knew living there was Ron.

When they arrived the Chief Inspector came over immediately. He was very upset, his face ashen and his distracted manner even more pronounced.

'Good morning Inspector, we have a terrible situation here I'm afraid. Captain,' he nodded at Moses clearly surprised that they had arrived together. 'I'm glad you could make it.' He looked around at the entrance to the hotel and back to them. 'We should go in, better prepare yourselves.'

They followed him in silence into the foyer where Grace, the formidable receptionist, was talking in a low voice with Mohammed, the hotel manager. There was a group of staff standing around unsure what to do. Two of the maids were crying, and from the restaurant Gloria could hear one of the guests loudly demanding to know if there was going be breakfast any time soon. The Chief gestured to Mohammed to accompany them and they squeezed into the lift.

When he pressed the button for the top floor Gloria looked at Moses. She remembered Ron saying last night how he loved the view from his room on the top floor. The knot in her stomach tightened.

'Has something happened to Ron, sir?'

'I'm afraid so Gloria. Mohammed called headquarters this morning and the duty officer sent me a message when she heard what had happened. I was the first officer on the scene.'

The lift doors opened and she saw a young policeman she didn't recognise standing outside a room at the end of the corridor with a handkerchief over his mouth. As they walked up the corridor she knew why. The smell coming from the room struck her and she stopped briefly until she felt Moses put his hand on her elbow. 'Easy boss, don't breathe too deeply.' They both got out their handkerchiefs and followed Kamara into the room.

It was a scene which was both strange and also totally familiar to Gloria. Death, its smell and sight, had become almost commonplace for everyone who had lived through the war but it was still shocking. Especially when it was someone they knew, someone who had been helping them just a few hours ago. Ron Miller was sitting in an armchair in the room still in the clothes he had been wearing yesterday, but that was the only recognisable thing about him. Although his head had been covered by one of the hotel towels, the amount of blood around it and its odd angle spoke of terrible violence. Moses and Gloria stood in silence for a few moments until they heard the Chief Inspector give a polite cough.

'Are we sure it's Ron Miller, sir?' Gloria asked. The silence told her everything.

'Yes it is him and we are in big trouble, Inspector. We have a UK national, a professional police officer, over here training our re-formed police force and he is killed in his hotel room. Everyone is going to run with this story and none of it is going to look good for us.'

And it's certainly not good for him, she thought, although she understood what he meant. Everything in Liberia was political and there were a lot of people who would try to use this murder to further discredit the police or to get the Chief and 'his' people moved out and their own people in. But that wasn't Gloria's biggest concern right now. Ron Miller was someone she had grown to like and respect in the last few days. She had been looking at a photo of his children hours before, for goodness sake, and now he had been killed. And brutally killed by the looks of it. Killed soon after talking to her and Moses about their investigation. One look at Moses told her he was thinking along the same lines.

Moses gently lifted the towel off the face and even he gasped. One eye stared up at them, the other one glued shut with blood. Half of his right ear had been torn off and there were burn marks on his cheeks. His top lip had been hacked off and his throat had been cut. It was truly horrible. Gloria looked and then turned away and Moses quickly dropped the towel again. The CID would have to deal with this.

'The guest next door is an American lady who is working with Global Vision. She says she heard noises around three this morning but was too scared to investigate. Her organisation's security guidelines require her to phone their security officer if she wants to leave her room during the night, and she didn't want to bother him.'

No-one even commented on the strange Western ways.

Gloria said, 'That means he was attacked as soon as he got in, because he was with me until after two this morning.'

The Chief Inspector's worried look meant she had to explain the attack on her apartment last night.

'Ron was discussing these child murders with us at Mickey's last night then some people broke into my apartment and tried to attack Abu. Ron stayed with us helping to put things back together. He would have reached here maybe around two-thirty this morning.'

'So it looks as if they were waiting for him,' Moses said. 'That could mean someone on the staff saw something or that it was an inside job.'

The Chief shook his head glumly. 'No, that would be too straightforward. Look,' and pointed to a corner of the room where the ceiling tiles had been removed. 'The roof is on the same level as the rocks.' The Mamba Point Hotel was built onto the side of the rock face. 'It would have been easy for anyone to get into the roof space and then into this room. They were waiting for him to get back and then they surprised him.'

'Are we sure it's more than one, isn't that a bit risky?'

'Look at the body, no ropes or restraints. Someone held him while someone else did the damage. The big question is why? His laptop is still here, his watch and money are still on him. This was a personal attack.'

'Or a warning,' said Gloria. 'Ron was talking to us about those murdered boys, giving us advice, or at least discussing different points about the case. We are dealing with people who feel very threatened and very angry.'

'Don't jump to conclusions, Inspector. I had no idea you were working with him. We need to investigate more before we decide what happened here. Anyway I just brought you down in case you knew of any links between Ron Miller and anything else your department is working on.'

Gloria realised what he was getting at. A few weeks ago a foreign consultant at the Ministry of Finance had been attacked and beaten up. It turned out he had been very fond of the young girls at the brothel on the beach and some of the neighbours had decided to teach him a lesson.

'No, Ron wasn't connected to our work, the only thing he was guilty of was trying to show us how to be better police and although some people took exception to that I don't think any of them would be driven to this.'

Her attempt at humour barely hid the rising anger and fear she felt. Moses looked at her and suggested they get out and leave it to the CID. Gloria stared at the battered body again and for a few moments she hated her country and the people who had made such violence commonplace. A fleeting thought of Abu's scared face overlaid the scene in the room and she shivered. It could have been Abu's fate too. She had no doubt these were the same people, they had to be. Maybe she should get Abu out. Many of her friends had sent children and family members out of the country. She had always resisted the idea but perhaps she should reconsider. If this was the new Liberia she wasn't sure she wanted it.

Neither she nor Moses was ready to go to the office but they couldn't face going to their respective homes either.

'What about some food?' Moses suggested.

Gloria was surprised she felt hungry but realised she had eaten very little yesterday. They went to the Daybreak Mouth Open Food Centre at the end of Randall Street. It was a bit of a risk as the quality of the food depended on how long the party had gone on for the night before. But today it looked as if it had been a quiet night. The place was open with the chairs set out and they could smell fried fish before they got inside. They both ordered the cassava and fish with the very milky tea. Gloria had learnt from previous experience not to even attempt the coffee here. The food was hot and delicious and they ate in silence, there was just so much to take in.

She really hoped Moses wasn't going to say anything about how Ron's death wasn't their fault and that the attacks were a sign they were on the right track. But when he didn't she found herself saying those exact things herself. For the first time since examining Aloysius's body in the morgue she wondered if they really were out of their depth. Four deaths, attacks on her family, threats from the highest and most dangerous levels of government. Maybe she should have accepted the inevitable, forgotten about Aloysius and turned her attention to cases she could have solved.

'Although you're not going to ask me I just want to say that I think we should stick with this. If we back down now this unit will be forever relegated to dealing with family disputes, parental rights, teachers abusing pupils and badly behaved foreigners.' Before she could speak Moses went on. 'I know all those things are really important boss and we will deal with them but the fact is if we focus on those alone the big people in this town will carry on doing exactly as they want. We need to start changing the system that allows these people to do what they want to whoever they want. Our investigation is obviously upsetting some powerful people like Prince Julu so that means we must be getting close and they know it.' Moses paused to drink and wipe his mouth.

'Come on, Moses, don't stop now, talk it!' She sat back in the shaky plastic chair.

'When the Chief Inspector said this was a test case I'm not sure he knew just how much of a test it was going to be. We have to win it and that means taking risks. We didn't know Ron that well but it's clear to me that no matter the consequences he would never have been able to abandon an investigation just because it was difficult and dangerous. We owe it to him to get the people responsible for his death as well as that of the children.'

Gloria nodded. 'You're absolutely right but it is just not easy-o.'

They both laughed quietly at her exaggerated accent, Liberians were always good at laughing in the face of the darkest circumstances. 'But are we even on the right track? Think about what Ron was telling us last night, all that stuff about diamonds being a symbol of power or even magic, and how Aloysius's death looked to him like a sacrifice and not just a warning. When you put all that together with the prayers it doesn't sound like the work of Julu's boys does it? But the actual killings and the attack on my house so soon after his threat and now this execution of Ron, that is clearly Julu's work. So are there two groups involved here, do they know each other or are they working together and if so then who is the other group?'

They had no answers to any of those questions yet.

It wasn't yet nine but the February sun was already beating down on them. The cooling harmattan winds had come and gone very quickly this year and they seemed to be permanently bathed in this sticky heat. It didn't help that she was exhausted from worry about Abu, lack of sleep from the attack and now angry and guilty about Ron's death. They needed a breakthrough and that just wasn't the Liberian way.

News of Ron Miller's death had reached the headquarters and the place was buzzing with rumours. By the time she got to her office she had heard her name mentioned three times and realised she was going to be linked to this death no matter what. She had a quick word with Paul and Alfred before they set off for Harbel, warned them to take time, to keep in touch with Moses and to make sure they kept their phones topped up in case of emergencies. There were three new reports sitting on her desk but without even opening them she called Izena in.

'Please go through these Izena, see what we need to prioritise and let me know before your meeting this afternoon. You are still meeting all the agencies today aren't you?'

'Yes ma'am, they have all said they are coming.'

'Good. I will look in at some point as well.'

Her phone rang just as she was getting up from the desk. It was Sr. Tony. 'Hey Gloria, I just heard about the attack.' Gloria didn't bother asking how. 'Are you and Abu ok?'

'Yes, we're both fine, just a bit shaken. He's got his friends staying now as well.'

'Is the attack connected to this case you're working on? I guess it must be?'

She should have been a detective not a nun thought Gloria.

'Thanks Tony, we really are fine although it was scary for Abu, not that he'll admit that now. But worse than that. . .' and out came the whole story about Ron. She could feel the tears welling up but she really couldn't afford to start crying, not so early in the day, and not in her office. Tony must have sensed it too. She didn't waste time with too much sympathy.

'That's too much for any person. Do you want me to come over to stay with you tonight?'

That made Gloria laugh and broke the tension. Sr. Tony was tough but she was also tiny and middle aged. What a great pair they would make if they had to face down marauding ex-rebels.

'No Tony, thanks, I will be ok and, as I say, Abu has his friends over so there really isn't a lot of space. In fact I suspect I may be organising an attack myself when those boys have been around for a few days.'

Now it was Tony's turn to laugh. 'Well don't be a stranger and promise you'll call if anything happens. Oh and by the way, two more children have gone from that shelter at Westpoint. Drake says he will check it out but he reminded me my services aren't needed any more. He's got all the children in a temporary shelter while he rebuilds the old one and he says he doesn't need any medical help. The man is a fool.'

With that she rang off.

The rest of Gloria's morning was taken up with report writing, being interviewed by the CID about Ron and fielding calls from her mother, uncle and other friends who had heard about the attack. Flomo was particularly annoyed when she eventually took his call.

'Gloria I vex-o, I am too vex. You get attacked and now you fill the house with those small pekins, those friends of Abu, to protect you. You know you supposed to call me.'

Flomo really wanted to come and live at her house but Gloria was not having it. If he moved in with her she would never get rid of him. But of course she couldn't say that so instead she told him the boys were not staying for security but to keep Abu company and so they could study together. He wasn't convinced but she was saved further explanation when Flomo's credit ran out.

By the time she had gone through similar conversations with her mum, her uncles, two friends and the lady who sold food down in the entrance lobby, Gloria was beginning to understand why crime victims were always so tired. If they had to go through this grilling from people supposedly trying to help them, while trying to get on with their jobs and lives, she was surprised people reported crime at all. Apart from Sr. Tony not one person had made any offers to help, they had just offered 'advices', as her uncle had kept saying, about what she should be doing. She knew they would come round if she asked but was loath to fill her private space with the noisy Sirleaf family and besides she would have had to buy several months' salaries' worth of food just to keep them going.

At two thirty she told Moses she was going to the meeting room to see how Izena was getting on with the centre managers.

She could have done without it but she suspected that Izena might need some help. She could hear raised voices all the way along the corridor and sighed. The people and organisations that ran centres and shelters for street children were a mixed bunch but they had some things in common – none of them wanted any interference in their work, after all weren't they nobly doing what the State was failing to do? Asking them to submit numbers and names and keep track of the children in their care was like insulting them.

Opening the door she could see almost twenty people in the room, and they all seemed to be talking at once. Izena, standing at the front, looked very young and was clearly having trouble controlling them. When Gloria walked in there was, if not silence exactly, at least a lessening of the noise. Two voices however continued to sound – from the only two white faces in the room. Marcus Drake she knew, and the other one had to be Richard Bennett. The others in the room, all men except for Clementine from St. Lukes, were Liberians ranging from the thin young man who represented the Alpha project, which ran a whole network of shelters and training centres and who worked closely with them through their own Child Protection Unit, to old Albert Frimpong who ran the Boys Town Outreach programme.

Marcus Drake looked up and started addressing his remarks to her. His accent struck her as rough and the sour expression on his face matched it exactly. He was sitting next to Richard Bennett in the front row with one arm out the window as if keeping contact with the outside world, and putting an invisible barrier between himself and the others in the room.

'It is clear to us, Inspector, that you do not understand our work. You come to us demanding numbers and even names and forget this work is unstable, these *people* we work with come and go as they please, they are like small animals scurrying around in the dark. We put out the food and they eat and then run back to their holes.'

The horrified expression on Richard Bennett's face and the sniggers from the others in the room told Gloria that whatever Drake had been saying before had not been quite so graphic. Before he could continue Gloria cut in.

'Ok Mr. Drake, let me tell you a few things. In my opinion anyone who thinks these children are small animals is not a fit person to be working with human beings.' Drake's expression hardly changed except his top lip curled even more. 'But for the moment what we want are the names of all the children who attend your centres or live in your shelters. That goes for all of you.' She looked around the room. 'I think you were told in advance this is what we wanted so I expect you to have that information with you. We need the information to solve a murder and, potentially, prevent more murders, so listen. I know you all have different tactics for getting funding from organisations.' The Liberians in the room laughed. 'I am not interested in your tactics, I just want an honest list, as best you can, so we can stop the killings.'

A hand went up at the back. 'Are our children in danger, Inspector? And if so what should we be doing to protect them?'

'Good question, people. I thought that was going to be the first thing you asked. The answer is, work with us, help us. Keep your eyes open for anything strange or different, people hanging around your centres, or children disappearing – and warn the children that they need to be more vigilant. Izena will be your contact person, you can get in touch with her any time.' She looked over at Izena who simply raised her eyebrows.

'Right, get those lists to Izena now and I think you can leave after that. However' – the rustle of departure stopped – 'we will be making a visit to all of your organisations when this murder investigation is over. Don't forget that you have a duty of care to the children you work with and the government wants to know what your philosophy is, what it is you are really trying to do for these *children*.' She emphasised the word while looking at Drake. She nodded to Izena who stepped forward and in her best convent English told them to pass their lists to the front and assured them of complete confidentiality.

Despite Drake's words of opposition everyone in the room, apart from him and Bennett, had some kind of register to hand in. Boys Town's photocopied handwritten files. St. Luke's memory stick. Untidy looking registers from Mission of Hope, Children's Rescue Centre and Liberian Children's Trust. And some very scrappy piles of papers from the Princess Diana Home for Girls, Healing Hands Outreach and the Thunder of God Mission. Izena ignored Drake and turned to Bennett who was clearly embarrassed at being seen as an ally of Drake.

'Oh, I say, I am awfully sorry. I'm afraid I am new here and I didn't really understand what was going on.' His bluster was gone completely. 'I will bring the lists in tomorrow morning first thing. We only have two centres at the moment so we don't have that many children.'

Izena nodded graciously and then addressed the group. 'Before you go, does anyone have anything to say, has anyone noticed any disappearances?'

Despite what Drake had said, it appeared that most organisations had fairly stable populations. The representatives of some of the smaller agencies immediately shook their heads and even the bigger organisations like Boys Town and St. Lukes could say quite clearly that, apart from two or three children who were currently languishing in the cells of the very building they were in and a few who had gone back to their families, there were no disappearances.

Gloria turned to Drake and asked him the same question. He looked at her and said that no, there had been no children coming and going from his shelters. He didn't seem to be bothered that this clashed with his earlier statement that it was impossible to keep track of the children. When she pushed him on it he just shook his head as if he had nothing more to say. It wasn't until she mentioned Sr. Tony's name that he started squirming in his chair a bit. He continued to assert that she was wrong but not as forcefully. Bennett could say nothing except that his manager, who he hadn't brought along, would have said something if children had been disappearing and, so far, he had said nothing.

When the meeting broke up Gloria and Izena compared notes and they both agreed that Marcus Drake needed more investigation. Even in a room full of some, quite frankly, strange organisations he had stood out by his complete detachment, coldness even. Even the most batty organisations seemed to care about the children, but he just didn't.

'Get back to Ambrose, tell him we need that information on KVG quickly.'

When she got back to her office Gloria realised it was almost four o'clock. There was no further news from CID about Ron and she and Moses were both exhausted.

'Before you say anything I don't need protecting tonight, I will be fine.'

Moses didn't argue, there was no point and he knew it. 'Just phone me if there is even a hint of trouble.'

'There are so many people threatening to come over and keep watch that I might not even be able to get in the apartment myself.'

She told him about Sr. Tony's offer and Moses grinned. The sisters were some of the few Westerners who'd earned his approval.

'Well if it was Margaret who had offered I could see the sense in that.' Margaret was big and loud and even Abu described her as 'impressive'. Gloria hadn't worked out if this was street slang for something or if it was just the impression she made on him but thought that 'impressive' was a pretty good description.

She promised to keep her phone on and to be cautious. . . Honestly, the whole victim thing was not as easy as she thought.

Grateful to escape she went out to the car park only to find two of her 'boys' leaning on the car. Although she reckoned they were only twelve, Pascal and Boyes had already been living on the streets of Monrovia for a few years. They knew every trick in the book and could have written a Guide to Street Living and awarded gold stars for the quality of food, accommodation and hospitality offered by the numerous agencies working with street children. Gloria had first met them a few years back in one of the lulls between the fighting when they had been living in a night shelter on Benson Street operated by St. Luke's. She had kept an eye on them since then trying to help them stay out of trouble and, as far she could tell, they were involved in nothing more serious than petty theft and the occasional bout of cane juice drinking.

Over the years they had also been a source of useful information which Gloria had learnt to trust. She hadn't seen them for a few weeks and could see that although they had the tough but undernourished look of street kids who had found a way to survive, they were now clearly in the twilight place between child and man. A particularly dangerous time for these children when they often fell into real criminal activities. And for these two, smart and funny, she really didn't want that to happen.

'Eh, old ma, how you keeping? Long time-o, you really lost from us since you got your big big job.' Gloria couldn't help smiling as Pascal delivered the standard lines with his trademark grin. Boyes, as usual, was much quieter and just a step behind him.

'Auntie, we just came to tell you sorry, we hear the people do bad to you last night. That is very terrible. Abu told us the people tried to kill him but when they saw his karate they were scarey and run away.'

Gloria knew that the boys didn't believe that for a second but kept a straight face and nodded gravely as if in gratitude for Abu's secret martial arts skills which had saved their lives.

'And how about you two, how you keeping?'

'Just the struggle, ma, you know, but we wan talk different thing today. We know you're the big woman for protecting all the small-small pekins and they just getting missing from the streets, especially in that Westpoint place.'

Gloria stopped fiddling with the car door keys and turned to Pascal. 'What are you saying, which children are missing? How is it that when I ask the people running these centres they just tell me everything is ok? They can't all be lying.'

'Look ma, some are lying and some not lying, tha life there. But we know some people are stealing the children. And not the regular gronna boys, these are different ones. That boy you find on the beach, he not from nowhere around here, and it's the same ting wi' all the others. They come on the street just one-one day or week and then they disappear – most of them are country children, some just from the bush, they no even speak no English or nuttin.'

Gloria was inclined to take what they said seriously. It supported what she thought and her exchange with Drake a few minutes ago supported it as well, plus the fact the boys had no reason to lie. These boys lived with, and to a large extent accepted, violence and injustice but it was somehow familiar to them and had a reason. This strange killing and these random disappearances had obviously made them scared. It was too unpredictable, to be safe on the streets you had to know what was coming and be able to avoid it or use it to your advantage.

The last few weeks had been the opposite and now it was affecting all of them. That would explain the fear they had picked up on among the street child population.

'Ok guys, you need to tell me everything that's going on but' – she caught the look on their faces – 'I know you can't do it now.' She knew they had a busy schedule of which centre to be at at which time to make sure they got food or a sleeping place. 'Can you come here in the morning, or come to my house early and eat, and then I'll bring you here.'

'No problem auntie, we will be at your house all night anyway with some of the boys to make sure they don't attack again.'

Gloria's heart fell. At this rate between crowds of street kids, off duty police, middle aged nuns, family members and, no doubt, the rest of Abu's football team or classmates – he was their president after all – her entire apartment block and the neighbouring streets were going to be packed with people trying to protect her.

'No Pascal, thank you, thank you too much but I will feel better if you get a good night's sleep and can give me information in the morning, that will be much more useful, really.' She rarely called them by their names so they knew she was really serious and they just nodded.

'Ok, ol' ma, but if anything happens and Abu's karate doesn't scare them this time' – street kids could be ironic she thought – 'send the houseboy to come call us.'

Gloria had told them many times that she didn't have a houseboy, just the old lady who dropped in to do some cooking and a bit of random cleaning, but they refused to accept this. She promised to send the phantom houseboy if there was any trouble and told them to be at her house early. Since she had mentioned food she knew she could rely on them for an early appearance.

The conversation reminded her about Lamine and the Rock Gang and she gave Moses a call to ask if Lamine had found out anything useful. There was a slight pause on the other end of the phone.

'Ok Moses. Tell me the story, what's happened?'

'Well boss, the truth is that Lamine has kind of gone native.'

She loved hearing Moses use an expression he usually found quite disrespectful but she didn't like what it implied.

'Please tell me he hasn't joined that gang, we can't lose one of our new recruits in the first month.'

'Not quite that,' said Moses, 'but he turned up at the office wearing shades, smoking and in jeans and a t-shirt. He says he's in character for the 'stake-out' as he called it, and he just can't get out of it so easily. In the end I had to send him back out before anyone saw him and started asking questions.'

She understood. At Headquarters stealing might be tolerated but sloppy uniform, or in this case a lack of uniform, was considered a serious offence.

'All right, I will go down to the Rocks and see him tomorrow if I have time.' Tomorrow was already filling up. 'Let's catch up first thing then but have a word with Izena if she's still there, she can fill you in about Drake and the meeting today. And get onto Ambrose, that research into KVG is really important. I don't know if it is just Drake or his whole organisation but there is something very suspicious about them. What about Paul and Alfred, any news?'

'They're fine boss. It was the boys' funeral today so having them there looked really natural. They said the checkpoint has disappeared and the rebel pekins haven't been seen since you were there. They haven't been able to see Banks yet though.'

'So they haven't seen or heard anything unusual at all?'

'The most unusual thing is that no-one wants to talk to them, even after a drink. People are friendly enough until they ask anything about Banks, the police or anything really – and then they just go quiet.'

'That might just be natural suspicion of strangers. And they're probably not very subtle.'

'No. The funeral lasted about four hours or more and you know what those two are like about things like that so I suspect they were too tired to be subtle. But they did say Famata and her family are ok, boss. Apparently the little girl said they had to tell you, thank you.'

'That's something at least.' Gloria yawned. 'I am too tired now. I need to go and sleep, Moses.'

Gloria made her way home, feeling her brain fog over as she parked the car. At least there were no groups of vigilantes gathering to protect her as far as she could see and for that she was grateful. She didn't think she would be able to perform even the simplest task now. All she wanted was a shower, some food and to relax with a book. She met Rohit at the top of the stairs surrounded by his crew.

'Inspector ma'am. I hope you had a good day.' Gloria nodded and then, tired and worried, found herself telling him about Ron's death. He had heard about it but still looked really shocked.

'These are still dangerous times, Inspector, and it means you can't take any chances. That poor man and his family though, it is too bad and is a shame on all of us. Can this country never get enough blood?'

They stood for a moment in silence and then she thanked him again and his crew of builders/wrestlers and went up to her apartment.

As she opened the front door she smelt cooking which was unusual. Usually her food was left to be reheated but the noise from the kitchen indicated some live cooking going on. She put her head around the door and found Abu, Leo and Morris all doing things. She couldn't quite see what as every cupboard appeared to have been emptied and there were bits of prepared and unprepared food everywhere, but it smelt heavenly. The boys just smiled and carried on with their conversation about an upcoming football match that weekend. Abu told her to go and relax, the food would be ready soon. So she did that and after a shower and a half hour with her book he called her to come and eat.

They had set the table and after a quick bow of the head and a prayer Abu proudly revealed two large dishes of jollof rice and gravy. It tasted as good as it smelt and there was a long ten minutes during which everyone tucked in. The shower, the food and the company all helped Gloria to relax and the fact that Abu seemed unaffected by yesterday's experiences also helped enormously. She decided not to say anything about Ron. Partly because they hadn't known him very well but also because she felt it would spoil the atmosphere of normality.

'I saw Pascal and Boyes on my way home, Abu, they said you had spoken to them.' Abu nodded.

'They were around the area this afternoon.'

'Mmm, they told me you went through the whole story with them.' He nodded again and shrugged. 'But they were really impressed with your karate skills and how you managed to fight off a gang of robbers.' Abu looked at her suspiciously but Morris and Leo were already laughing. Morris slapped the table.

'Eh Abu, you still telling those stories. Karate, I beg you.'

Abu was lost for words for once and looked around the table. Morris especially loved a joke and for the next ten minutes found a hundred different ways to bring karate into the conversation. Abu finally started laughing but claimed Pascal and Boyes were just gronna children who knew nothing.

'All right, that's enough, Abu. Don't insult the children, they're not gronna, not yet anyway.' She got up from the table.

'Anyway, thank you guys the food was too sweet' – sometimes only a Liberian compliment worked – 'but it's getting late. You better go study your books and then sleep because it's back to school tomorrow.'

12.

BY SIX the next morning Pascal and Boyes were at her door. That they managed to do this without anyone stopping or questioning them was a tribute to their skills, Gloria thought, rather than evidence of poor security. Luckily there was more than enough jollof rice left over from the previous night and by the time Abu and the others came out the boys were already tucking in. There was enough for them all as Gloria declined the offer and stuck to her coffee.

She liked the fact that neither Abu, Leo or Morris was surprised to see the two boys sitting eating at her table. There was a kind of equality among young people, whatever their circumstances, that you didn't find in any other part of Liberian society. Gloria didn't know if it was the same everywhere but in Liberia which was so divided by tribe or money it was very noticeable. The subject of martial arts was tactfully avoided by everyone except Morris who insisted on referring to Abu as 'Karate Boy', but Pascal and Boyes were focused on their food and Leo and Abu were discussing some referee who had just been suspended for taking bribes, so no-one took him up on it. The three of them were soon out the door to school. As she shouted 'And no going walkabout after school' at their departing backs, it struck Gloria that she was now responsible for three teenagers instead of just one. She made a mental note to get Leo and Morris back to their own homes as soon as possible before they settled in her apartment permanently.

When the rice bowls were completely empty Gloria got the boys in the car, although to stop them washing everything, which would have taken another half hour, she had to insist they leave the dishes and the pots for her fictitious houseboy. They got to the office without further incident and Gloria asked Izena to have a word with the boys and see if she could get any more definite information out of them. Izena was great at working with victims of abuse and families who were having a hard time but she really didn't like street children. She was a bit scared of them but also repulsed by them and secretly thought they didn't deserve much help. Gloria knew this and her answer was to now keep her in contact with street kids and their lives as much as she could. It wasn't changing her attitude very much but it was improving her confidence and the kids, strangely enough, liked her and responded to her.

An incident at the St. Luke's street children shelter a few weeks previously had been dealt with promptly and fairly by Izena. She had managed to investigate thoroughly and had established that the children's complaints, that the centre manager was selling their food and beating them, were all true. The manager had been sacked and the organisation had put a new system in place to make sure it didn't happen again. Not a bad result in Monrovia's murky waters, if only Izena could show some warmth to the children, and a bit of trust in the people who worked with them, she could achieve great things. Maybe that would come.

Gloria had just reached her office when Moses came to tell her that they had a visitor. The Minister of Defence was here to see them. She checked her watch. Ten past eight, he certainly didn't waste any time!

'Any explanation as to what he wants?' She was already angry.

'I haven't seen him. Not sure if I should go down with you after our last encounter, but there's no-one else who could go, except Luseni, old Alfred or Ambrose.'

Not a great choice in facing down a rebel-turned-minster who was also their chief suspect in four killings. But she didn't want to expose Moses to any more contact with him and thereby make him even more vulnerable.

'All right, I'll take Ambrose. At least he's smart and you can be in the room next door so if it sounds like it's getting out of control, you come in. How many men has he got with him?'

'None, he's on his own.'

'Interesting, right let's go and see what he wants. Maybe he's come to confess.'

As she went down the corridor to the meeting room Gloria found herself in a real quandary. She was going to face the man who she believed was responsible for several deaths and threats against her and others. She was torn between anger and apprehension. She heard running steps behind her and Ambrose reached her by the time she got to the meeting room door. He looked his usual impassive, slightly sullen self.

'Your job is just to listen. No speaking, no comments and no heroics.'

Ambrose nodded. 'It sounds like life in the seminary so that should be no problem.' And he smiled.

They went in and found Prince Julu looking very uncomfortable in the drab room.

'I requested a private meeting, Inspector.'

Gloria thought that 'requested' wasn't the best description but didn't respond to his comment and sat down opposite him.

'I thought maybe you had come to confess, sir. This young officer is just here to observe. Just proper procedure.'

'Oh the priestling.' Julu turned his attention to Ambrose

'First the gown, then the gun and now the badge, that's quite a progression for a young man.'

Gloria thought it was all overly dramatic. I mean 'priestling', was that even a real word, she didn't think so. She should have guessed he would know all of her team and no doubt thought he could intimidate them. Ambrose didn't move or even acknowledge Julu's presence, much less his words, and they fell flat in the room. Gloria felt an unexpected giggle rising in her.

'Not as good a progression as yours, Minister, university lecturer then rebel leader and now Minister of Defence. At least this young officer's progression is going up.' She let that hang in the air a bit but Julu didn't respond.

First round to them.

'So why are you here, Minister? We are investigating several murders as you well know so we don't have any time to waste.'

He stared at her for a moment but broke eye contact first. Gloria thought he looked more defeated than anything else and his initial aggression seemed to have evaporated.

'Inspector, I heard what happened to you the other night so soon after you were in my office with your colleague. I am very sorry and I was glad to hear that neither you nor Abu were hurt. And the murder of a British policeman, that is very bad news. But I wanted to tell you that no matter how it looks I had nothing to do with any of those attacks.' There was a line of sweat developing on his brow and his upper lip. 'I hope you believe me, for several reasons. I never threatened violence, just that Abu might take a sudden urge to join the army. I would never have anything to do with killing a British policeman, I know that will have very serious consequences, and lastly. . . believe me if I organised an attack on your apartment it would have ended very differently from the way it did.'

Gloria held his gaze. 'Well it's interesting that you have come all the way here to deny something no-one has even accused you of, Minister. In fact I heard this morning that the investigation into Mr Ron Miller's killing has already been closed and has been attributed to a random robbery gone wrong. I believe they have arrested half the staff at the hotel, including the manager, to find out who was the inside contact. Considering they took all that time to torture the poor man and then didn't actually steal anything I think it's a pretty flimsy conclusion, to be polite. But I would have thought you would be very happy with that result.'

Julu looked as if he was about to burst.

'You really think I am so crass, Inspector. I am no humanitarian but I am a good soldier. How else would I have survived the war? This whole sorry story has all the signs of people who have resources but no strategy. In fact it looks to me as if they don't even care. This cover-up over Ron Miller's death – yes I know it is a cover-up – will only last until the British investigators get here today. They will see in an instant this was no robbery. But that's for your boss to worry about. I didn't come here today to plead my innocence but to warn you again. Whoever is behind this, and it's not me, is clearly ruthless, well-resourced and determined that nothing will stand in their way. I hope you know what you are up against and that you're taking it seriously.'

He stood up.

'Wait a minute,' she jumped in. 'None of this helps me, this is just more veiled threats. You obviously know a lot more about what's going on here. If you're not guilty of anything then give me the information I need to get whoever is.'

'One thing I learnt in the war, Inspector. If the message is clear then there's no need to dig any deeper. How do you think I survived when so many of my colleagues didn't?' He stared at her for a few moments. 'There is a time to stop asking questions and just walk away. You have to accept this is Liberia, this is

Africa not the rural England of those detective books you love so much. Things work differently here.'

'It's true, Liberia is not England' – he even knew what books she read, that made her even more uneasy – 'but a death is a death anywhere and if your war experience enables you to accept a child's death as a price worth paying for whatever you're hiding then my war experience has taught me the opposite.' Gloria knew she sounded preachy but she couldn't stop. 'The only thing worth hanging on to is the value of each one of us.'

He was clearly very frustrated and moved towards the door.

'Enough of the lectures, Inspector. I have warned you and you won't listen so you have to accept the consequences and that,' he turned to Ambrose, 'is definitely not a threat, in case you're witnessing, it's a friendly warning. You are on dangerous territory here.' He wrenched the door open and banged it shut behind him. They could hear the clatter of his boots on the corridor as he stomped out.

'The Minister of Defence is afraid of something ma'am. It must be very big to make him afraid. Maybe it's better for us not to know, before we get scary too.'

'You're right about him being scared, Ambrose. But believe me, it's always better to know what you're up against.' She moved to the door and held it open for him. 'Well, we need to get on, and thanks for your help in there.'

'What help, ma'am? I just did what you told me and said nothing.'

'Yes, but you did it so well, Ambrose,' she smiled at him, 'and that's what makes the difference. But it was an odd meeting altogether. I'm not sure I believe him entirely but some of what he said made sense. And let's face it, if he had organised an attack on my house the results would have been different. Also, it's true what he said about Mr Ron's murder. These were amateurs or people who don't care. He is not an amateur and he cares very much, even if only about his political career. So we are still in the dark about a lot of things.' She ushered him out. 'Oh, and I need to see your research on the KVG urgently. I hope you've been able to finish it. Go and get it now and you can talk me through it.'

'Yes ma'am.' He was just out the door when he turned back. 'By the way, if you were wondering, there's no such word as 'priestling'. It's not even a very good made-up name.' And he smiled again.

Moses was coming in as Ambrose left. 'Did I see young Ambrose smiling there?'

Gloria nodded. 'It's his second time today, if he keeps this up he might actually start enjoying the work.'

She briefed Moses on the interview and he reluctantly agreed with her that Julu was probably telling the truth. He hadn't tried to present himself as a shining example of anything, just as a pragmatic strategist. His last statement, that they would have known if he had been behind the attack because it would have been successful, was chilling but had the ring of truth. So there had to be some other force at work here. What it was they didn't yet know but they were getting an idea of its shape and its power. What force could intimidate even Prince Julu, one of Liberia's most feared rebels?

On the way back up to the office Moses asked her if it was true the CID were trying to close the file on Ron.

'I heard they are trying to say it was a robbery that went badly wrong, I mean. . .'

'I know Moses, it is so clumsy and makes no sense. Someone is panicking. I'm going to speak to Ambrose now and then go and see Lamine. I think we should tell Paul and Alfred to focus on Banks and finding his family. They should leave the investigation into the Harbel children's murder to Sampson Moore, for now anyway.'

When she got in her office Ambrose was already there waiting with a whole pile of papers. As always he waited in silence for her to sit down and make the first move. She indicated to him to start talking and without looking at the papers he gave her the rundown on the KVG, at least what he had been able to research from the internet.

'Ok,' he cleared his throat 'first of all, the name itself. KVG stand for Kinders Van Gud, it's Afrikaans for Children of God. This was a movement which started in South Africa among the Afrikaners just after the end of apartheid. They are a group who resisted all the changes in the new South Africa and could not accept that they now had to live side by side as equals with black people.' He looked down at his papers and shuffled them. 'They have some very rude names for black people.' He looked at her again and smiled. 'Honestly ma'am, some of the language is so bad it is almost funny, but it certainly makes it clear that they believe black people are not just inferior but sub-human.'

'Sub-human?'

'Yes, it is extreme, even for South Africa. It sounds as if it's a kind of quasi-religious movement you know the kind of thing, quoting the bible to prove their superiority and their place as the 'Chosen People' – which justifies their attitudes and actions. They lobbied for an independent homeland within South Africa but that got nowhere and then they tried to undermine the new ANC government for a while with some guerrilla tactics.'

Gloria frowned. 'Bibles and bombs eh, a dangerous combination. Strong beliefs, capable of violence and, presumably, well resourced. They are starting to fit the profile of our killers.'

'I thought that ma'am but the thing is that in the last few years, although they haven't changed their philosophy or beliefs, they have toned down the violence and the racist rhetoric. They have now positioned themselves as a very right-wing political movement advocating change – mostly by constantly pointing out the corruption and failures of the current South African government as far as I can see. But they have publicly disavowed violence as a means to their end.'

'Disavowed means what? That they don't support violence publicly but might still see it as legitimate?'

'That's the impression I get. The website and any writings I could find present their right-wing views now as a reasonable alternative to South Africa's current problems. But anyone who thinks of other people as they do – less than human basically – is capable of doing anything to them.'

All of that tied in perfectly with Drake's behaviour and words. She told Ambrose what Drake had said about the children being like animals scurrying around in the dark and how he managed to be in a room full of Liberians but still put up some kind of invisible barrier between him and them.

Ambrose just looked pained. 'As if we don't have enough problems without people like him working here. Can't we check up on these people before they come here opening centres? And why is he doing it anyway, why spend all this money running centres for children you don't even think are human beings? Why isn't he back in his own country doing something?'

'Well that might be the first twisted clue, mightn't it? As you say, he's working with children he thinks are no better than animals, the reports we are getting about children disappearing are all from his centre, or that area anyway, and he's denying it. I suppose he is capable of violence but it still leaves the question of the diamond. And the bigger question of 'why'. Why do any of this stuff? Kill and torture children. What is all that for?'

'Oh I was just coming to that,' Ambrose broke in. 'I found a tiny reference to diamonds in a pamphlet written before the end of apartheid. The writer claimed that all the diamonds of Africa were given by God to the Afrikaners as a sign of his favour and their pre-eminent position, and more or less claimed they were entitled to take control of them any way they liked. It was the only reference I could find so I don't know how widely that belief is held but there are a lot of references to their 'birthright'. I suppose that could include ownership of all diamonds.'

'They sound crazier than some of our mad rebel groups.' Gloria had spoken the words before remembering that sober, earnest Ambrose had been part of those mad groups. She just couldn't connect articulate Ambrose with the violent out-of-control children she had come across during the war. He showed no reaction apart from nodding in agreement. Maybe he was distancing himself from it all. She wouldn't blame him for that.

'Well it doesn't make logical sense yet, Ambrose, and crazy as they might be, there will still be logic to what they do. It won't look that way to us but it will make perfect sense to Drake. Obviously we need to investigate Drake further and immediately. There could be more children at risk.'

'I would really want to be part of that investigation, ma'am. I don't know why you always leave me in the office. Even Izena gets to go out and investigate. Unless you think I am not good enough.'

Gloria was a bit taken aback by his words and his tone. 'Come on, Ambrose, you are as good as anyone here, as far as I know. But you also happen to be better educated and better organised than most of your colleagues so it makes sense to have you here bringing the information together, looking for connections, building up the bigger picture.'

'Oh, is that what I was supposed to be doing then?' The aggrieved tone of voice annoyed Gloria more than it should.

'Hey, don't push me, Ambrose. If you want to be a good police officer you take every duty you are given and do it to the best of your ability. Use the skills you have to help the whole team.' Ambrose's seminary and military training didn't allow him to shrug off what Gloria was saying but he wouldn't meet her eyes. 'Look, your insights led us to Bomi and to Aloysius's name and family, and now this information on the KVG is very valuable. That is a lot. Don't frown your face on me, we *work* for children Ambrose, not *act* like them.'

He finally laughed and relaxed a little. 'Ok, ma'am, thank you. But I would still like to do some field work.'

A few minutes later, with the team assembled Gloria ran through the updates emphasising that Julu was no longer a prime suspect for the death of Aloysius but was still considered implicated in the deaths in Harbel. She asked Ambrose to tell them what he had told her about the KVG – first advising him that 'disavowing' was probably an unnecessary word to throw in and might not endear him to his colleagues. This was followed by Izena's account of her discussions with Pascal and Boyes which had revealed, as far as she was concerned, absolutely nothing except their insistence that children were going missing from that area. Gloria told them that with this weight of evidence they needed to urgently investigate Drake but with some care so as not to upset him. They were quite a small team with Alfred and Paul away, Izena already overworked with the new cases and Lamine so deeply immersed in his 'stake-out' that he couldn't even be seen around the office.

She appointed Moses to head up the investigation into Drake with Ambrose and old Alfred supporting while she went first of all to get Lamine back. She was also going to pay a visit to the Minister of Social Welfare to alert her to the possible dangers facing children in the KVG centre and try and get her to do something about it.

'We meet back here at two, except if there's an emergency. And get thinking about connections, we have a lot of clues and leads now, we have names and information but we need to see how they join up. Don't just go about your own assignment. Try to keep up with what everyone else is doing. Talk to each other and share whatever information you manage to collect. No-one is going to solve this one on their own.'

When the others had gone she asked Moses where Luseni was. She couldn't recall seeing him for a while. Moses took her over to the board, away from the open door.

'Oh he's transferred, didn't you know? I just found out about it from the guys in CID. I think there's a letter on your desk about it.' There were a lot of letters on her desk, she just never seemed to get around to opening them, never mind answering them. 'Apparently he decided his skills would be better used in CID than here with us. And his uncle or cousin arranged it for him.' Neither of them stated the obvious about that. 'But I hear' – Moses always heard a lot more than she did – 'he was full of praise for you, I believe he described you as a dynamic and dedicated leader, so I don't know what you did to scare him but it worked.'

Gloria laughed 'What do you mean? I am dynamic and dedicated – or is that hard-headed and hard-mouthed?' Moses raised an eyebrow but said nothing. 'Oh I didn't scare him Moses, I just know too much about him. I think he'll do just fine in CID, and at least there aren't too many 'chopping' opportunities there as it's mostly dead people they deal with.'

'Well that's the worry. There's already talk that our case should be handed over to them as it's a murder investigation and we don't have the experience for it.'

'Well, we don't have much experience but it will be over *my* dead body if they try to take it off us. If CID gets it everything will be closed in a week to nobody's satisfaction but with the added benefit that no big people will be upset and everyone can carry on with whatever schemes they're involved in. On the other hand, if we keep it. . .'

Moses grinned. 'I know, we might even bring the right people to justice and upset a few more gangsters.'

'Right, but it does mean we need to get moving. Come on, Moses,' she stood up, 'let's get back on it. Why were the three children and Ron killed and who killed them? These are the main questions.'

She left then to look for Lamine but said she would be back for the afternoon meeting. The Polo was very hot and she was sure the air conditioning wasn't working again. After fiddling with it for a while she abandoned it and opened the windows. The air was warm and heavy and it neither cooled nor refreshed her, but the drive didn't take long and the mournful stretch of beach soon lay in front of her again. It seemed an age since she had been here at the start of the investigation but it didn't look as if it had changed much. If anything it looked emptier than her last visit, even the Haven of Refuge looked abandoned.

Up on the rocks she could see a few figures and walked towards them. The sand was burning even through her shoes and in her uniform shirt she could feel the sweat gathering at her neck and running down her back. She was not going to look very composed when they met. By the time she reached the base of the rocks Lamine was already standing there although she didn't recognise him at first. In dark wraparound sunglasses, a bandana and a loud t-shirt she got an idea of what he must have looked like in the war – quite intimidating.

'Lamine, good to see you. You must have seen me coming. How are things with you?'

'Well boss, this is not easy but I think I am onto something here. It took a while for the people to accept me so that's why I am dressed like this.' Gloria managed to look surprised as if she had just noticed what he was wearing. 'Once I did that it got easier and now they accept me as one of their own.'

I bet they do, Gloria said to herself. 'So what have you found out?'

'I think that better wait until I'm out of the way, Inspector, don't you think?' She turned to see the leader of the Rock Gang coming down towards her.

'Hi Francis.' He looked a bit taken aback that Gloria knew his name but kept on coming.

'If you need any further information about us, Inspector, just come and ask for it. There's no need to send your officers along. But I think you are more interested in the murder of that child than in us. I told you we were not involved with it and we are not involved with the people who did it. If we acted like that the locals would drive us out, you know that. And we don't act for anyone else, we are independent.'

'So we will cross you off the suspect list, Francis,' said Gloria, 'but what can you do to help us find the people who did it? I am pretty sure you know more than you told us.'

'Ok, Inspector, it's like this. That night we were not inside, the caves get very hot during the day and don't cool down until the early hours of the morning. We were sitting outside listening.' He paused as if sitting outside listening was a normal Liberian pastime. 'And we heard those people arrive. We didn't know it was a child they were burying, most of the bodies get dumped here for a good reason and we don't interfere. Then we heard them say that they were worried about being found out and the tall one with the funny accent said to them, "Don't worry, no-one can harm us, just as his own father couldn't save this poor child." Then we knew it was a child and went down to see.'

Lamine looked startled, obviously hearing this for the first time. Gloria just nodded. It made sense. They knew exactly what they were doing and it was one person leading them. The only thing that jarred a bit was the description of the man. Drake was a small man, but that could have been a trick of the light.

'Thanks Francis, it would have been useful to know this the first time we met.'

'Well I didn't know you then, Inspector, but I know I can trust you now.'

'How do you know that?'

'Well Lamine has told us all about you and he convinced us you are someone we can trust.'

Lamine looked completely baffled. Obviously the stake-out had worked the opposite way with Lamine giving information rather than collecting it. Anyway, it had had a positive effect and she could also see it was not going to be a problem to persuade Lamine to return to normal duties.

'Francis, if you trust me you will let me know if you hear anything else. Remember I am in the Family and Child Protection Unit so I am not interested in your thieving, or anything else, unless it hurts people.'

Francis Bryant nodded and smiled at her. 'It's a deal Inspector. Lamine, nice meeting you. Keep in touch, and remember to keep reading those books I gave you.'

Lamine just muttered, took off the bandana and sunglasses and started walking back to her car. Another great Liberian headline she thought, Gang Leader Teaching Police Recruits to Read.

She didn't refer to his experience on the way back to the office, Moses could deal with that. She told Lamine to get changed and be back in the office for the meeting in the afternoon. He agreed meekly, his attitude gone along with the sunglasses and the bandana. Well at least he knew he had been fooled by Francis Bryant, that was a start.

At two o'clock the entire team, apart from Paul and Alfred who were on their way back from Harbel, assembled in the office. Gloria welcomed Lamine back and told them about the valuable piece of information he had got from the gang after winning their trust and assuring them of their safety. She saw Lamine straighten up from his slouch at the back of the room at this praise which he knew he didn't really deserve. Moses reported that they had started looking into Drake and his work. He had an office on Gurley Street and appeared to run just one shelter, the one which had been damaged in Westpoint. From the outside it seemed like a classic street children's programme providing shelter, health care, education and protection. The day-to-day activities were overseen by two volunteers who were young, inexperienced Europeans although they said Drake visited the centre almost every day. Moses said he planned to go back and talk to the volunteers and also the children in the centre.

Ambrose had already picked up from Fr. Hilary, who ran the Star of the Sea parish in Westpoint, that KVG kept themselves to themselves. This was very strange for Westpoint where, despite its reputation for roughness, there was a strong community which would support you if you were actively part of it. Fr. Hilary had also said that no-one knew who the children at the centre were. The local children, the kids who worked with the fishermen and 'hussled' in the market, were taken care of at the St. Luke's shelter at the other end of Westpoint. The children at KVG were all outsiders.

'Drake is not telling us the real story boss. I think we need to have someone around the centre for a few days and nights to get an idea of what is really going on.'

'I agree Moses, what about Lamine? He's got some experience of that kind of work now.' They had already discussed this. Moses thought it would help to boost his confidence and they could see if he was learning from his different experiences. Lamine looked surprised but very happy. Moses said he would brief him afterwards.

Izena suddenly looked animated as if she was finally making some connections.

'Ma'am, I am just thinking. We also have two other reports which came in yesterday and today, both of them are about children who have disappeared.'

She outlined the stories of two children whose families lived in Voinjama and Ganta. One had been approached by an organisation called Families Together which claimed to link poor families living in the rural areas to their relatives in the city, and the other by a representative of the Ministry of Social Welfare making the same claim.

'They promised to bring the children down to the city to these relatives and make sure they were sent to school. The parents showed me the papers they signed, they looked very official, and the address and contact numbers they were given. They sent four of their children with these people and at first it was fine. They received messages from the children in the first week saying they were ok and going to school but after that the messages stopped and they've heard nothing since.' A few people shook their heads. There was a sad inevitability about the story.

'So these poor parents have come all the way from Ganta and Voinjama, ah, that would cost plenty.'

'They tried calling the numbers but they either couldn't get through or the phone would be answered by someone who was just rude to them, ma'am. That made them even more worried.'

'What about the Ministry? Did they try there?' Moses looked really angry now.

'They did, Captain. The papers from the Ministry were false and the other organisation 'Families Together' doesn't exist. Even the relatives know nothing about it. The parents are at their wits' end.'

How old were these girls?' Gloria asked.

'No that's the strange thing, the ones we know about were boys aged between ten and fourteen.'

Gloria's first thought, of course, had been that the children were being trafficked out the country but the fact they were all boys put paid to that. The trafficking of boys from Liberia was almost unheard of.

'Do we have their names?'

'Yes, and I've checked all the centres' registers and they are not there.'

'Well check with KVG, that's the obvious one, and maybe the reason he didn't want to give us his lists. It could even be why he has stopped Sr. Tony from working there. But if KVG is going to these very elaborate lengths to get a few children what is the reason? Aren't there enough children right here on the streets?'

'Body parts?' Again Ambrose had been doing his research. The sale of body parts for juju was a thriving industry in the region but this seemed like a very elaborate way to get them.

'It's a big operation for only a few children,' said Gloria.

'Well, ma'am,' Izena went on, 'we don't know the numbers. The parents who have come to look for the children are probably rare, most just don't have the resources to do that. So it could be a much larger number of children who have been brought down and no-one will ever know. Unless we do a radio campaign to ask people to come forward but even then. . .'

The war had destroyed so much of Liberia's infrastructure and, outside the few major towns, people were living in very isolated villages. Added to that, the war had created so much suspicion and mistrust that many people would probably not come forward even if they heard the announcement, fearing some kind of punishment.

'No, I think we are going to have to get this at the source which seems to be Drake and his outfit. But we need some urgent action. Moses, you start putting more pressure on him. Lamine, you have to watch for all movement of children around that centre and report anything you see. Do not talk to them.

Ambrose, go back and talk to more people in the Westpoint community, see if we can get any idea of the numbers of children involved. I will go to see the Minister. She will at least want to avoid a scandal, and there could well be someone in the Ministry involved in this. But I still don't see what makes it worth all this effort.'

On the way out she asked Izena how she was coping with Pendle. 'I think he's bored but waiting for his real story, whatever that is. He just follows me around everywhere and then keeps disappearing. He is very close to Drake though. I've seen them together a number of times along with that other one, the tall one.'

'The tall one. . . of course, Kopius.' The tall one, now that was a familiar phrase, Gloria thought. Could Kopius be involved as well? 'Well keep a close eye on him and his friends.'

13.

GLORIA'S MEETING at the Ministry went pretty much as she expected. First of all the Minister herself was too busy to see her so she had to meet the Deputy Minister, Peter Dennis. Peter was known to be the real brains behind the social welfare reforms anyway so she knew he would take the situation more seriously. A former social worker who had been recalled from his job in Ohio Child and Family services in the States, he had come back full of ambitious plans to make Liberia a model of childcare in Africa. His long absence from the country, however, had dimmed his memory of Liberia's social and cultural minefield and his plans had been quickly modified then modified again to try and find a system which the country could afford and which was acceptable to local people.

Gloria walked through the empty reception area – Deputy Ministers were clearly not accorded much respect in the ministerial hierarchy – straight to Peter's office. He shouted for her to come in and when her eyes adjusted to the gloom (the electricity had failed again) she was a bit startled to see he was wearing a cream silk suit, with a matching waistcoat, and a red bow tie which looked a bit incongruous against the background of his rather decrepit office.

'Are you going to a wedding Peter?'

He laughed briefly. His months of working with a broken

down social care system in a factionalised unity government had taken its toll both on his health and his humour. But Gloria liked him, he was an honest man trying to make the system work against impossible odds.

'Have a seat, Glo.' He was the only one apart from Abu who called her that. 'Have you come about the new Juvenile Justice Bill? I know we should have completed the first draft by now but it's still on the Minister's desk.'

Gloria didn't set a lot of store by Bills and Acts but her position meant she was on a number of these committees.

'No, it's something a bit more urgent. Why has it been on her desk for so long anyway, she's not actually reading it, is she?'

The Minister was a political appointment whose only question on social welfare reform was 'What will this do for my career?' She had taken the job under the misapprehension that social welfare was the warm caring side of government and, Gloria believed, had pictured herself kissing babies and opening orphanages. The reality was very different. She quickly realised that real social welfare reforms affected all kinds of people, including business people, local leaders and even her Cabinet colleagues, who used Liberia's lack of system to prey on and exploit children in hundreds of different ways. Every new piece of legislation which made it harder for people to abuse children had been met with huge opposition. Only the week before the new Children's Act had again been sent back from the House of Representatives with questions about whether all this talk of children's rights would affect their African traditions and customs. It would get through, pressure from the international community would see to that, but it was a fight. It meant that the Minister was unwilling to take on any more controversial issues and so the draft of the new Juvenile Justice Bill was likely to be severely delayed. The rumour from Moses was that the Minister was trying to get a move to a less controversial Ministry.

Gloria explained what was going on. Peter had heard about the murders and been appalled by them but he didn't know the background. His face grew longer and longer as she explained everything they knew so far. When she had finished he stared at her in silence for a moment.

'Poor children.' Liberia's violence never failed to sicken him. 'And what a story that will make for the press. We will be destroyed in the media if they get wind of this. Gloria, you have to solve this before we all suffer the consequences. And you know I don't mean my job,' he added hurriedly, 'this will be the excuse some of those politicians are looking for to stop the reforms and go back to a system they call 'traditional'. He rolled his eyes. 'And we all know traditional just means that the more power you have the more you can get away with.'

Gloria nodded. Both of them also knew that if accusations were made it would not be the Minister of Social Welfare or the Director of Police who would take the blame – it would be them.

'What can I do?' Gloria knew that Peter was quite isolated within the Ministry, resented by the old guard who didn't want anything to change but feared by the new gang who thought his zeal for reform was going to hurt too many influential men in town.

'I just need you to know what's going on. Whoever is behind this has already tried to hush up Ron Miller's death. They obviously have a lot of influence.'

She told him about the Chief Inspector's warning. 'If they can intimidate him then they are very powerful. But they must have people helping them from within your Ministry. If you can find out who they are that will be a great help.'

'You know how it is Gloria. Our payroll had over three hundred ghost employees on it last month. The place is still in chaos although Taiwo' – Taiwo was the Assistant Minister for Administration – 'is making a difference. But I will make some enquiries.' That was all he could do. They were fighting a forest fire with thimblefuls of water.

By this stage Gloria couldn't stop herself any more. 'So are you going to a wedding or is this how you dress for work?'

He smiled 'I know, it's too much eh! Maybe I should have worn something darker but it will give my enemies something else to talk about.' He could see Gloria was still puzzled. 'We have all been called to the Executive Mansion this evening for the release of the report into the fire on Inauguration Day. Surely you have to be there, weren't you investigating it?'

Gloria sighed. She vaguely remembered being told something about this but it hadn't registered. She felt wrong-footed by being reminded like this. She would really have to get organised, she couldn't afford to miss events like this, not if she wanted to have any influence. There was probably a memo on her desk informing her about it but as she hadn't really sat at her desk in the last week, she couldn't say for sure.

'Thanks for the reminder, Peter. I better get home and make sure the uniform is smart enough. What time is it starting?'

'In about forty minutes.'

Where had the day gone? she thought. There was definitely no time to go home and get back, she would have to go just as she was.

On the way out she called Moses and told him to meet her at the Mansion. She was not sitting through this on her own. She then called Abu who sounded quite wary.

'Aunt Glo, what's up? Something happen?'

'No Abu, it's just that I will be back a bit later tonight. What are you doing?'

'I've got practice after school, I have to go, and we've got a big game at the weekend. I can stay with Morris tonight instead of coming home.'

'Ok but no walkabout, remember. Practice and then home

and I will call you when I get in. And by the way' – she looked at her watch – 'shouldn't you be at home now anyway?'

'No, we are having the elections for my council.'

'Your council?' Her mind went blank for a few seconds. 'Oh yes, the student council. Are Morris or Leo running for any position?'

'Well not Leo, auntie, as he goes to a different school.' She could hear the exasperation in his voice. 'He attends CWA, I told you that ages ago. You never listen to anything I tell you.'

'Of course, I remember now, sorry, there's a lot going on here. Right, well I have to go now. See you tomorrow then.'

'Ok Aunt Glo, see you, and tell the old ma, hello from us students.' Gloria didn't promise to pass on his greetings to the President.

At five sharp Gloria and Moses were sitting together on the fourth row in the Parlour of the Executive Mansion waiting for the press conference to start. There was no sign of the President and the room was beginning to heat up. It was packed with government, press, diplomats and security and the air conditioning was doing very little to cool them down. Gloria thought for a moment how funny it would be if they spontaneously combusted during a press conference about the last fire. Sitting next to her, Moses looked even more uncomfortable and kept whispering about needing a Club beer. She said they should go for one as soon as they could escape from here.

'Where's Hawa?'

'She's still at the airport, she'll be back later. They're having an initial inquest.'

A Nigerian plane from the Mid Flight Company had overshot the runway the previous day and crashed into some trees. The only casualties had been two goats which had been travelling as cargo and had mysteriously disappeared after the crash landing.

There had also been some pictures in that day's papers of the cabin crew elbowing passengers out the way to get off the plane first which, of course, had caused much amusement in Monrovia. The Ministry of Transport had opened an inquest about safety and aviation standards in general.

'The first thing they should do is change their name,' Gloria said, 'I mean Mid Flight! The name doesn't exactly inspire much confidence!'

'Well it's not that but the fact that after the crash it took an hour before any kind of fire service vehicle could get there, by which time the fire had gone out by itself. Questions are being asked.'

Gloria was just glad the questions weren't being asked of her. They stood as Her Excellency Madame Helen Sirleaf entered the room and went straight to the podium. The President was alternately portrayed as the Nation's Grandmother or as the Iron Lady depending on the circumstances or who was reporting but one thing was sure, she definitely was a survivor. Gloria thought about all those men, the warlords who had terrorised people or the old elite who tried to impress and intimidate with their money and education, and she had outdone them all, even beating the national football hero at the election. That was only the start but it was a good start. She had so many enemies though, many of them sitting in the Senate and the House of Representatives, it was a wonder she managed to get anything done.

The President smiled benignly at the room and told them to please be seated. Tonight she was the Nation's Grandmother obviously. There were no introductions just a prayer led by the very good looking pastor from the Global Healing Temple, and then the President. Her speech was very precise, outlining the events of the fire, the scope of the investigation and its conclusions.

'There was no conspiracy or plot to kill me, just bad wiring and poor maintenance.' They laughed dutifully. 'As you can imagine, I am delighted with that but also saddened it has taken so long to get to that conclusion. We have no more time to waste in Liberia. We cannot afford to go down any more blind alleys, to spend any more time looking inward at government and fighting ourselves.' This was a reference to the political bickering that had plagued the new government. 'We must, and we will, look outwards to the people. The poor who need jobs, the sick who need hospitals and the students who need schools. We will press ahead with re-building our country, healing our wounds and creating a free and just society. If there are some of you listening to me today who are not prepared to do this' – she scanned the front row where the Ministers of Defence, Health, Education and Social Welfare were sitting – 'then you should leave. We have to put Liberia at the heart of our politics not our politics at the heart of Liberia.'

Someone at the back of the room started clapping and it gathered momentum until everyone was applauding. Liberians loved a rousing speech and the President had tapped into the mood of the country. People were fed up and hungry for real change. The President ended by thanking all those who had supported her in office so far and urged everyone to come together and work for the common good. The brief ceremony ended with the national anthem and in just under forty five minutes they were all outside again.

'At least it didn't take long,' was Moses' only comment. 'How did you get on at the Ministry?' She told him as they drove down the road to one of the many small bars on the beach. It was empty and they sat under an umbrella and ordered two cold Clubs.

'I'm going to have to stop drinking and take up some exercise.' Gloria's resolutions on exercise and healthy lifestyle were made two or three times most months and often didn't last longer than the beer she made them over. Moses didn't even respond. A few minutes later Gloria broke the silence.

'Is Lamine watching Drake's place?'

'Yes, and Ambrose is still there. I've got a feeling he's going to stay around with Lamine. Funny, they are so different but they seem to get on.'

'We need to get a move on. This case is just dragging on and on. We need to nail Drake and stop this. Friends or no friends. If there is the slightest move from his centre tonight we bring him in, and then see what his friends will do. I just don't see how he can have influential contacts here, he can hardly bring himself to talk to black people. I can't see him being able to sit down with our big people and bribe them. It doesn't make any sense to me. Is there any more news from Paul and Alfred?'

'They're back and want to meet you tomorrow morning. They sounded very excited.'

Gloria stood up abruptly, feeling tiredness wash over her. 'I'm going home Moses. I need to sleep. Do you need a lift back?'

Moses shook his head. 'I'm going to walk back. I need a clear head to deal with Mammy Pepper,' which is how he always referred to Hawa's mother. 'She's on the warpath again because we are refusing to send the children to extra school on Saturday. We pay enough for that school they go to already. They should be learning everything they need to during the week. Anyway I'll see you tomorrow.' He got up too and then turned back to her. 'Why don't you come for something to eat? Hawa will be back and she will be happy to see you.' Gloria hesitated and then decided she needed some company tonight and it would be good to catch up with Hawa.

In a few minutes they were at Moses' modest house. The

redoubtable Mammy Pepper gave Gloria a great welcome and Moses a glare. The house was quiet as the children had been put to bed and when Hawa arrived home they sat down to eat almost at once. An unspoken agreement meant they did not discuss work, well at least not in any detail. Hawa told them there was complete confusion at the airport with everyone blaming everyone else.

'Honestly Gloria the pre-assessment meeting went on for five hours with everyone talking different-different things. So-so nonsense the whole business. And to make it worse all the people's things went missing from the plane so the Nigerians are calling us thieves and the Assistant Minister said if we were thieves then they should stop flying their yama-yama planes into our country.'

They all roared laughing. It sounded like a very typical regional discussion. Gloria and Moses did not discuss their work but Gloria found herself relaxing a little and enjoying the warmth of being with friends. She could have stayed much later but knew she would be no use the next day if she didn't get some sleep so she took her leave and drove up the quiet road to her apartment.

She spent the night half asleep but alert to every noise. The satisfaction of having her apartment back to herself hadn't lasted very long. She was no longer sleepy, now she felt over-charged. She phoned Abu, who was fine, made herself some tea, tried to read her book and finally gave up and opened her notes again. This was a puzzle and a half. The only way it would all make sense, as far as she could see, was if they were all working together in some giant conspiracy. But who had the influence and power to bring all these different people together and if they did what was the purpose? To smuggle a few children out for body parts? The scale of it was all wrong. They were going to solve parts of this case but she couldn't see the whole story and that gnawed away at her.

Eventually she fell asleep in the chair and awoke sometime later in the dark, the faces of Aloysius and Ron and the two boys in Harbel floating around her. She opened the doors to her balcony and the night breeze blew the images away. She hadn't been involved in many murders but she could remember the faces, and the gruesome details, of every victim she had dealt with. She worried that if each case left this mark on her what was she going to be like in a few years time. She would be completely haunted, and the little space she had in her life at the moment for family, relationships and fun would be completely squeezed out. But another part of her knew she didn't want to lose any of them either, not yet, not until they were at rest. She went to bed but the night was long and hot and she woke in the morning tired and heavy. These killings were getting to her, although she would admit it to no-one.

She was in the office before seven that morning but only had half an hour to herself before Paul and Alfred bounced in, eager to report back.

'Morning ma'am. We wanted to tell you everything before the day got too busy.'

She nodded, her head feeling as if it was stuffed with cotton wool.

'Did you see Banks' son then?'

'No, he told us the boy was still with the aunt and had had a relapse but neither were his wife or his other children back. It was just him in that big house. He looked even worse than when we saw him the last time. He's like a ghost and people say he never leaves the house, he just sits on the porch all day.'

Alfred continued with the story. 'The police there have done nothing to investigate the murder. They are saying it was heart men, so they will never be found and that it's the same community people who know who the heart people are and should tell them. As far as they're concerned the investigation is closed. I would say they didn't try very hard. In fact I don't think they ever leave that fine police station.'

'What about the families?'

'Oh yes, they are ok. Apparently your promise is like some kind of magic so they don't need to worry. Famata says hi and wants to know when she will see you. She's very smart I think, but she is too small to be taking care of the old people. It's not correct.'

'I don't know about magic,' said Gloria, 'but I did try to tell all those big people what I would do if anything happened to them. And you are right about Famata but there's nothing we can do about that. It is too bad though that those guys have done nothing to investigate the murders or even to make a show of investigating. Anyway, thanks guys, good job. Go and write it up straight away and then I want you both back on duty here.'

She was just finishing when a noise drew her out into the corridor. Lamine and Ambrose were standing in the corridor with Marcus Drake and he was furious.

She couldn't tell which was making him angry, that he had been arrested or that the arrest had been carried out by two young black men.

'You people will be sorry for this,' he hissed at her as he was escorted down to the interview room. At least he called us people thought Gloria but she said nothing until he was safely inside.

'Right Ambrose,' she looked at him with a neutral expression, 'you better come into my office and explain what's going on, and it had better be good. Lamine was told to observe Drake, you were supposed to be making enquiries in the community. You were not supposed to do anything more than that without permission.'

Ambrose looked tired but energised, 'I know ma'am but last night I decided to stay with Lamine. We sat in a cook shop across from Drake's centre for hours and nothing happened. Then, just when it was getting dark, we saw him come out of the centre with five children. He put them into his pick-up. After that nothing much happened so we kept on observing, as you told us to. When it was fully dark Lamine and I took turns walking past the pick-up to check on the children, just to make sure they were ok.'

'That's all good so far Ambrose. But you should have called someone, Moses or me, for further orders.'

Ambrose looked sheepish. 'We didn't have a phone or a radio between us ma'am, well nothing that worked anyway.'

'Right, we'll talk about that later. What happened next?'

'Well as far as we could see the children were lying on a mattress in the car sleeping, I mean it was dark and we couldn't stare in but they looked peaceful enough. Then just before daybreak we heard all this holler-holler, it was crazy. Drake was shouting, there was screaming and then crying.' Ambrose was animated now. 'Drake then came to the door of the centre and started shouting at these two young girls that the project was finished, he was closing the centre and they should find their own way back to their countries. He was like a crazy man, they were crying and the neighbours were beginning to wake up. He had his suitcase and was obviously going to leave so we thought it best to stop him.' He finished and sat back shaking his head. 'What a night ma'am.'

'You did ask for some field experience Ambrose. You certainly got some. What about the children?'

'Oh yes, we found they were actually tied up and I think they had been drugged but they are not harmed. We brought them in as well. And the volunteers.' He grimaced. 'The desk sergeant is not happy. Oh, and by the way, ma'am, one of the children he had in the car was your friend Pascal, all tied up like a chicken.'

'Pascal? How did he get there? What about Boyes, did you find him?'

'No, he wasn't in the car and the centre was empty. It looks as if Drake really was closing his operation.'

'That is worrying, but good job Ambrose, really good work. You and Lamine have done well. I think we've got him this time. We'll tell him we are going to charge him with attempted kidnapping and suspected murder and then leave him to cool off. See if that has any effect on him. Where are the children now?'

'They're in the conference room.'

'Ok well, get them some food and make sure someone stays with them. See if any of them match the description of the children who were reported missing. And get someone to explain to them that they are not in trouble.'

Gloria went into the interview room and looked at Drake. He was literally shaking with rage and she thought she could see specks of foam at the corners of his mouth. He didn't respond when Gloria told him what the charges against him were. He just glared at her. She sent for Moses and after half an hour they went back in to see Drake together. As they had no equipment to tape the interview they called in Izena to take notes.

Gloria opened.

'Mr Drake you were arrested by my officers who found children tied up in the back of your car. Can you explain what you were doing?'

No response.

'Right Drake, let me explain how it works here. If you refuse to answer you should be detained here but as we have no secure holding cell you will be taken down to the Central Prison and held there. We will bring you here for questioning every day and take you back there every night until you start answering. Is that clear?' There was a slight twitch around his eyes. 'Before you ask, there is no official South African representation in the country at the moment. I believe the nearest is in Nigeria, and it could easily take a week for us to contact them so they can come visit you – if they decide to visit you at all.'

Drake's expression had changed completely now. The mention of the Central Prison had clearly scared him. It was infamous for overcrowding, violence and disease. Gloria knew that Drake could hardly bear to be in the same room as black people never mind sharing a cell with them. He actually found them abhorrent. Right at the moment he looked as if he was going to be sick and then he started talking very quickly, words bubbling out.

'Look, it was a misunderstanding. I was taking the children to meet someone who could help them get a new life. That's what my organisation does.'

'Which person? Where were you meeting them?'

'I don't know. My job was just to select the ones who would most likely succeed if trained properly, and then bring them up to the border with Sierra Leone and hand them over to someone who would then take them to their new places.'

'You had them trussed up like animals. What kind of new life were you giving them? Forced conscription in some awful war, or maybe forced labour somewhere, or were you just going to sell them for their body parts? Maybe you are a heart man after all Drake.' Gloria was on a roll. She had waited a long time to confront him.

But Drake looked genuinely baffled. 'I only tied them to

stop them hurting themselves, the same way we would do with cattle or goats.'

Gloria could feel Moses tensing, getting ready to pounce.

'See, I don't understand Drake. Your organisation is called Children of God and yet you treat these 'Children of God' as animals. It doesn't make any sense to me.'

Drake had relaxed a little and even started to smile. 'Oh they are not the children of God, we are, we the members. We are just called upon to treat them as you would any domestic animal. You must know that story in the bible, God gave them dominion over the whole earth etc. That's us.'

'And why then do you come to places like Liberia if we are no better than animals, why not just stay in your own country.'

Drake had no idea Gloria was leading him on. He seemed to be relieved to finally talk about his true thoughts and philosophies as if they made perfect sense. As if the months of holding himself back could now be rolled away. On and on he babbled about their superiority, dominion, quoting bible verses and other sources as if they were having a school debate.

'And to answer your question about why do we come here, well we have been given dominion over the earth, over Africa. We are the only ones who can bring order out of the chaos. And we are always looking for a place where we may have to settle in the future.'

Truly, spectacularly mad. His xenophobic philosophy just kept on coming. He admitted that for many months he had been accepting children into his centre who he had then moved on by taking them up through Bomi and to the border. He only knew they were going to be trained for something better. He asked no more questions than that, in fact wasn't even interested. All his orders came to him in letters or by email.

In answer to questions about where these orders came from,

Drake looked blankly at them. 'Well, from my headquarters in South Africa of course, the same people who sent me here.'

'The people who sent you here to kidnap children?'

'No, the people who know we have a duty to rescue some of these creatures and try to turn them into something useful.'

'Did it never occur to you these were children with families who would miss them, that these children belonged here in their own country and with their own families?'

Drake just laughed. 'A government made up of people who willingly gave guns to ten year olds and taught them to fight and destroy their own families and villages? Families who are only too happy to hand their children over to strangers, probably expecting some money for them? I don't think so, Inspector. You may try to talk like civilised people but you're not, that's the fact.'

And then Moses punched him hard sending him flying backwards off the chair and bouncing off the wall.

'You'll have to excuse me Mr. Drake, it must be my lack of civilisation.'

Gloria pulled Moses' arm. 'Enough Moses, let's take a break.'

They left Drake searching for his broken tooth and went outside. Gloria didn't even mention the punch.

'What do you think?'

Moses looked at her. 'I know what you're thinking. We've got the kidnapper but is he cold and ruthless and sufficiently well-connected for the murders and the intimidation. I don't think so. And, unfortunately, I think he genuinely believes what he's doing is right.'

She nodded. 'Exactly. Let's try him with Aloysius and see what we get.'

But by the time they got back Drake had retreated into himself, sitting and rocking quietly on the chair. They waited and then Gloria spoke.

'Ok, Mr. Drake, we are ready to take you to the prison now.'

He looked up panicked. 'I thought you wouldn't do that if I answered your questions and I've done that.'

'Well not all of them, not yet anyway. What about this child, do you recognise him?'

She placed a photo of Aloysius in front of him. He stared at it for a while and then said, 'Yes I do.'

'Was he ever in your centre?'

'My centre? Of course not. He lived in Bomi. I used to see him at the border sometimes selling peanuts and sometimes he would bring me a note or a message about where to take the children.'

'Are you sure?'

'Of course, he was unusually smart and polite. I remember him well. But why are you showing me this?'

'Because he was killed on the beach not far from here a few days ago by people speaking in a strange accent, an accent something like yours.'

Drake looked genuinely confused. 'But why would I kill him, why would I kill anyone, it's against my religion you know. And this little boy was from Bomi, what was he doing down here?'

She told him the story of the diamond and the prayers and he looked more and more baffled.

'Look Inspector, I've told you what we believe, and got punched for it,' – he glared at Moses who just grinned back at him – 'but this other stuff, child sacrifices and diamonds is all mumbo jumbo. We don't do any of that. I think someone is fooling you.'

'What about these children then?'

She showed him the picture of the two boys from Harbel but he looked blank.

'Are these from Bomi as well?'

'No, these boys are from Harbel, out near the airport'

'Well I'm sorry but I've never been to Harbel, only to the airport.' When she finally asked about Ron, Drake started laughing, albeit quietly and with one eye on Moses.

'It sounds to me as if someone is weaving a very intricate story to pull you in the wrong direction Inspector. I am no killer and I would have no motive for killing children or foreigners. I admit what I was doing may have looked like kidnapping and I will defend my actions in court but this, no, for this you will have to look elsewhere.'

'I suppose you will be expecting your friends in the government to get you out.' Moses joined in.

Again he looked blank for a moment and then seemed to come to his senses a little.

'My friends in government? I'm afraid, Inspector, your sources, or those children you have in uniforms out there, are filling your head with nonsense. I've got no friends in government here, wouldn't want any either. I was just obeying orders about what to do with the children at my centre. I can show you the emails and letters, I have everything filed away. But for the rest, it sounds as if you have a murderer on your hands and. . .' he faltered now, 'and it is not me, do you understand it is not me.' He shouted the last few words and then slumped in the chair as if the effort of thinking and speaking had drained him.

Their big breakthrough was turning out to be just another piece of the puzzle, not even a key piece either by the sounds of it. If what he had told them was the truth they were no nearer to understanding who was behind this and what it was all about. Clearly Drake had been a conduit for children being taken out the country but Gloria was willing to bet there was no way to trace where they had gone and for what and that his mad stories would all turn out to somehow be true. Her frustration which she had kept under control until then was boiling over and now she wanted to punch someone or something. As she was marching up the corridor she met Izena coming down with an old lady and a young boy in tow. Both of them were crying.

'Inspector, this is Florence, you remember I told you about her coming from Ganta to look for her son. And this is her son Friday. He was one of the children in the car, we got him just in time.'

Gloria shook the lady's hand. She was crying and smiling at the same time and holding on to her son with her other hand in a tight grip.

'What about the other boy?'

'Friday identified him. Drake moved him out last week, Friday would have been moved too but he was sick. I have to tell his mother the bad news.'

'No leave that to me. I will talk to her. Take Friday and his mother for something to eat and then see if one of those centres can get them new clothes and arrange for transport back home.'

'What about Pascal? He's still downstairs and he's quite shocked. I've never seen him so quiet. He says Boyes was taken too. They were grabbed by some men right off the street soon after leaving here and taken to Drake. That same night Boyes was put in a car and taken away. Pascal feels really guilty about that. He says it was his job to protect Boyes.'

'Thanks Izena. I will talk to him too. What a mess, what a terrible mess.'

She went down to the main conference room which now had the four remaining children including Pascal. As soon as he saw her he started crying. Tough little Pascal crying, she had never seen that before. She gave him a hug and then told them all to sit down while she talked to them. They all had shocked faces. The youngest was a tiny little boy who looked about eight or nine.

Gloria explained as best she could probably what they already knew, and told them they should not be afraid. They would be going somewhere safe until their parents could be found. She was going to ask Izena to take care of them and find them a decent shelter to go to but decided to ask Ambrose instead. He seemed much more sympathetic and the way the children were sitting around him told her they trusted him too. Izena's brisk efficiency was not what they needed at the moment, she could do the write-ups instead. She told them to work together but to make sure the children were safe.

Gloria's next task was to talk to the old lady whose son they had just missed rescuing. The mother listened in silence as Gloria explained what they knew so far and didn't react even when she had finished. Up close Gloria could see she wasn't really old at all, probably in her late forties but her lined face and stoop told the story of years of poverty and war, of running, being scared and sacrificing herself for her family. To have survived all that only to hand your child over to these people didn't bear thinking about. At the end she stood and shook Gloria's hand.

'Thank you, Inspector. I have to go back to the others now but if you hear anything you can contact me through my uncle, he works at the Ministry of Rural Development. The lady officer has his name.'

Her English was clear and educated and not the accent of a country woman at all. Gloria promised they would continue the investigation although her words sounded hollow even to her own ears. She left the woman feeling even angrier and more useless than she had felt at the start of the day.

Upstairs, Ambrose was on the phone calling the different centres. Pascal was sitting next to him and had cheered up a little. He was advising Ambrose which centres he should contact and outlining the comparative advantages and disadvantages of each of them. Boys Town Outreach – too tough, Healing Hands and Thunder of God – too religious, Lost Child of Liberia – good food but too strict, St. Luke's – the home in Larkpazee was fine but the Hostel in Vai town was very rough, and so on. In the end, the two boys who were friends were taken to the Mission of Hope Centre in Old Road and the small child, on Pascal's advice, was taken to the Princess Diana Homes for Girls on Snapper Hill. Although it was a home for girls Pascal said they also took in small boys, and the women who ran it were very kind. Thank goodness for inside information. Pascal himself refused to go anywhere for two reasons. He was used to taking care of himself but also he said he had to find Boyes.

Ambrose left with the other children and Gloria sat with Pascal. She had already dispatched Moses along with young Alfred and Christian, the latter recently returned from a bout of malaria, up to Bomi to the border to see if they could get any more information on the children and possibly even stop the last group from crossing over. Paul had been sent back to Harbel with old Alfred to bring Banks in for questioning, he was clearly involved somehow. And she also had the Chief Inspector demanding to see her immediately to know what was going on. At least they had one full day before the press would be able to print any story so they had to get it sorted by then.

'Pascal, can you remember anything else about Drake or that centre, anything at all? Did anyone else come to visit or did you hear them talking about anything? What about the two people who worked there, the two volunteers?' Gloria also had the volunteers in custody but they seemed totally bewildered.

Pascal thought for a moment. 'No, those girls there were more scarey than me. They got plenty fuss, all day just so-so crying and crying.' He shook his head, mystified by the ways of foreigners. 'Everything made them scarey, the children, the community people and that crazy man most of all.'

So the girls were afraid of everyone, thought Gloria. Drake isolated them and made them scared as a way of controlling them.

'Da' one say she tire of everything, even da mosquito bite scratching them too much.' Pascal laughed. 'The girl say she will go look for her country people. She asked me' – he attempted to imitate the high nervous voice of the volunteer – 'where I could find the embassy.' He looked up at Gloria. 'I no tell her nuttin, I tell myse'f say her one must go look for it.' He sucked his teeth in contempt. 'After that one different person came one-one time. He just see us but he not speak, except to Drake.'

'Did they touch you, or beat you or try to do anything bad to you?'

He shook his head. 'No, no beating, no cussing. They give us good chop and just left us in that place locked up. That last night the chop was too sweet and everyone ate plenty. When we woke up we were in the back of the car, with the rope all round us.'

Drugged of course, she thought.

'Ok Pascal, listen. I've sent the other officers back up to Bomi to look for Boyes and the others. It's not safe for you to even try and go there. Promise you won't try. You can come here every day and I will tell you what's going on.'

'But I have to do something. I the one suppose to mind him.'

Gloria knew that friendships on the street were all these children had and that friends were family, advisers, companions and protectors all rolled into one.

'Well why don't you ask around, see if you can hear anything more about what happened to these children? And why would they want to take these boys out the country?'

'Ok auntie. I will go to the St. Luke's, that's the nearest one.'

Gloria had been to that particular shelter which was in a disused warehouse in Benson Street. It was literally a shelter, with a few mats on a cold cement floor and nothing more.

'Good. But don't take any risks. There are still some very bad people out there.'

She left Pascal eating his egg and bread and went back to her office. There was still the Chief Inspector to deal with and then the press release which she would have to write herself to be sure it didn't contain too many inaccuracies.

14.

IT WAS LATE afternoon by the time Gloria had finished briefing the Chief Inspector. His initial enthusiasm at the thought that they had caught the killer quickly leaked away to be replaced by a lot of gloomy head-shaking as Gloria completed her story.

'Great,' he said, 'so now we have a British national dead, a South African national in custody for kidnapping and we still don't know who is behind the killings. The press are going to eat this up.'

Gloria couldn't think of anything comforting to say – and didn't really see why she should – when the Director of Police himself walked into the office. The Director of Police never walked to anyone else's office. In fact he was seldom in the building at all as far as anyone could tell. Rumour had it he'd been a taxi driver in New York until the opposition members in the senate had pushed through his appointment to prevent the President's preferred choice, a man with a lot of police and political experience, getting the job.

Given his lack of experience of real policing, his absence from the country during the worst years of the civil war and his complete lack of ideas on how to deal with the post-war crime wave in the capital, the story was that his only qualification was the fact he looked very good in the uniform. The gaudy, quasi-military uniform suited him and everyone admitted that he cut a fine figure on public occasions standing next to the President. He did not look well now though, somewhere beyond flustered and just before panic. Ignoring Gloria, he rattled off a series of questions about the arrest of Drake at the chief, who sat in silence until the questions finally petered out.

'Director, this is Inspector Gloria who is heading up the investigation, she has just been briefing me and I'm sure can answer all your questions.'

The Director looked at her as if noticing her for the first time. 'I haven't really come to ask questions, I know what has happened and I know what the consequences will be if we don't find a solution.'

As he continued to talk Gloria realised that 'finding a solution' for the Director, was not the same thing as finding the killers. It was, in fact, almost the opposite. He was telling her to close the investigation, release Drake and move on to something else. But Gloria could see he was on the verge of panic. He was afraid, deeply afraid of something or someone. She knew direct disagreement was not going to work but she needed to get him out of the picture.

'That would be the best thing, sir, the best thing for all of us, if we could just close this down.' The Chief Inspector, who had clearly been expecting a firestorm, looked bemused but only for a moment. 'The only problem is we have Rufus Sarpoh on our backs.'

The Director, who had briefly looked relieved, was now speechless. Rufus Sarpoh was Monrovia's greatest investigative reporter – according to his own by-line – well known for his tenacity in investigating rumours of corruption and his delight in running with a story which embarrassed the government. If there was any suggestion of a cover-up he would be on to it. The street kids and the neighbours in Westpoint had already told him some of what had happened. And he was waiting downstairs for more information – which inevitably meant he was soaking up the whole story. There was no need for phone hacking here, just hang around the right corridors and give the key people some 'cold water' as it was known, and you could get all the information you wanted.

The Director knew that any suspicion of a cover-up would ruin him completely.

'You misunderstood me, Inspector.' He sounded like a man under enormous pressure. 'I was just giving you some advice. For all our sakes you would do well to complete your investigations as soon and as efficiently as possible.'

He left them as abruptly as he had arrived and Gloria felt the now familiar wave of weariness wash over her. It really felt as if they were being sucked further and further into a morass of lies and deceptions but without getting to the heart of anything. Who had killed Aloysius and the other boys? With the Director now being added to the list of powerful people trying to guide the investigation, she wondered just how deep the corruption went.

'Gloria,' the Chief interrupted her thoughts, 'you could hand the whole business over to CID you know, without any shame. And it might be safer. Even I can't protect you from all these forces you know.'

'I'm sure CID would have the whole thing wrapped up by this afternoon, Chief Inspector. Drake would be free and some person we've never heard of dragged off to jail for the murders. No thanks. If this unit is going to have any credibility we have to see this through to the end and make sure those children and their families get justice.'

She was aware she was beginning to sound more like a crusader than a policewoman. She also knew that the office had started referring to her as 'Mother of the Station' in mockery of

206

the President's 'Mother of the Nation' title, but she couldn't help it. She would not be beaten by this cabal of powerful men and their leader – whoever that was.

She stood up, anger bringing her a new rush of energy. 'Thanks for the advice, Chief. I appreciate it but I have to get back to work. I have a press release to get out before someone starts spreading the wrong stories.' She left the room.

At the top of the stairs a figure stepped out of the shadows and shoved a piece of paper into her hands. 'The Director sent me to give you this Inspector.' Gloria recognised the Police Director's personal assistant but the woman had already turned and was hurrying away in the opposite direction. Gloria read the note as she went down the stairs. 'Inspector, please come to meet me at my home tomorrow evening at 9pm. Come alone and discreetly. We can close this case together. Please destroy this note.'

Despite the seriousness of the situation, Gloria had a little laugh to herself. The Director had been reduced to passing notes and arranging secret meetings like a fourth grader. She hoped they weren't going to have to climb into a tree house or crawl into the roof space or something. She wasn't built for that any more. But she knew he must be seriously worried to organise a meeting like this, unless it was a trap to lure her to a lonely spot. But he must know that there was no way she was going to come alone to such a meeting. And if it was so urgent why had he not arranged it for today. Ignoring the note's instructions she folded and put it in her pocket. It might be useful as evidence.

Back in the office the atmosphere was heavy. With the children gone and most of her team out in Harbel and Bomi there was nothing much to do except wait. Gloria spoke again to Izena who had already reported that the two volunteers from KVG had provided no useful information at all. They were scared half-to-death – as most of the people connected with this case seemed to be – and could only repeat how they had been recruited through an advert for volunteers in a student magazine. They had been expecting to 'bring love and happiness' to poor grateful orphans. Instead they found themselves living totally isolated in a hostile community – that's how Drake had described Westpoint to them. The bewildered, terrified children they worked with refused to speak to them, arriving and disappearing with depressing regularity.

'But even so, Izena, they must have thought something was going on. I mean anyone could see that wasn't a normal situation.'

'They knew ma'am yes, they knew something was not right but those girls are straight from school. They had no friends, no-one to talk to, only Drake. They said it felt as if they were in jail with the children. Drake always managed to send them off to the warehouse when anyone came to the centre. In four months, in the first girl's case, they have spoken to no-one except Drake and some of the market women. Unbelievable. You might be able to charge him with something on that as well.'

'Ok, so what are we going to do with them?'

'I've contacted their embassies but the UK one is in Cote d'Ivoire and the Australian embassy is in Nigeria. They weren't that interested to be honest, but they said they would try and send someone in the next week or so.'

'A week! Great, what do we do with them till then?'

'Well, I thought we needed somewhere safe, and not expensive, so I contacted Sr. Angie. She's my old teacher you know, and the sisters said the girls can go there until their embassies come and talk to them.'

'Well done, Izena, good idea. I will try and arrange for an officer to stay with them as well until we are sure who is involved in this.'

It seemed there was nothing much more to do now except wait for some results from Bomi and Harbel. So many possibilities swirled around her head that she couldn't get her ideas straight. And for the first time in her life she couldn't see any way forward, she had no ideas and no inspiration.

These dark thoughts were interrupted by Paul's return with John Banks in tow. She didn't ask how many traffic laws they had broken to get back so quickly, she was just relieved that they were here and she could busy herself with something. The trouble was she didn't know how she was going to approach this interview and, without her usual conviction, she was worried it was going to be a poor interrogation.

'Paul, you can come with me.' They went down the hall to the interview room. 'How was Mr. Banks? Did he talk in the car?'

'No, ma'am, he said almost nothing. I thought he might refuse to come, you know with him being a powerful man, but when we said he was needed here to answer questions he just came with us.'

As soon as they went in Gloria saw what Paul meant. Banks looked like a broken man. He was slouched over the desk with his arms on the table, clenching and unclenching his fists, and when she sat down and said his name he looked at her with an empty stare. Gloria said his name again and when she had his attention she thrust a picture of Aloysius in front of him, without saying anything. It was the same picture she had shown him in Harbel. He looked down at it and, without any noise or any change of expression, started to cry. Great big tears rolled down his cheeks as he continued to stare at the picture and, once started, it seemed they were not going to stop easily. Gloria and Paul sat in silence until eventually Gloria handed him a paper tissue and sent Paul for some water.

'Ok Mr Banks, tell us the whole story, it's the least you can do for Aloysius.'

It was as if he had been waiting for the opportunity to pour it all out.

'It is my son, it is Aloysius. And they killed him, they took him from me and his mother and they killed him and left him lying on the beach. I can't get the picture of that out of my head.' He looked directly at Gloria. 'And I did nothing to save him.'

Finally, thought Gloria, a breakthrough. She was too tired to feel anything more than that. But even that sense of satisfaction was short-lived. Ten minutes later Banks was still talking, or rambling really, but Gloria realised they were not actually getting any hard information out of him. He was simply repeating the same recriminations over and over.

'Mr. Banks, I know this must be very difficult but the hardest part is over. You've told us you know who did this to your son, you've admitted that, now you need to give us some names and some details about why they did it.'

This, however, proved to be more difficult. Banks shook his head. 'These people abducted Aloysius when we were living in Bomi. We heard nothing, no ransom demand or anything like that. The next thing we know is that our son turns up dead on a beach in Monrovia.' The tears had stopped now but Banks looked gray and exhausted. 'I moved my family to Harbel for safety. When you came around asking questions I lied to you. If I say any more than that the rest of my family will be in danger.'

'But Mr. Banks, you are here in the police station, if these mysterious people know that then they will assume you have talked to us, your family will be in danger anyway. Better give us the information and we can stop them.'

Banks looked at her for a few moments before answering. 'You really have no idea who you are up against Inspector. These people will know exactly what I have said to you. There is nothing they can't find out. Now lock me up or let me go, I don't care which, but I can't say any more to you.'

He leaned back in his chair and it was as if the shutters had come down. They had been in with him for an hour now and were obviously not going to make any more progress. He looked as if he had switched off. Once again they were left with more questions than answers. Why had Aloysius been abducted and killed? How had Banks managed to move from Bomi to his current prominent position in Harbel? And most importantly, who were the people behind it?

Before Gloria could decide what to do next she heard raised voices and then the sound of people running up the corridor. There was a lull and then more hurried footsteps outside and urgent voices asking questions and giving orders. She looked at her watch and saw it was after nine. Usually, by this time, the building had slipped into a light doze and was quiet and still.

'Stay here Paul. I'll go and see what the noise is all about.' She left Paul with Banks and went into the corridor. There were people standing in little groups in a dazed way, looking lost, waiting to be told what to do. A lady she recognised from the Records department was crying quietly by herself near the far door.

'Doris, what is going on?'

'Oh Inspector, it's terrible.' She sobbed and pointed down the corridor to the far end.

Gloria followed the noise until she got to the Communications room. The door was half open so she went in. It usually held nothing more interesting than a few operators and some crackly radio equipment but it was full now and there were even more people jostling for space to get in. The strange thing was that the room was quiet, no-one was talking, they were all listening. She paused and then over the loud static of the radio she distinctly heard the voice of the Police Director. He was shouting orders of some kind but the panic in his voice was quite clear. She pushed her way through the crowd to where Chief Inspector Kamara was standing with the chief radio operator.

'What's going on, sir?'

Kamara looked round at her. He looked tense, his left eye twitching. 'Ah Gloria, as if things couldn't get any worse around here. The Police Director left from here, from my office actually, to fly up to Zwedru and address a group of new recruits, you know the kind of publicity thing he does so well.' Gloria nodded, that's why he wasn't able to meet her today. 'Well it seems they set off just before dusk to fly back and they are now in their descent to the airport. The only problem is the landing lights have not been turned on at Robertsfield, and no-one can find the technician.'

It sounded like a very bad joke but Gloria knew how serious this was. No international flights landed at the airport at night because visibility was so poor and landing conditions so tough. Robertsfield airport, and the whole Harbel area, had been heavily shelled during the war and although the airport had been reconditioned recently it certainly didn't meet international standards. She knew that private flights and internal government flights, usually smaller, lighter planes, could arrange for the landing lights to be switched on. With the lights on any reasonably competent pilot could land safely. But in the dark, and without the landing lights Robertsfield was very dark, it was nigh on impossible.

'Why are they not re-directing to Spriggs-Payne then?' This was the small airfield in the city itself. During the war it had been the main, the only, landing point for all craft. It had a small but serviceable runway and was always lit up.

Kamara groaned. 'I suggested that, in fact I tried to speak directly to the pilot but the Director has panicked. He says they don't have enough fuel to reach Spriggs-Payne.'

Over the static of the radio Gloria could clearly make out the voice of the Police Director, high with anxiety, shouting to someone to switch on the lights. He had panicked alright.

'The pilot managed to patch their distress call through to here when he was getting no response from Robertsfield. There doesn't seem to be anyone at the airport.' Kamara bent down and whispered to Gloria. 'The Director was making threats. He has his gun out and is ordering the pilot to land. He has lost it completely Gloria. This is not going to end well.'

Gloria's mouth was dry. This was appalling. How could they be listening to a disaster unfolding in front of them but be powerless to do anything. 'I presume you have sent people out there sir.'

Kamara nodded. 'Yes, of course, but they will never reach the airport in time.'

As if to back up his words the voice of the pilot came back over the radio. He sounded remarkably calm for someone who was probably only minutes away from his death. 'Control, this is Jackson. I am going to have to circle the airport again. Conditions are impossible. If I try and land here now the casualties will be huge.' There was a hum of agreement in the room. The area around the airport was heavily populated. 'I will circle one more time and then,' his voice broke a little, 'if there are no lights on I am going to head out to sea.'

There was a collective gasp in the room. Jackson, whoever he was, was going to make that sacrifice to ensure no-one else was killed or injured.

The radio controller, more used to dealing with traffic accidents and thefts, responded calmly. 'Jackson, this is Control. We have your message and approve your decision.' He shrugged and turned to Kamara, unsure if he was saying the right thing, and Kamara nodded.

It was then that the Police Director's voice broke in. 'We

can't circle again, look, the tanks are empty. Are you stupid man? You have to land the plane now.'

Jackson's voice, explaining his decision, was drowned out by a babble of noise. It sounded as if all the passengers were crowded into the cock-pit. In contrast the silence in the radio room grew heavier. Gloria and Kamara looked at each other. Kamara's prediction was coming true. The babble of noise from the radio got louder and louder until, over the noise of the hysteria, they heard what was clearly a gun shot. There were screams and then another gun shot followed by louder screams, echoed by screams and shouted prayers from the people in the radio room, the spell of silence broken. Some people covered their ears, it was so painful to listen to. And then the radios went silent except for the static of the empty airwaves.

The silence was broken almost immediately by a mobile phone ringing, then another and then the office phones started to ring as well. News had spread very quickly. It was only a few minutes before the leader of the team dispatched to the airport called. They had arrived just in time to see the plane crash alongside the airport runway, ploughing into the remains of the war-damaged terminal building and exploding in a spectacular ball of flame. She was sure there would be no survivors.

Chief Inspector Kamara took control calmly and decisively.

'Listen everyone, we need to act quickly now. We will set up an Emergency Response team in the main conference room and you,' pointing to a junior officer, 'will handle any calls, together with our radio operator.' He was the weary-looking man slouched over his receiver. 'You and you,' singling out two more officers, 'will go and meet the Ministers of Defence and Transport and the Speaker of the House, and brief them. I think Inspector Gloria has already called the hospitals.'

He looked at her quizzically and she nodded. 'Medical teams

are on their way from both Catholic Hospital and ELWA Hospital, sir.'

'Good. I will go and brief the President myself. At the moment all we can say is there appears to have been a technical fault leading to the crash. It is not expected that there will be any survivors but we will confirm that later. We cannot comment on causes of the crash or assign blame. Is that understood?' They all nodded. 'That will be the responsibility of the Aviation Authority under the Ministry of Transport.' There were more nods. Good luck with that, thought Gloria. The newspapers would be full of stories tomorrow. She was sure of that.

Gloria wandered back up the corridor. The Police Director dies in a freak accident on the same day he sends her a note asking for a secret meeting. Was there a connection or was it just a very unlikely coincidence? She had mentioned the note to Kamara, after he had finished giving orders, but he had been, understandably, preoccupied. He had read it and then handed it back to her with instructions to 'follow it up', whatever that meant. She fingered the piece of paper in her pocket. The net was closing in alright, but was it closing in on the murderers or on them?

Paul was tense when she found him again. He had heard the news, of course, and she remembered that his mother and sister lived very close to the airport.

'Have you called them?' she asked him.

'All the lines are busy, ma'am, I don't know if that's a good or a bad sign.'

'Come on, I'll get you on to one of the details going out there and you can check for yourself.' She locked the door behind them. 'They will need all the sensible people they can get out there so if the family don't need you make yourself useful.' He nodded quickly. 'What about Banks? How did he take the news?'

'Yes, that was odd, ma'am. He shrugged and that's all. I mean he's the Commissioner out there.'

'Well, he's a strange man altogether.'

'Oh, and his wife arrived, wants to take him back with her.'

'Ah really? I think I'll have a word with her then, since she's already here.'

She found Banks and his wife together in the interview room. Bennetta, the wife, was at least twenty years younger than Banks and quite beautiful. The age difference was not so unusual and her deference – she sat with her head bowed as if waiting his next command – was fairly common in traditional marriages but there was something more here. Gloria looked at her closely, she looked somehow familiar.

'Excuse me, Mrs. Banks, but have we met before?'

The lady kept her head down but shook it.

'The funeral. The day we buried your son, Bennetta. Were you not there that day, across the road?'

Another more vigorous shake of the head.

'That's not possible, Inspector,' Banks interrupted, 'my wife was in Kakata until a few days ago and then she came back to our home in Harbel. Didn't you, my dear?'

Bennetta looked up, not meeting Gloria's eyes, and nodded agreement.

'After what I have told you, Inspector, there would be no need for us to lie about something like that, would there?' Banks was holding his wife's hand now.

'You have told us very little, Mr. Banks. You confessed to being a coward and allowing strangers to take and kill your son, but then you continue to act like a coward, hiding those people from us.'

'I have explained why Inspector. I have to protect what remains of my family. If I tell you anything more you will not be able to guarantee my safety, will you? I mean you people are not even able to protect your own Director, how could you keep poor people like us safe.' He sighed and grasped his wife's hand harder.

'What about you, Bennetta, do you not want us to catch the people who killed your son?' Bennetta started to cry. She whispered something Gloria couldn't hear. 'What was that?'

This time her voice was just audible. 'We will see our son in the next life, for now we have to get on with this life and the children we have left to us.'

Frustrated and tired, Gloria stood up. 'Ok, you can go but please come back here tomorrow. We have to talk some more. Think about what I've said, please.' She didn't think there was much risk in letting them go. They had no legal grounds to keep them anyway, and if they treated them like criminals they would never trust them.

She noticed they didn't speak as Bennetta supported him down the corridor. Banks looked like an old man as he left. She had heard how guilt and fear could physically weigh you down and Banks looked like a man who was carrying a lot of both, but if he was too scared to tell them who was behind the killings what could they do? However, Banks seemed preoccupied with his suit, smoothing out wrinkles, picking at his cuffs and collar. This struck Gloria as a little odd. She couldn't help noticing that the suit was very expensive, not locally made. Unless it was an extreme response to stress, this jarred a little with the picture of a man broken down by grief.

She sat at her desk in the dark listening to the muted sounds of the building. It was very late when Moses arrived back and he looked exhausted. It had been a long drive, in the dark, on the infamous Bomi road and he was worried about Hawa, having heard on the radio about the crash at the airport.

'She called me,' he said. 'She's at the airport now, along with every other official. She says it's like a bad joke, you know, how many airport officials does it take to work out why the bulb didn't work.' Gloria smiled for the first time that evening. 'Except the real reason they're all there is to decide who is going to take the blame for it.'

'I thought there would have been talk of plots and assassinations by now. Surely the death of the Police Director is going to be seen as a direct attack on the new government – at the very least.'

'I agree, but Hawa says it's being made very clear to them that the crash was the result of incompetence or individual negligence.'

'Really. So they have decided on a result before the investigation even starts.' Gloria pursed her lips. 'More big-people politics. Or maybe it's because the Director didn't exactly cover himself in glory in the last minutes of his life. Did you hear?'

Moses nodded. 'The story is all around the place already. But what do you want to bet that it's the Director and not the pilot who gets all the praise in the official press release. . . noble sacrifice and all that.'

'Well, they will need a victim now to take the blame and Paul tells me the technician who was supposed to put the lights on, and the airport Duty Manager, have disappeared. I hope Hawa is safe from all that.'

Moses didn't think Hawa was in any great danger. She worked on the administration side of the airport's operations and, although it was a senior position, it was surely far enough removed from the technical side for her to be safe from blame. It was true what they said here, the higher up the ladder you went, the further you had to fall, and they would definitely want someone from very high up to take the fall for this.

'Please give me some good news because at the moment, Moses, we are not getting very far.'

'The first thing. . .'

But Gloria had put her hand up. 'Wait a minute Moses. I've just thought of something. Banks and his wife heard me talk about burying Aloysius, they both swear that Bennetta was not the woman I saw standing across the road at the cemetery – but neither of them asked me where their son was buried. Surely that would be the first thing you would want to know.'

'Maybe they really are so afraid or, they don't want to think about it.'

Gloria shrugged. 'Maybe, anyway go on with your report.'

'Ok, the first thing that surprised me was the guards at the border. They talked about Drake quite freely and they remembered the children well. Regular groups of them crossing over but they claim the paperwork was always correct.'

'Maybe they've been bribed?'

'I thought of that boss, of course, but it turns out the commander there is a cousin of my late father.'

Gloria laughed. 'Extended family right enough.'

'No, I know this man well, boss. He still visits us in the holidays, my children call him uncle. But, more than that, I trust him. He's a proper soldier, from the old days. That's why they've sent him up there. They don't want to take any chances.'

The border crossing with Sierra Leone was a sensitive one as feelings still ran high on both sides about Liberia's involvement in their civil war. It was inspected regularly, well patrolled and tightly controlled. The last thing the new government wanted was accusations that they were still facilitating the trafficking of guns across the border, or that they were benefiting from diamond smuggling.

'I'm not saying he doesn't take a dash one-one time but, that border post is well run. He even got me copies of the papers used to take the children across and they include lists of the children and their ages.' He brandished a sheaf of papers triumphantly.

Gloria was taken aback. Lists, names and ages, official papers – this was almost unheard of and the last thing she had been expecting. Even Moses was still shocked to find that the papers existed and in such detail. They were all signed by someone from the Ministries of Foreign Affairs and Social Welfare and stamped. Although the signatures were sufficiently wild to be illegible the stamps all looked authentic.

'Right, give me those Moses, what a find.' She started to look through them and then looked up at him. 'What are you waiting for, I thought you were going to the airport to Hawa?'

He nodded gratefully. 'I'll see you tomorrow boss.'

When he left Gloria flicked through the papers until she found the lists of names, she skimmed them looking for one name in particular and there it was. The most recent list from a few days ago had one Boyes Sipor listed as being thirteen years old and an orphan. She had never asked for his surname but she was sure it was the same Boyes. So he had definitely been taken over the border. She found another set of papers detailing the routes and the places the children were being taken to.

The destinations on the forms were all different; Boyes had, apparently, gone to the KweKwe Training Centre in Bo but some of the children had gone to the Margai Academy in Lunsar, and a few to the Mohammed Bah Football Academy in Freetown. On paper it all looked organised and legal. In fact it looked exactly as Drake had described it, an opportunity for very poor children to make something of themselves. Maybe Drake had been acting in good faith. Perhaps he wasn't evil, just crazy!

Anyone with any professional training would have asked questions, of course. Many of the children listed were younger than twelve and who sends children off to training institutions or football academies in a foreign country at that age? But the papers were good enough to satisfy a group of border guards. If it was official however, there should be additional paperwork at the Ministry of Social Welfare detailing the children's safe arrival at these institutions and their progress. She was willing to bet that didn't exist. At least the names seemed to be real though, that would be a big help in tracing families.

Gloria stretched, it was late but she didn't want to go home, there was too much simmering here. She went down to check on Drake. She had kept her word and not sent him down to the prison but he had been very agitated, walking around the small cell and talking to himself. She had sent for her friend, Dr. Bartu, and he gave him some injection to help him relax. The effect had been dramatic. Drake had gone from frenetic activity to a catatonic state. He was now lying on the small bed staring emptily ahead but Bartu assured her he would be fine in the morning.

She wandered down to the main office and looked again at the rather tatty display of photos and leads they had posted up. It looked nothing like the shiny smart displays they had all seen on the TV shows. Theirs consisted of a few photos and bits of paper with scrawls on them indicating various ideas and pieces of information they had discovered. Most of it was now hanging off, the adhesive tape already losing its sticking power in the dank humidity. In spite of that, and the late hour and the lack of sleep, Gloria stared at it, convinced the answer was there. She knew when they unravelled everything they would find all the major parts of the story already there on the board. She just hoped it wouldn't be too late by then.

In the small side office she could see a light still burning and found Ambrose hunched over a laptop.

'It's Drake's,' he said without looking up, 'and it has almost no security on it but unless he has another one somewhere I would say he has been telling us the truth.'

'What do you mean?' Her irritation at having to speak to the back of his head put an edge on her voice. As if sensing her disapproval Ambrose swung around in the chair to face her.

'I've been through all his documents and there is nothing on here which contradicts his story. It's full of papers and articles about their organisation and what they believe. It's got the project plans for the shelters, and others like it, and it's all exactly as he said. Their strange mixture of paternalism, racism and colonialism is all there in his documents. I've got some addresses for their headquarters in Pretoria which might be worth following up on. I also sent all his emails over to a friend of mine' – Ambrose seemed to have useful friends all over the place – 'he's a Nigerian at the ECOMOG base who is a computer expert and who, unusually, only uses his powers for good.'

Gloria laughed. Ambrose had read her mind accurately.

'The thing is, ma'am, he got back to me very quickly and all those emails giving Drake instructions about where and when to take children, came from right here in Liberia, not from his headquarters. I would say he has been well and truly fooled on a grand scale. . . by a 'simple native' too, most probably.'

They both laughed again, despite the seriousness.

'This Nigerian friend of yours can say that for sure?' Ambrose nodded. 'So we know for sure this is a Liberian affair, not an international conspiracy. Well done, Ambrose, an excellent piece of work. You can follow up in the morning with the Pretoria connection. But you should go home now and get some sleep.'

Even as she said it she knew it wasn't going to happen. The war had so disrupted their living patterns that in any kind of crisis, or for any excuse really, people would happily not sleep, preferring to be together. It was also a good excuse for the many of them for whom sleep simply meant a return to the nightmares of the last years. Each one on their own reliving the terrible things they had seen or done which they could never talk about or even refer to in the light of day. Add to that the scarcity of electricity, the stifling heat, and the fear of armed robbers, it was surprising anyone slept at all. All things considered, it was probably a better option to be part of the dark excitement of the plane crash, however remotely.

Gloria went back to staring at the board, going over again and again what the bits of information might mean. There was something flitting around her mind, a piece of information or a connection, just on the edges of her consciousness. Her thoughts were interrupted by Ambrose who appeared to be offering her a cup of coffee. She had been desperate for a coffee for hours but she didn't know where to get one in or near the building, and especially after midnight. She took the cup and sipped it. Strong and sweet. This was an answer to prayer.

'Should I even ask where you got this from?'

'It's only coffee ma'am. I just happen to know that the Chief keeps a supply in his office along with a kettle. He says there are some things you never get used to living without and coffee is one of those things for him.'

It was the early hours of the morning when Pendle and John Kopius turned up. It took her a few moments to focus on them and try to pull her thoughts together. Pendle, she presumed, was after the story of the crash but it turned out to be Kopius who did most of the talking and he seemed only interested in the arrest of Drake. She had never seen him so agitated, and she quickly realised that he was extremely worried that he was going to be tainted by his association with Drake. Every question was also a statement putting more and more distance between Drake and himself, making it clear he knew nothing about Drake's activities or his philosophy.

'I knew he had some strange ideas but then you meet all kinds of people in this work.' That was as much as he would say about the KVG. Drake's total collapse seemed to give him some comfort, writing him off as a lunatic who slipped through the net would be the best line to take. Pendle, on the other hand, just sat there saying nothing.

'I expected you to be busy getting your story about the crash out first.'

He just looked at her before drawling. 'It's not hard. My story is already written and sent, it will be a few lines in the international section, read by a few people.'

'But we don't have the details, how could you have written and sent your piece already?'

'It's not difficult. Police director's plane crashes at night due to human error. I know what everyone is already saying, the theories about plots and coups, jealousy and revenge. You think the events in your little country are so important but I could have written this story yesterday before it had even happened and still have got all the details right.'

She had known he was a cynic but this was of a different order. His tone had something of the contempt she had heard in Drake's voice when talking about his mission. She stood up.

'You had better go, it's been an extremely long night and my judgement is shot to pieces. There's no knowing what I might do if I have to listen to any more outsiders passing judgement on my country. We may look just like a corpse for all you international vultures to pick over but believe me the heart is still beating and the brain is still working. You stopped listening to us years ago but we may just surprise you one day soon.'

She stopped. Pendle was still smiling.

'Good line Inspector, I may use that in my next piece.'

'As for you John. I may as well say it too. I am deeply disappointed. I thought better of you and what you are trying to do but you haven't shown any concern about the kids who were murdered or asked one question about the children caught up in this mad KVG scheme. You are only concerned about how it will reflect on you and your organisation. You could have offered to help us find the missing children or asked about the welfare of the children we rescued today, isn't that your work? Isn't that what all your press releases and reports say? But you only wanted your organisation to get out of this with no mud sticking to you. You're not much different from Pendle.' She turned back to the notice board. 'Now, you should leave. I have work to do.'

She was tired of them all. She knew she was being a little over-dramatic but she didn't want them hanging around now, either justifying themselves or engaging in an argument. But her words seemed to have struck home and there was no more to be heard from either of them. They just got up and left. It was Ambrose who wondered if it was possible that Pendle and Kopius couldn't know what Drake was doing. After all, Drake must have talked about it, he wasn't embarrassed by his work. In fact he really believed it was the right thing so how could Kopius and Pendle not have known?

15.

THE NEXT MORNING was one of the gloomiest Gloria could remember since the end of the war. Although she had managed to dash home and change her clothes she felt no fresher by the time she got back for the general meeting called by Chief Inspector Kamara. The meeting was held in the training room with its memories of Ron still fresh in their minds, his poster sheets with the three Ps on them still stuck to the walls. Kamara invited her and the heads of CID, Traffic, Fraud and the other departments to join him on the dais while he addressed as many of the force as could squeeze into the room. There was a minute's silence in memory of the Police Director and the others who had been killed in the crash and, as if taking his cue from the room, the Chief remembered to mention Ron as well.

'I wanted to talk to all of you this morning about the tragic events of last night. At any time this would be a tragedy, and our thoughts are with the families of the Director and the other passengers who were killed last night, but of course we also have to be on our guard while the investigation into the crash is taking place. We need to make sure people don't take advantage of the situation to cause trouble. There will be rumours, there already are, you have to ignore these and get on with your work. The military are on full alert and they have increased security around the town but the President is anxious not to start a panic so she wants an increased police presence around the Executive Mansion rather than bringing the army in. She wants to emphasise that we are a civilian democracy – besides, the army restructuring and re-training is not yet completed.'

For that, read 'Julu is a suspect in the coup plots', thought Gloria. After all, the police restructuring and re-training was nowhere near completion either and not likely to be with Ron dead and the investigation into his murder being brushed over. As if reading her thoughts she heard the Chief continue.

'We also have the delegation from the British Embassy arriving today. They are not satisfied with our investigation into Mr. Ron Miller's death and will be examining all the evidence again.'

What an admission to make in public. Gloria saw her colleague in CID squirm in his seat.

'So, we all have to be on red alert for the next few days until these investigations are complete. A calm professional presence on the streets is what people need at the moment.' He paused dramatically and looked around the room.

'Now is the hour for all of us to prove to the Liberian people that we can be trusted and relied upon.' He paused again. 'Right, I think we should all get on with our work.'

The Chief marched off with more resolve than she had seen recently but the other inspectors milled around analysing the Chief's speech and taking care not to be seen to be too close to Inspector Barton from CID. He had been publicly humiliated and clearly was not going to last in his post much longer. Gloria's main ally and one of her best friends was Lawrence Boakai, the Head of the Traffic Division. She saw him coming over to her, pushing his way through the throng of police, most of whom didn't seem particularly anxious to get out and spread peace and professionalism on the streets.

'How is it Gloria? Long time-o.'

Gloria was delighted to see Lawrence. He was a year older

than her but they had been in the Police Academy together and had been friends ever since. They shared a passion for reading and good coffee and they both enjoyed a good laugh.

'I hear you've been having a time of it. I thought the Family and Child Protection Unit was going to be all community meetings, committees and babies but it sounds like you've got murder mystery on a grand scale. How are you managing?'

Lawrence was just back from Accra where he had attended a conference in 'Post-War Urban Planning'. He had missed all the events of the past days.

'It's mad Lawrence, the bodies are piling up, the suspects all have alibis and the whole establishment seems to be involved in hushing it all up.'

As they walked downstairs she outlined what had happened so far and when she had finished he looked so serious she began to feel bad for him.

'Gloria,' he said, 'I'm concerned about your safety. I heard about the attack on your house but I thought it was just one of those random things that seem to happen all the time now. I didn't realise you were at the centre of this madness. Is there anything I can do to help?'

Apart from closing the roads in the morning and in the evening and accompanying the Presidential motorcade, Lawrence had a fairly flexible schedule.

'I could do with some extra transport actually,' replied Gloria. The two things Traffic had were good vehicles and smart uniforms. 'To get up to Bomi as quickly as possible.'

'Hey, that's easy. I'll send a car round right away and some officers if you need them. We do have one or two who know something about police work.'

Gloria smiled. 'Thanks, but I have enough officers, if I can just get them on the road to speed up this investigation.'

'Ok, but let me know if there's anything else I can do. I'll ask around and let you know if I hear any more.'

Lawrence had always been the biggest collector of gossip on the force and it had proven useful on a number of occasions. In fact, knowing what was going to happen ahead of time was a necessary survival skill and Lawrence had it perfected to an art. Where Gloria could read the signs and work out what was happening, Lawrence just knew lots of people from many different walks of life – secretaries, tea sellers, taxi drivers, street boys, minor officials to name but a few – and he was able to get information from them that no-one else had access to.

'Did you hear that Julu has been placed under house arrest?'

Gloria shook her head.

'They will announce officially that he is taking time to grieve – his cousin was on that flight you know, she was a junior reporter on The Courier – but the whiff of the coup plot hangs about him. And Barton is being arrested, even as we speak, on corruption charges, but I bet you worked that out.'

Gloria nodded. She hadn't thought about Julu but it made sense now that Lawrence said it. Whether it was the 'whiff of the coup plot' – or just a way of getting rid of an enemy who was too powerful, it could cause serious problems.

'What else do you know, Lawrence? You've probably got the name of the murderer as well haven't you?'

Lawrence laughed but said no, on that all his sources were very quiet.

He had to rush off then to organise the arrival of the British Embassy delegation who were being accorded the highest levels of respect, and who would accompany Ron's body from the morgue to the plane that evening for transportation home. He did the funny 'I'll call you' sign with his hand which always made her laugh. He was the only person in town who used it which made it a bit useless as a way of communicating. She watched him disappear into the crowd.

Gloria called the team together. It was already mid-morning and they had a lot to do. Unfortunately both she and Moses had to stay and meet the investigators from the embassy so it meant dividing the team up. Paul and Christian were to go back to Bomi to find out everything they could about Banks. Izena was to check around the shelters, inform the NGOs what they had found out and make sure the children were safe. Izena also needed to go through the forms they had received from the immigration office in Bomi to help trace the families of the children who had already been taken.

'The problem is that nothing really adds up,' said Gloria. 'We have all these people but no connections and no clear evidence. Does nobody have any ideas?'

She knew it wouldn't help to get irritated but she couldn't help it. The events of the last few days and the heat seemed to have left everyone paralysed. She let the silence hang there, determined that someone else would speak. Unexpectedly it was old Alfred who put up his hand as if they were in grade school.

'Ma'am, we have some of the answers. Drake was part of it, whether he knew it or not. Banks is part of it. Julu and the late Director knew enough to be afraid.'

The others were nodding.

'And we know it was being organised from inside Liberia,' said Ambrose.

'So there is someone working it all, pulling the strings and making everyone else dance. The question is, is it someone we have already met or someone else? And why? What was behind this elaborate set-up, surely not just to traffic some children out the country? It hardly seems worth it.'

A few days ago they had an array of suspects and now none of them had the look of likely masterminds. The Director dead. Julu under house arrest. Drake in shock.

'We are still missing some vital links,' said Gloria, 'maybe even some vital person.' She paused.

'Ok, Ambrose will follow up the leads with KVG in South Africa and start contacting the centres in Sierra Leone which the children are supposed to have gone to, as well as contacting the Ministry of Social Welfare to find out if they had any contact with these children. Alfred, I want you and Lamine to ask around about Pendle and Kopius. Nothing specific, just check out what's being said about them. Moses and I will stay here and deal with Drake, and Banks when he comes back in.'

She looked around the room at her team, most of them young and inexperienced – or old and tired like Alfred.

'Remember that it's going to be even more tense than usual,' she looked at Paul and Christian. 'The army will likely be very angry about Julu being arrested so take your time in Bomi and think about how and who you ask. And the town will be simmering as usual. The only slight bit of good news is that the plane crash has knocked our investigation off the front pages so that gives us a bit of space. Ok then, off you go but I want everyone back here by six this evening at the latest. Paul, Traffic division have lent us one of their cars so you and Christian take it and' – she whispered to him – 'keep Christian out of trouble.' She paused. 'Old Alfred is going to be here co-ordinating our movements today.'

Alfred looked exhausted from the previous day's events but she wanted to avoid offending him, he already didn't approve of her. 'Alfred will be checking in with you so make sure your radios are charged and you report in every hour. There's one in the car you'll be taking Paul so that goes for you as well. Make sure Alfred hears from you every hour.' She looked at them all. 'I want to know where you all are at all times.'

That got a buzz of excitement out of them. The new radios had been promised for months but last night's events seemed to have been the impetus needed for the Supply Department. No-one wanted the finger of blame pointed at them for anything, not at this sensitive time, so the radios had been distributed that morning. They all had one now and Gloria knew it was going to be noisy today, in spite of them being given detailed instructions on how to use them. But this were the only practical way of keeping in touch.

By the time they had finally left, tripping out like children going on an outing, it was already noon. No matter how hard she tried time just seemed to slip away from her. It felt like days since she had seen Abu, although he sounded happy enough on the phone. She felt the urge to gather all the people she cared about around her to help keep them safe – or at least to keep them in sight. That was one of the things that made this situation so different from the war. The war had been terrifying and dangerous, and sometimes dull and interminable, but at least they had all been together. It was so much harder worrying about Abu, and others connected with the investigation, when they were all scattered in different places and when the danger had no face. Her thoughts were interrupted by the crackle of the radio and she heard old Alfred start the call-in to all the officers. They hadn't even got out of the building yet. Yes, it was truly going to be a noisy day.

Moses decided to take the next interview with Banks, who had come in on time and had been kept waiting for several hours. Banks didn't know him and that might help in the interview process, although Gloria didn't hold out too much hope. She had agreed to sit with one of the doctors while they tried to get through to Drake but she was already feeling that this was old stuff. What she needed were some new leads, some new energy. She found herself looking at the photos on the board again and caught that fleeting strand of something in her head, the connection she was missing. The phrase Ambrose had used about the Chief yesterday, 'there are some things you never get used to living without', had come back to her again and again but she couldn't grasp its significance.

It turned into another of those days where the hours just slipped away. She had meetings with Drake and the doctor, with the people from the embassy and with the Chief – all with background radio noise and Alfred's incessant questions to the teams. The doctor had recommended that they sedate Drake and leave him to recover but he seemed more agitated and, even while dozing, he was still muttering about being tricked by worthless people.

In his lucid moments he told Gloria that following the instructions he believed to be coming from his headquarters in Pretoria, he would take the children to cross the border where they would be met almost immediately by a man and a woman in a white pick-up truck. The children were handed over to be taken on to the different places and he would return to Monrovia. No, he maintained, he hadn't thought it strange that the children were always met by the same people in the same pick-up even though they were apparently going to different institutions all over the country. Nor did he think of asking who the people were or what their organisation was. He just followed his instructions. Gloria didn't think Drake was someone who could ever change his mind or his prejudices but the fact that he had been tricked for months and months was hurting him and had shaken, at least temporarily, his belief in his own superiority. That, and the realisation there was no international organisation coming to save him, made him a little more co-operative.

'What about Aloysius then? Tell me what you remember about him.'

'Ach, the checkpoint was always busy, noisy, and usually we had to wait while the guards checked the papers, counted the children, sometimes they even phoned back to Monrovia, or at least that's what they said they were doing.' He closed his eyes again and sighed like a man exhausted.

Very thorough, thought Gloria angrily. They did everything, except speak to the children. How many times had Drake crossed over and not once had anyone, except perhaps Aloysius, spoken to the children?

'The child was smart though, that was clear.' His eyes were open again, staring at her intently. 'He was always asking me questions. Where were the children from, where were they going? He even persuaded me once' – Drake smiled weakly at the memory – 'to let him ride in the bakkie over the border to see the handover.'

'When was the last time you saw him?'

'I don't know, I can't remember. The boy changed, he was rude. I came back one day and he was talking to the children.' As she thought, Aloysius had spoken to them. 'I mean he couldn't understand what they were saying but he could see they were upset, crying. After that he gave me no peace, every time I drove there he would be around telling me the children looked unhappy and asking why I was taking them from their families.' Drake's eyes clouded over. 'He didn't understand, he was just a child. In the end I told him to stay away. I said if he came around I would tell the soldiers he was stealing from me and they would beat him.' This was as much as Gloria had got out of him. He kept talking but became more and more incoherent until it was obvious they were not going to get any more sense out of him for a while. Anyway, it was time to meet the people from the embassy.

John Tidworth and Marie Lang managed to live up to all of Moses' prejudices about the British. They were formal, arrogant and aggressive. Marie Lang did most of the actual questioning with Tidworth sitting to one side, writing in a notebook and occasionally asking for clarification. It hadn't started well.

'Thank you for meeting with us Miss. . . eh,' she consulted her notes.

'It's Inspector Gloria Sirleaf actually.'

'Oh right, Inspector then. Let me start by saying that Her Majesty's government is not satisfied with the investigation into the death of one of our citizens. We believe there is more to this incident than has been reported yet. We want to get to the bottom of this. Firstly, the theory that this was a robbery. . .'

Gloria held up her hand, stopping Marie mid sentence. 'We agree with you. No way this was a robbery. So we don't need to go through all those bits.'

They both looked surprised, and a little thrown, as if Gloria had departed from a prepared script. Gloria explained in detail how she had known Ron and the events of the night he had been killed. They had little to say so she continued, explaining the details of the children's deaths and possible connections with Ron's death.

'This is all very interesting Inspector,' Lang actually looked at her watch, 'but we don't want to get involved in your investigation. We need to concentrate on completing our investigation into Mr. Ron Miller's killing. I'm not sure that all this other stuff is relevant.'

'I thought you wanted to find out the truth?'

Tidworth butted in at this point and made a speech about the difficulties of working in West Africa, how volatile the region was, risk management and the high incidence of random killings in post-conflict countries.

'So, you have a plane to catch, is that what you are saying?'

Tidworth didn't deny it. Gloria realised they simply wanted a more plausible story than the one cooked up by the CID. Links with international child trafficking and murder had no interest for them and the thought of a protracted and complex investigation away from the comfort and security of the embassy obviously worried them intensely.

But she wasn't letting them off the hook so easily. She talked for another twenty minutes suggesting people they should interview, links to follow up on, people they should be putting pressure on and places they should visit.

Lang joined in the head-shaking now. 'This has been very useful Inspector, very useful. Unfortunately we have to balance the need to investigate with an appropriate use of embassy resources and time.' She looked at her watch again. 'Our security people are inclined, on the basis of the evidence we have so far, to conclude that Ron Miller was the victim of a random killing, perhaps a robbery gone wrong. I think our investigation will come to the same conclusion.'

Gloria was stunned. 'Why did you even bother coming here? That is exactly the same conclusion our CID reached.'

They smiled at her again. 'Let's just say that we needed to satisfy ourselves that everything had been done properly.' They closed their books in unison. 'Thank you Inspector.' She had been dismissed. They left with the promise to keep an open mind and perhaps return later. Gloria decided she wouldn't be holding her breath waiting for that.

16.

IT WAS LATE, dark and hot and nowhere was hotter than their office at this time of night. With the windows closed to try and reduce the number of mosquitoes, and the few fans they had managed to find blowing a hot breeze over everything, they should have been a tired and dispirited team. But, hey, this was Liberia where you could never quite predict what was going to happen. It had been late by the time everyone had managed to come together and Gloria had been inclined to let everyone go home and start fresh in the morning but the team had been adamant: they wanted to stay and press on. They were all energised by their day's work but even more by the fact that, with the CID under investigation and Traffic and Fraud unchanged since the war, they now looked like the most professional department in the police – and they loved it. After months of taunting about being a 'nursery' service, or being referred to in meetings as 'childminders', they were now at the forefront of the police force.

Having worked their way through the jollof rice Gloria had got her mother to prepare and Flomo to deliver, they finally settled into the report-back session. She deliberately started with an account of their interview with Drake to fill out the picture of Aloysius that was emerging and then asked Izena to report on her progress. Although she managed to convey her disappointment at being kept back to do paperwork, Izena had approached it with her typical logic and thoroughness.

'Right, I went through the papers and the first of them dates back just over a year, when the war had really just stopped and the new government was starting to exert some control outside Monrovia. The first groups of children were large, thirty or forty, and in one set of papers from last July, sixty three children in one go.' She got a gratifyingly surprised reaction from the team. 'The more recent groups are much smaller though, on average twenty children at a time. They seemed to go almost every month at the beginning and not only from Drake's shelter. There were at least four other organisations mentioned in the earlier forms, none of which exist any more. The total number of children taken out of the country, according to these lists, is three hundred and forty one.' There was a buzz of talk around the room. That was a lot of children. 'But guys, and ma'am,' she added hurriedly, 'that's just the official number. I think this has been going on for a long time, while the war was on, maybe even before when there was no need for papers. The real number could be in the thousands.'

Ambrose jumped in at this point. 'Just to confirm what we already know. I tried to contact the Sierra Leonean institutions referenced in the various forms and of the eighteen different places mentioned ten of them no longer, or never, existed. Of the remaining eight, I managed to get through to three of them and they claim they have never heard of KVG, or received any children from Liberia. They all said that they don't have enough space for their own children so why on earth would they be taking children from Liberia. And, two of them added, especially since we caused their war. I think it will be the same with the remaining five places but I'll keep checking to make sure.'

It was a depressing picture but certainly made more sense. The trafficking of children on this scale made it a very lucrative business and definitely one worth fighting, and killing, for. But how, wondered Gloria, could they all have missed this going on under their noses and in such high numbers. Alongside the violence, unemployment and general corruption this showed just how big the cracks were in their society. No wonder so many people had been desperate to hush everything up. To no-one's surprise Ambrose added that the Ministry of Social Welfare had not been able to identify the signatures on the papers, although they said the stamps all looked genuine. The Ministry had heard nothing from anyone in Sierra Leone about any of the children but had promised to launch an inquiry immediately.

Gloria could see Paul and Christian fidgeting like children, bursting to tell their story. She really hoped they had managed a more professional demeanour when in Bomi.

'Right.' Paul had obviously appointed himself as the senior officer. 'Bomi was different today, completely different. Today there was just a wall of silence.' He paused for effect, taking in the whole room. 'The soldiers did not want to speak to us, no way, they tied their faces bad way.' There was a quick burst of laughter. 'When we pushed them, my man here, Christian, just kept on asking questions, they got tough. One of them wanted to fight. They say since their commander, Julu, has been arrested they will do something. Mmm, they are serious, we could be in for trouble.' He paused again.

'Eh, Paul,' Gloria had had enough, 'politics aside, we are trying to solve several murders here, so if you could just give us the rest of your report. Did you manage to find out anything useful for us?'

He frowned, but before he could carry on Christian started speaking.

'The soldiers were not going to tell us anything so I just went over to some pikens who were kicking around an old football made of rolled up t-shirts. I showed them a picture of Aloysius and as soon as they saw it they started talking about him. Aloysius was young but they all knew him and they liked him, he was kind of their leader. But,' he shrugged, 'they said they didn't know what happened to him but I think they were afraid.'

As they were walking back to the car one of the children came after them. 'Alo, he had a photo,' he said. When they pressed him the boy just repeated that Aloysius had often talked to the children who were being taken across the border, and that he was really angry about what was happening to them. A few weeks ago he said he had found a photo that would help the children. But he wouldn't say any more than that and he wouldn't show them the photo. When Aloysius had disappeared they had come to the border every day just to see if they could see him but the market women, who criss-crossed the border at will, had told them to stay away, that it wasn't safe.

Paul and Christian had spent the rest of the time asking around the town about Banks and the family. But Bomi was like a huge army camp with everyone watching everyone else. There was a subdued feel similar to the atmosphere in Harbel and soldiers everywhere, just lounging around. Paul said it felt as if their every move was being watched and their every conversation overheard. Christian, who had some first hand experience of course, said it just felt wrong. It was as if the rebels had never left, as if the war had never ended. The uniforms may have changed but the rebels were still in control.

When they went back to the mission compound to ask some more questions the catechist again claimed he had been there a very short time and recommended they speak to Fr. Garman who had been in charge of the mission for years. Unfortunately Fr. Garman was out, actually he was usually out, in some remote part of the county and there was no saying when he would be back.

In the market they eventually found one woman who

240

admitted she had taken goods across and had got a ride in the pick-up on the other side on a day when there were not many children. When they pressed her for details she had clammed up and when they were distracted by a fight between two other traders she had disappeared in the crowd.

So what did they have now? A reference to a missing photo and a few other people they needed to talk to.

Moses had very little to say. Banks had admitted his 'usual' name was Cooper but he had changed it when he moved to Harbel because he was afraid. As to how he had managed to get such a good job in Harbel he wouldn't say anything except 'it wasn't as it looked' which wasn't very helpful. By this stage Gloria was thinking of wrapping things up until Alfred and Lamine chipped in. They had been trailing behind Pendle and Kopius all day and there had been nothing very strange to report until they followed them to the Sudden Food Grill on Gurley Street. This was an unlikely place for either of them to frequent but that's where they had met up with a policeman, none other than Sampson Moore. Although they couldn't hear what was being said, Kopius had been very angry and had looked as if he was going to shake his fist in Moore's face, like some cartoon figure. Moore had grabbed his arm and twisted it back, spoken very intently to the both of them and then got up and left.

Gloria decided enough was enough. It would be waste of time to try and piece this together tonight. They knew who they had to talk to and where the follow-ups were. Now they all needed some sleep. Before she could say anything she realised the team had already organised themselves to make sure everyone got home safely and in a few moments there was only her and Moses in the office.

'Is it making sense to you yet?' she asked him and was surprised when Moses replied that it was.

'We are on the right track, we must be and if we keep going

along it we will get the answer. You know the thing here is that nobody expected we would keep on investigating. They, whoever they are, thought we would get tired of the threats and the dead-ends and close it down. So now all this panic is an attempt to cover up and you know we Liberians are just not good at cover-up. Threats and bribes we can do but cover-ups. . . we like talking too much, we just can't help it. Whatever this story is we will find it out.'

Gloria laughed for what felt like the first time in days. It was true but her other worry was the children who had already been taken. It would be a hollow victory if they found the murderers but were unable to help the hundreds of children who had been taken out the country.

'How are things with Hawa? Have they worked out who they are going to blame yet?'

'The official line is the technician in charge of the lights got drunk and there was no back-up as the Director's flight was the only flight due in that night and even that was arranged at the last minute. But the reality is they can't even find the technician. An old lady said she had seen him on the airport road talking to some men in uniform earlier in the evening but by the next day she had changed her story, said it was dark and she wasn't sure what she had seen. The problem is, with Julu under house arrest and the CID director also under arrest, no-one wants to point the finger at anyone else. Too many vacuums in the power structure. . . not good for our fragile democracy!'

They parted on the steps of the police headquarters. Although it was now after one in the morning there were still people coming and going and even some of the traders still selling. She had read about New York, or was it London, as the 'city that never sleeps' and it had always sounded quite glamorous and interesting. Monrovia was also a city that never slept but only because it was a city so ill-at-ease with itself. It didn't dare turn off the lights and close its eyes.

She was getting fanciful again, really she needed to sleep.

17.

TO HER SURPRISE Gloria woke to find she had slept for six hours when she thought she would never escape the thoughts and theories dancing around her head. The flat was quiet with Abu still away and, although she missed the noise, it did help her to think. She needed to speak to this Fr. Garman and one person who would know how to contact him would be Sr. Margaret. If she hurried she might even get some breakfast there.

She arrived at the convent just after eight. The smell of fresh coffee hit her as soon as she entered the house and she could hear Margaret's voice above all the others. Did these ladies never just sit quietly? Even her very noisy family tended to just grunt in the mornings but clearly not this crowd. She was greeted like one of the family and before she had even sat down there was a coffee and fresh croissant in front of her. The conversations around the table never faltered and Gloria was able to explain to Margaret what was going on and that she needed to speak to Garman.

'I hear he's a difficult man to track down but I thought you might know some way I could meet up with him.'

'Well you're in luck actually. He'll be here along with all the other priests for their meeting with the Archbishop. If you wait here we could catch him before the meeting starts.'

Gloria phoned and told Moses what she was doing and asked

him to organise the rest of the team and arrange for the travel documents they would need to cross the border. She had made up her mind they were going to go and look for these children.

Fr. Garman turned out to be very quietly spoken and a lot more thoughtful than she had expected and was happy to give her the time. He had stayed in Bomi for a lot of the war, only moving out when things got too dangerous. When she showed him a photo of Banks he remembered him immediately although he knew him as John Cooper.

'Yes, it was very odd. He came to Bomi while the war was on, when most people who could were running away. He came with his son and. . .'

'Well maybe I could ask you about his son first. Aloysius must have been very young when they came back.'

Fr. Garman frowned. 'Oh Aloysius is not his son. He was the child of Esther's first marriage. No, John Cooper's son was already seventeen or eighteen when they moved in with Esther and the trouble he caused is still talked about.'

Gloria sat back. Aloysius wasn't his son after all? And where was his son then? He must be a young adult by now, if he had survived the war.

'What was his own son like?'

'I didn't really know him. Esther and Aloysius used to come to church but John and Sonny Boy didn't. There were stories around the town at first that the boy was odd and then that he was dangerous. Young as he was, he got into trouble for beating up a girl who refused to be his girlfriend, and not just beating her but torturing her really, even slicing off part of her ear because she 'refused to listen to him'.

The whole thing was hushed up as John Cooper seemed to have quite considerable influence even though he was a newcomer and in dangerous rebel territory. The stories about the boy continued until everyone was thoroughy scared of him.

In another setting he would have been diagnosed as a psychopath or a sociopath but in Bomi he was just dangerous and evil. And then six months after they had arrived he disappeared. Cooper told everyone he had sent the boy to a traditional healer to get rid of the demons.

'We have never seen him since in Bomi and he is not missed. A few months after that Cooper took Esther and the family and moved them out. Then we heard about Aloysius being killed. It's all been really strange. Are you any nearer to finding out who killed him?'

Very strange, thought Gloria. She explained that it wasn't just Aloysius but two other boys in Harbel and that they were confident of getting a result – well if you were going to admit to not being confident there wasn't much point carrying on. Fr. Garman looked really distressed when she explained about the children who had been taken out of the country across that border and she knew he would feel responsible, although he couldn't possibly be. She knew his slightly paternalistic attitude was just the way he showed his real care for the people of Bomi. She had heard all the stories about how he lived very simply and of the huge numbers of people he had helped, saved even, during the war. The fact that children were being trafficked out through 'his' territory would be a real blow to his pride, as well as to his principles.

Unfortunately he wasn't able to give much information about Cooper's background prior to his arrival in Bomi. There had been rumours of course but all he was sure of was that Cooper had come from 'abroad', some people said it was South Africa, others that it was further afield but no-one knew for definite. He had discouraged any discussion about his past but had referred to having studied abroad. And it was obvious that Sonny Boy had never lived in Liberia. It was as she was leaving that Fr. Garman dropped his final bombshell.

'The strangest thing was that all this was going on while we were under the control of the IFLL and you know how brutal they were, especially our beloved Defence Minister, well before he re-invented himself anyway.'

'I didn't know Julu was in Bomi.'

'Julu was in command of the whole region by the end of the war, from Bomi down to Monrovia and all the way to Voinjama. And he led the attacks into Sierra Leone as well. He will never admit it but he was the mastermind behind much of this destruction and given his background it makes it even worse.'

Gloria hadn't realised just how powerful Julu had been – and probably still was – he must have known what was going on. All the leads take us back to him, thought Gloria. He controlled the area, was extremely influential, had access to Sierra Leone and his deputy, Moore, was still clearly acting on his behalf both in Harbel and around town. But how could they touch him, especially now he appeared to be under house arrest. The thought occurred to Gloria that maybe his house arrest was a double bluff, something he had organised himself. It wouldn't be the first time that had happened. Previous presidents had organised pretend coups whenever their popularity was waning or they wanted to get rid of some opposition. She remembered the bullet-ridden jeep that had been put on display at the Mansion a few years before the war, as proof of a supposed attack on the then president, and the huge number of rising politicians who had been arrested and executed on the pretext that they were plotting to overthrow the government. No-one had believed it was a real attack but it had given the President the excuse he needed to clear out the opposition which fed the resentment which had contributed to the war. So Julu could well have organised his own arrest which meant he was planning some power move. Or was she getting ahead of herself?

'When you say 'his background' makes his subsequent career

even more disappointing, what do you mean?' Gloria was aware she was talking in stilted formal sentences – it's the effect priests had on her.

'Julu came from a good family. He was educated at St. Patrick's and then won a scholarship to study in the States. His undergraduate and postgraduate studies were all paid for by the government. He was supposed to be part of the new Liberia, young, smart and professional. Instead he became a warlord, or a Dr. Warlord as I believe they are referred to on the street.' That was how the city wags had christened the young elites who had studied abroad at the taxpayers' expense and then come back and headed up warring factions. The Dr. Warlords.

'What did he study?'

'I have no idea. I suppose Business or Accounting, you know, something that would give them a desk job with access to money or influence.'

Gloria left as Archbishop Francis Gray arrived laughing uproariously at some remark he had heard. Clearly they were going to have a noisy day as well.

When she got to her car she found Pascal leaning on the door picking his ear with great concentration. When he saw her he straightened up and asked if there was any news.

'Not yet, Pascal. Didn't you see Izena yesterday? She was supposed to tell you what was going on.'

'Yes I saw her ma, but she doesn't like us so we can't be sure about what she tells us.' Mark that one for Izena's next performance review, she thought.

'Well, what she said is true. We are still looking and when there's any more news I'll let you know.'

'Ok, but me, I coming with you to the office just now, ma. I will sit down there and wait if you need any help.'

Gloria hesitated and then decided it wasn't worth fighting. One of these children had bitten the Archbishop's finger a few weeks back when he had wagged it out the window at them while telling them to move out of his way.

'Get in the car and when we get to the office you must sit in the lobby and not cause noise.'

'I will sit in the lobby until you need me.'

She noticed he had made no promises about not making any noise but left it. If he tried anything on the market women who sold food around the entrance they would deal with him a lot more effectively than she could.

She left him sitting with Auntie Fata, a huge old lady who sold roasted meat and who freely dispensed advice to Gloria, whenever she got the chance, about finding a man and 'borning' some children. Let her try her life coaching skills on Pascal she thought. . . two immovable objects meeting each other.

Upstairs there was an atmosphere of quiet industry which only seemed to happen when she let Moses organise the team. But in her office she found Moses and Hawa huddled together. Hawa, who was usually very smartly dressed and very sure of herself, looked as if she hadn't slept for days. She was wearing a lappa and slippers with an old blouse and a black head tie. No jewellery – Gloria had never seen her without her gold chains – and no make-up. She looked old and tired.

'It's going badly at the airport then, Hawa?'

It was Moses who answered her with a vigorous nod of the head.

'They've run out of scapegoats. As I told you yesterday they can't afford to blame any of the big men. The President has made it known that any more prominent arrests or resignations might affect national stability – I think she means the unity government is not so united any more.'

National stability. The catch-all excuse for governments to forget about their democratic principles. Not a great time to be on the radar. Suddenly Hawa's senior management position made her an ideal target – important and with responsibility but not of national importance.

'My boss came to see me last night, Gloria, a man whose mistakes I have covered for on many occasions,' she added bitterly, 'and he says it is very likely I am going to be arrested and charged with criminal neglect.' Hawa looked defeated.

This was serious. If she was found guilty, which she probably would be if they were setting her up, she would face a long jail sentence. She shuddered at the thought of the graceful Hawa behind bars. The bright competent façade was already peeling away under the shock and the betrayal. She didn't waste any more words.

'What's the plan?' She knew Moses would have one.

Moses and Hawa had already accepted the inevitable. This was Liberia where your safe normal life could be torn away in a matter of moments.

'We have to get her out the country, but they will be watching the airports of course and stopping all cars at the borders. I want to take her with us when we go into Sierra Leone to trace the children.'

It was a good plan. A police car with senior officers would not be searched. But it was also a terrible plan. They were using their police authority to aid a fugitive from the law. She could see the headlines already but pushed that thought away.

'How far along are we to getting the papers we need to cross?'

'It's been slow,' said Moses, 'but I think they will be ready by tomorrow. I said we were not sure at this stage who needed to go so they are making out a general pass for the department.'

Hawa hadn't said another word during this exchange. Gloria sat next to her and gave her a hug.

'I'm so sorry Hawa but we will get you out. You can't go back home but you need to send someone you trust to pack your things, just the valuable ones, the rest will have to stay. At least it's not the war, they're not going to send soldiers to ransack your house and nobody will touch your children. Once you're safe, the children will follow.'

For the first time Hawa looked up and even smiled. 'You're right. I ran an international airport for goodness sake, I think I can manage to get my things and outwit these fools. Thanks Gloria. Take care of Moses.'

'Whoah, slow down Hawa. We won't be going just yet and anyway, if you and the children go, I don't think Moses will be staying here on his own. But you can't go back home so I think you will have to come home with me tonight.' Hawa nodded gratefully.

An hour later they had finalised the details. Hawa's niece, a trainee midwife at Sr. Margaret's nursing school, agreed immediately to go and pack some clothes and Hawa's jewellery. She would wear her uniform so no-one would ask her any questions. Hawa would stay hidden in Gloria's office, its lack of windows and air conditioning suddenly making it a good place to hide a fugitive.

Meanwhile Gloria was itching to get back to work. She called Ambrose in and explained to him what was going on. Moses was trying hard but he was clearly distracted by his wife's predicament.

'We need to get more on these people's backgrounds, find out who they know, where they are from. If Julu had a government scholarship someone has to know about it, even if all the paperwork is lost.'

Gloria knew that the National Archive Centre had been looted so there would be no paper trail but there had to be people who remembered. There hadn't been many scholarships given out to real students, especially after the troops had been sent onto the university campus in the late 80s. All academic activity had been viewed as potentially subversive after that.

'Rufus Sarpoh might know,' Ambrose chipped in. 'He has been covering stories for years and has been a thorn in the side of all authorities. He also has a near photographic memory which makes him even more devastating. He might remember something.'

Rufus Sarpoh, yes, if he didn't know he would know someone who knew someone. And he owed her a few favours.

'Find him Ambrose, and tell him I'll meet him at that small place on the beach at Randall Street, where it's more private.' Ambrose looked surprised at being given another task that didn't involve the phone or the computer. To find Rufus before lunch would mean trawling the ghettos of the poor and offices of the powerful. He was delighted and headed out.

As she was going back to her office she saw Izena with a huge pile of files diligently making lists of some kind.

'What are you working on?'

'I'm just trying to cross reference the children. If the records are correct, and I suspect Drake at least tried to keep accurate records, these children were deliberately selected group by group. Each group was made up of children from different regions, many of them speaking their dialect and nothing else. The groups were designed to make sure these children didn't get to know each other, share information or even organise themselves. You know that's how the Small Soldier Units were organised during the war. They would put children from different tribes and regions in the same unit to make sure they couldn't really talk to each other or form any kind of bond except that they were soldiers. It made it much easier to control them and brainwash them. I think the traffickers used the same methods.'

Everything pointed back to Julu again. He had control of the area, he had access to Sierra Leone, and he even knew how to control the children. And if he had arranged for his own arrest to distract everyone from investigating him it was working. Dr. Warlords indeed, criminals with PhDs, they had to be the worst. The connection between him and Cooper wasn't clear but if Cooper had started to change his mind about being involved in the trafficking, and Aloysius had been heard asking questions, it would make sense – to Julu anyway – to kill Aloysius to make sure he didn't say anything but also as a threat to Cooper, which had obviously worked. And then arrange for him to get the job in Harbel where Sampson Moore could keep an eye on him. Were the other children murdered just as a warning to Cooper?

No wonder Cooper was terrified. Julu was a monster, and still a very powerful one. Even with the pieces of the puzzle finally coming together, Gloria felt a huge anger at the casual indifference towards these children's lives. Maybe Ron was just in the wrong place at the wrong time and that's why he was tortured and killed. . . she would never allow herself to forget how Ron had died, that would be too easy. And Julu was obviously making another power play now, which had to mean he was aiming to be President. Gloria was sure of it, total power and control, he would settle for nothing less. Was it too far-fetched to imagine a scenario where Julu, the popular leader, incites the army to take action against a government headed by a woman who, apparently, is not able to stop the corruption and death? Julu steps in, takes control and saves the day. It did seem very elaborate but still quite plausible.

She talked through her theory with Moses who agreed with most of it but thought the coup part of it was just too much.

'If you go to anyone with that story no-one will believe it. We need to find a way to trace these murders back to Julu and that will finish him. But we have to do it fast before he makes a move.'

'Right, you follow up on the papers and I'm going to meet

Rufus. I'm sure there's a clue to all this in Julu's history. Let's get moving, we should aim to get up to Sierra Leone tomorrow. Tell Izena we need any clues to the real destination of those children. We can't just drive around the country on the off-chance of finding them. I need to talk to the Chief but he's so busy I think he'll just sign off the trip.'

She was already moving as she was talking, the sense of urgency growing.

'Gloria, don't forget how dangerous these people are. They'll know who you've been talking to and likely who you are going to see now.'

When Gloria got down to the lobby she could see Pascal deep in conversation with Fata but he turned to her as she walked across the lobby. Fata spoke first.

'This is a smart one here, Inspector. He's just been telling me some of the tricks those boys use to steal from us, well not from me but from some of those other women. I will be advising them.'

'Well I'm so glad he was useful, auntie, but I wouldn't listen to everything he says. If he told you all their tricks he would put himself out of business.'

Pascal made a face and followed behind her.

'Where are you going?'

'I'm going to meet someone, you stay here. I'll be back soon.'

Pascal didn't argue or make any objection and went back to Fata – no doubt to offer her more words of advice. She had kind of hoped it would be the other way around, but there you go.

Rufus Sarpoh was already waiting for her. He got up to shake her hand and they both sat on the rickety wooden chairs. The restaurant was only big enough to hold four tables, three of which were empty. It was made entirely of corrugated iron with some wire mesh along the top in place of windows but it sat under some trees and faced the sea so it was both cool and private, the sound of the waves drowning out any conversation.

'I'm glad Ambrose found you so quickly.'

'Ambrose? I just heard you were looking for me and I guessed you would come here. You shouldn't be so predictable, you know.'

'And you shouldn't be letting me know that you have someone in my office passing on all the information.'

'Come on, Inspector, you knew that already. How else am I supposed to crack the big stories? What's it to be today then, the plane crash or the trouble at the National Bank?'

Gloria hadn't heard about the trouble at the Bank but didn't let on.

'No, I just need to pick that famous memory of yours. Prince Julu, what can you tell me about him? Not the war stuff, his earlier stuff. Where he studied, you know all those kind of details.'

Rufus stopped talking then and seemed to freeze. Just for a few moments and then his eyes came back into focus. When he saw her worried expression he said, 'Sorry, it's my recall method, everyone with a photographic memory has their own way of recalling information. I won't give away my secret but I do remember some details although I don't how useful they will be. I was working on the National Prophet at the time – it doesn't exist any more – and I remember the story quite well.'

Gloria sat back as far as she could in the uncomfortable chair. She knew Rufus was another Liberian man who loved an audience.

'What made the story interesting was that there had been no scholarship students since the army invasion of the university campus. It was only when the President wanted to get a degree that academic life began to open up again. After he received his degree in political science.' Political science, Gloria laughed to herself, a bit ironic considering the way the President's political career had ended – arrested at the port and executed the same day by a less well-educated warlord. 'He restarted the scholarships and Julu and his colleagues were the first (and the last, as it turned out) group to go. Julu and our recently deceased Police Director were two of them.'

Gloria sat up. 'The Police Director was one of that group too?'

'Oh yes, their families were well-connected politically. Of course the Police Director never came back. He could see even by then that the system was cracking open.'

So that was the connection. 'And the other two?'

'Well there was John Moore and Nathaniel Watson. They were picked because they were brilliant students, especially Watson, but they were not really high-profile. But I seem to remember something happened while they were there, we never really got the details and it was hushed up of course, but something. . . oh I remember, one of them died. There was some kind of terrible accident and Watson, I think it was, was killed. We never got all the details as I say, but they were the last scholarship group and by that time the war was starting here, so their story faded away a bit I'm afraid. Yes', he was almost talking to himself now, 'something happened while they were in North Carolina – that's where they were studying – and only Julu came back as far as I remember. He was working at the Ministry of Lands and Mines when the war started. Eh, I had forgotten all that. But tell me Inspector, how can any of this old history be of help to you?'

He saw her hesitating.

'Come on, Inspector, you know you can trust me.'

'Alright, it's Julu.' And she told him about the killings and their suspicions that Julu was behind everything including the four murders, although she left out her suspicions about his political manoeuvrings.

'He's the one with all the opportunity and the connections but I can't really prove anything yet and it could take a long time to collect all the evidence – and we don't have a long time.'

'If I were you, Inspector, I would focus on finding the children. If you do that will be a big enough headline, no-one will be able to ignore it. And it's clearly the right thing to do, to try and save some of them.'

Gloria thanked Rufus sufficiently to ensure she would be able to make return visits if the need arose.

'By the way, Inspector, if you wanted more information about those scholarships you should go and talk to Professor Andoh. He was in charge of that programme and he would know the details better.'

Gloria had heard of Andoh of course. He was a bit of an institution himself. He had taught at the university for years, had managed to be a radical without falling foul of any of the regimes. He had also managed to use his study of Liberian dialects – a subject most people found so dull they would only nod politely if they heard about it – to develop a 'paradigm of native liberation', which essentially meant challenging the Americo-Liberian assumptions about privilege and power. It would be interesting to speak to him but maybe that would have to wait for another time. She was now convinced that Julu was behind this whole mess and agreed with Rufus, they should concentrate on finding the children. And, she remembered, they had to get Hawa away as soon as possible. A double imperative.

18.

MOSES answered on the first ring.

'Any luck with the passes yet?'

'We will have the papers by this afternoon so that means we can leave first thing in the morning.'

'Very good. I'll be back in an hour and we can complete the arrangements.'

Gloria had already decided she needed lunch and to spend some time with Abu. Although it was against the school rules no-one was going to object if she fetched him from school to come and eat with her. Well, Abu might object but that didn't really count. Abu also answered on the first ring and she didn't know whether to be pleased or to ask him why his phone was on while he was in school. She had planned just to leave a message and then call back. She decided against any more questioning and was more than compensated by Abu's delight at her suggestion they should go for lunch which was now, she thought, looking at her watch.

Abu was outside the campus with Morris when she pulled up outside. Morris just waved and gave her a smile. They both looked so big and so confident. Surely, she thought, they couldn't have grown so much in the few days since she'd seen them. In her head she knew she sounded like her mother, this obsession with growing and eating but she had enough sense not to say any of it to Abu. He gave her a hug as he got in the car and started talking immediately as if he was finishing a conversation they had started at breakfast.

Half way through their burgers she gave up the idea of having a serious conversation with him about the events of the past few days. The politics of being the captain/manager of the football team and the class president sounded so complicated he had no time left to think about anything else. All things considered, this was probably a good thing. It was only at the end he dropped in the news that he had done so well in his exams that he was being given a double promotion. It would still make him older than he should be for his grade but it was great news.

'Aunt Glo, since I have done so well, and if I promise to be good, to really study, can I come back home now, please? If I do anything wrong you can send me away again, but I won't.'

Gloria blinked hard and was momentarily lost for words.

'Abu, I didn't send you away because you did anything wrong, what are you talking about?'

'Well, since we had the attack on the house and I wasn't really helpful and I was complaining about being stuck in the house and then brought Morris and Leo around, I thought you just got tired of me. . .'

'Oh Abu, I only 'sent you away' because I was going to be so late at night and I was worried about you being in the house, even with Morris and Leo. None of this is your fault, it's these crazy people. In fact the place is too quiet now. It's so quiet I can't sleep at night. That's why I wanted to see you, if you had let me get a word in. Come home after school today. Julu's under house-arrest so no-one's going to do anything to us now.'

Abu grinned, delighted. Gloria stared at him. She suspected Abu had just out-manoeuvred her again but at this stage she didn't mind.

'And then we can celebrate my birthday properly, because it has been kind of rough.'

Gloria just laughed. 'Don't push it Abu.'

It was just over the hour when she got back to the office with some food for Hawa. Hawa still looked thoroughly miserable.

'So it looks as if we are set for tomorrow, Hawa. Only one night to go now.'

Moses looked a lot more animated than he had in the morning. The papers had come through and they authorised the members of the Family and Child Protection Unit to extend their search into Sierra Leone for forty eight hours. The Justice Ministry had cleared it with their counterparts in Sierra Leone. They were all set to go.

'There's another piece of news boss. Cooper turned up here today.' He shrugged as if unsure what to think. 'He said he had heard we were going to Sierra Leone to look for the children. He claims he was taken over the border once before when he first started to have doubts about being involved in what they were doing. He still won't say Julu's name but says he was blindfolded and put in the pick-up and driven for about an hour. When they took the blindfold off, he was on a long road heading into the mountains. They said he should keep co-operating or Aloysius might disappear down that road. Anyway, he wants to come along tomorrow, he thinks once we're over the border he will be able to help find where the children have gone.'

Alarm bells were going off in Gloria's head but she said nothing. Moses was obviously anxious for his wife but trying to appear calm. It wasn't a good moment to introduce any new doubts she might have and besides it was the only lead they had and they might get more information out of him as they were travelling. She still wasn't clear what his role had actually been.

'Ok, we don't have a lot of choice. I don't see what harm he can do anyway. But I'm afraid it means Hawa will have to sit in the back so that Cooper doesn't get a good look at her.'

'That's the other problem. There'll be four of us going up and only three of us coming back after Hawa heads to Freetown. The border guards won't check us but they will count the numbers, how are we going to explain losing someone?'

That hadn't occurred to Gloria.

'So, we need someone to come with us, hide in the back on the way up and then put on Hawa's uniform after she goes, for the journey back. Do you know I think that would be perfect for Abu? He won't mind the rough ride there, and in a shapeless uniform and cap he will pass for Hawa on the way back, and it will be dark anyway. And we can trust him, which is vital especially since this place leaks information like an old bucket.'

Moses didn't look convinced but couldn't think of a better solution right at that moment.

'Well for lack of a better plan, I suppose we can go with this but it feels like the plot of one of those Nigerian movies – and look how they always turn out.'

'We'll both be there, what can go wrong? And I got permission for us to use Drake's vehicle. It's new and it's strong and it might help us at the border if the guards recognise it.'

'You mean like a horse, it will miraculously follow the scent and take us on the right path.'

'You're tired Moses, you should go home to your children and tell them something about their mother. I am going to see the Chief and then I'll take Hawa home with me. We will leave early, by six tomorrow morning. I'll bring some food. You need to find a uniform that will fit Hawa and bring it along.'

The Chief had agreed to see her in between his other very important meetings and he listened abstractedly to her explanation about the trip to Sierra Leone. He only asked if they had the correct papers and when she said yes he just nodded. His last question took her by surprise though.

'Are you around tomorrow?'

'Well no, I've just been explaining sir. I'm going to Sierra Leone, that's what we've been talking about.'

'Oh that's awkward, I didn't realise you were going to go yourself, I thought you said Moses was going. Surely it doesn't take two senior officers to go. Anyway it's out of the question. The President wants to meet with us tomorrow. She needs a briefing, in person, about what we're doing to contain the situation. You know there was a riot at Red Light market today about police corruption and the women have moved out of Nancy Doe market in protest as well. They are now selling right on the road, which is causing mayhem in Sinkor – the Presidential motorcade had to be diverted through Jallah Town which wasn't pleasant for anyone. They're protesting about price increases. But all of this on top of the plane crash and the British Embassy investigation has got her worried. So,' he smiled at her, 'sorry Gloria but we both need to be there tomorrow. There's only you and Boakai from Traffic that can string a sentence together, the others will just be there to swell the numbers. Tomorrow at one o'clock in the Mansion. No discussion.'

She left his office wondering if they could possibly delay the trip by one day, surely it wouldn't make that much difference. But her heart sank as she came back downstairs to find a man and a woman waiting there. She recognised Martha Dunmore from the Ministry of Justice, a thoroughly nasty piece of work, waiting for her. Infamous as the most ruthless female investigator at the Ministry she had recently been appointed a senior anti-corruption investigator with wide-ranging powers, powers she used to terrorise everyone she came into contact with.

There were no handshakes. 'Inspector, we are looking for Hawa Anderson. Do you know anything about her?'

'I'm not sure I understand the question. I know who Hawa is, of course, but I don't know where she is and' – she knew she had to head her off before they reached her office – 'I have a meeting with the President tomorrow morning which I need to prepare for so I can't talk to you at the moment.'

She saw Martha hesitate and then turn around.

'We'll be back tomorrow afternoon then, make sure you've got time for us Inspector. This woman is responsible for the death of a senior policeman. She will have to pay for that.'

Well, not if I can help it, thought Gloria. She watched them go and went in to find Hawa crouching down beside the desk and the cupboard.

'Come on Hawa, let's go home. Tomorrow you'll be out of this. I just need to speak to Moses first.'

She went into the other room and phoned Moses and told him what the Chief had said and also that Martha had paid a visit.

'We can't put the trip off.'

Moses agreed. 'That would be dangerous for Hawa.'

'And all the other arrangements are in place. No, you need to go ahead,' said Gloria. 'Take Ambrose with you. He knows Bomi and he can distract Cooper while you do the switch-over between Hawa and Abu. . . but please take care of Abu.'

She was beginning to regret involving Abu especially now that she wasn't going to be there. But what was the likely danger? At the very worst if they were caught smuggling Hawa out it would be embarrassing but hardly dangerous. And it was too late to find someone else who could be trusted.

'I'm off home. Pascal informs me that the lobby is clear. No, he doesn't know why I need that information but he says he's enjoying helping the police. I will be back here at six tomorrow morning, Moses. See you then.'

19.

IT HAD ALL gone very smoothly. They had got home, collected Hawa's things, fitted her out in a uniform and explained to Abu what his role was going to be. Once he had clarified that being Hawa did not involve wearing a dress he was excited about the trip and went off to rehearse – whatever that meant. She had thought of telling him he wouldn't need his karate but decided to drop that. Now it was just before six in the morning and they were all in the car pound at the back of the police headquarters. If the officer on duty thought it strange to see this odd mix of people and at this early hour he gave no signs of it. Their paperwork was all in order, all the right signatures and all the fancy stamps. As far as he was concerned that was all he needed and he handed over Drake's car keys. He went back to his post while Abu climbed in and arranged the mattresses Drake had in the back to make a comfortable nest in the corner which would be invisible to anyone looking in. Hawa in her uniform and cap got in and sat in the other corner and Ambrose climbed into the front. Moses got into the driver's seat without a word. If it hadn't been so serious it would have been comical, and off they drove to collect Cooper on their way out of town.

'I know, keep in contact,' he said to her, 'just remember that when you call me, Cooper will be here listening.'

And he was away to look for trafficked children, to smuggle

his wife into exile and spend the whole day with a criminal in the front seat beside him – just another day in paradise.

There was only one thing she could possibly do now at this time of the morning. Down to Ma Mary's for coffee. It might be the only thing that would help her through the day. Well that and some half-decent conversation. She called Lawrence who sounded bright and breezy as usual, even at that hour of the morning.

'Is it too early for us to meet? We need to think about what we want to say at the meeting with the President this afternoon.'

'Not too early for me, Traffic never sleeps you know. Are you at Ma Mary's?'

'Am I that obvious? I am actually. And how do you know about Ma Mary's I thought I was the only one?'

'Come on Gloria, you sound like a jealous wife. I'll see you in ten minutes.'

Lawrence arrived on time and full of energy. No-one in the area gave them a second glance, two officers in full uniform at six thirty in the morning drinking coffee at Ma Mary's was not a strange sight. Gloria filled Lawrence in with the rest of the story. He knew better than to comment on her decision to help Hawa escape or send Abu up to Bomi but she could tell he didn't approve. But she also knew, gossip or not, he wouldn't pass on a word of it to anyone else.

'Well, hopefully they'll be back this evening with the success of having found the children. Let me know though. My day is fairly free, apart from the meeting with the President. One thing I would say is, go and meet Professor Andoh. You never know, he may have some information that could really help to back up your suspicions against Julu. You can trust him. As you know he's survived all these years, so he knows how things work.'

She agreed to give him a call and maybe even see him today before the meeting. They finally agreed on some points they could make to the President, if they were even asked. You could never predict how these meetings would go. Lawrence was all for presenting a smooth picture while Gloria wanted to take the chance to hint at some deeper unrest.

'Come on Gloria, you can't 'hint at some deeper unrest'. They'll never let you out of the Mansion until you've spelled it all out for them, names and all, and without any evidence your career will be finished! Let's just get through this. You could suggest she make some price concessions to the market women, tell her she did the right thing by not confronting the crowd in Sinkor and advise her to do one of her walkabouts next week when it's safer. That's enough.'

She finally agreed and they arranged to meet up later and go to the Mansion together.

Back at the office Gloria tried to get the team going but felt a bit paralysed, frustrated at not being on the trip to Bomi and worried about the outcome. As a way of having something to do she found Professor Andoh's number and called him. At the third attempt she got through and sketched out for him what she was looking for, information on that group of scholarship boys. He was interested and told her she could call round any time. He didn't do much teaching these days but liked to go on the campus and see what was happening. He still lived in one of the university houses so was only ten minutes away from the police headquarters.

When she arrived he had obviously been doing some research, or he had been recently burgled. There were papers everywhere on the floor, dining table and chairs. She hoped this was going to be useful and not just some reminiscences of the good old days. She had calculated Andoh must be at least in his late seventies but despite his age, civil war, and political upheaval, he looked very healthy and sounded very sharp. Gloria explained to him what she was looking for, without going into too many details. Julu could have spies everywhere. It may have been his unusually sharp memory, or just the fact that there hadn't been many scholarships in the past years, but Andoh remembered Julu and his companions very well.

'They were the hope, you know. We started to believe that this was a sign of renewal, the beginning of a new group of trained professionals who could begin to change government from the inside out.' He paused. 'We still believed in dreams then. It took our recent wars to show us that our 'Land of Liberty' may have been founded on a vision but it was only going to continue by power and greed. Anyway, enough of that, what can I help you with exactly?'

Gloria explained she just wanted to know anything he could remember about them. Andoh talked about them being chosen to go and then the incident which had changed everything.

'What was the incident?'

'Well, we don't know all the details, the story was hushed up and back then communications were a bit more primitive.'

Gloria nodded. She remembered how it had worked then, having to go to the telecommunications building, pay $15 and then wait in a booth while an operator connected her to her friend in Canada for three minutes of very crackly conversation.

'Then the war started and everything else was forgotten. Julu was the only one back in the country at that time. He returned and took a job at the Ministry, you know. But the story as I heard it from different people was that they had been there for four years and were nearing the end of their studies when they fell out – over a girl. Watson was the cleverest of the group by far. His exam results were always better and he was more popular with the other students and the teaching staff. He moved out of the house they had all been sharing and into a house with a girl he had met. Three months later, and just before their final exams, the girl told Watson she was pregnant but not by him. It turned out that the father was one of his Liberian companions. That was all the girl would say.'

Andoh poured out some tea and handed it to Gloria. She looked at the gray liquid and sipped it gingerly. It was awful.

'Well, Watson went round to the house and confronted the other three who denied everything, and then they started to laugh at him. Clever Watson hadn't even known what was going on under his nose. It seems Watson finally lost it completely and out came the big secret. The other three had been running a racket. Both Moore and Julu had finished their courses the year before but had managed to stay on and were still taking funds from the Liberian government which they had invested in a lucrative drug business on campus. Your Police Director had dropped out in his first year so he had been taking money for three years under false pretences. Watson started screaming that he was going to report all of this back home to the government and under the current regime that would probably have meant the firing squad for them! He stormed out saying he had all the paperwork to prove what they had been doing. And he wasn't seen again. His girlfriend reported him missing and the university went through the motions of trying to track him down but with no success. In the end the university authorities put it down to final exam stress and nothing more was done about it – he was a foreigner after all and a surprising number went missing each year anyway – until they fished his body out the lake four days later. Despite the marks on his torso and his feet, the police said it was suicide and that was that.'

Gloria was fascinated in spite of herself. It was like an old movie plot.

'I hope I'm not boring you, Inspector.' Gloria assured him he wasn't. 'Well back here we only heard that he had died. The other details came out years later when his girlfriend, who says she was too frightened at the time, wrote to me with the whole story because she had found my name among Watson's papers. There was no evidence at all and it was such a long time ago. But she maintained she heard Watson threaten them and then he died. She believes they killed him.'

Gloria was stunned.

'Didn't you even try and tell anyone?'

'Come now, Inspector, what would you say if I came to you with this story? There's not a scrap of evidence and two of the suspects hold the highest offices in the police and the army. What chance did I have? However, I wasn't surprised to hear about the Police Director's death. These things usually come back to haunt us. One of them was the ringleader and I think he probably still controls them now.'

She nodded.

'Look, I've got a picture I can show you.'

He rustled around the papers on the table and pulled out an old black and white picture of four young men, blinking in the sun, full of swagger and promise. She saw a young Julu immediately, standing on the end, arms folded.

Andoh was still talking. 'That's him there, the most manipulative person I've ever come across.' But he wasn't pointing at Julu. 'John Moore, a really nasty piece of work.'

It took Gloria only a few seconds to focus and then as she recognised the face it hit her like a slap on the face. John Moore was John Cooper. He was the fourth member of the group.

She could hear Andoh still talking in the background but her mind was spinning. This revelation changed everything. Cooper was part of this scholarship group, he was the most manipulative, Andoh said, and the name. . . Moore!

'Was he the father of the child, do you know?'

'Yes, part of the reason Watson's girlfriend finally wrote to me was Moore returned to Liberia while the war was on and took his son back with him so she felt free enough to tell the real story. Up until then she was too frightened. The son must have been about fifteen by then. It didn't take him long to join in the fighting though, he must take after his father. I hear he's a policeman now out in Harbel.'

Gloria sat back. She felt as if all the wind had been knocked out of her. John Cooper was actually John Moore, Sampson Moore must be his son. So, who was controlling who? She spilt the story to Andoh and her theory about Julu being the mastermind behind the trafficking and the killings but Andoh didn't look convinced.

'Everything I've heard about this group then and since would convince me it's John Moore, or Cooper as you call him, who is behind it. I told you, he is a master manipulator, Julu might have a big job but I believe he was no match for Moore.'

The coldness she could feel in her arms and legs seemed to be spreading. All she could think of was Drake's car speeding towards the border with Moses, Hawa and Abu in it, all unaware of who Cooper really was. Cooper had insisted he should go with them. He had 'suddenly' remembered some information. He must have known she would find out and was trying to escape. It would probably give him a lot of satisfaction if he could arrange for the police to unwittingly help him escape. But having done so he obviously couldn't allow the others to come back.

'But that would mean he arranged the killing of Aloysius, his own step son and two other boys in Harbel, and Ron Miller. And tortured them first.'

Andoh was nodding sadly. 'I didn't know that but this kind of evil grows in a person. Unfortunately, nothing would surprise me.'

Gloria stood up quickly, the panic receding, replaced by the need for action. She took the picture and ran to the car. It may not be too late yet. One hand on the wheel she called Lawrence.

'Lawrence I can't explain. I need a decent car and a driver to go to Bomi now.'

He caught the urgency and didn't ask any questions except where to meet her. Then she called the Chief. 'Sir, you really need to listen to what I'm going to say. I am going to Bomi so I will miss the meeting with the President, please give her my apologies but tell her I am catching some serious criminals, if I'm not too late.'

He started to speak and she cut him off.

'That's the easy bit. You also have to get the CID together and send a detachment to arrest Prince Julu for accessory to murder, conspiracy to murder at the very least.'

She paused, waiting for the Chief's outburst but following his instincts he just said, 'You better be right, Gloria, otherwise we will both be finished.'

'Sir, if I don't get to Bomi in time I will not care what happens to me.'

By the time she got to headquarters Lawrence was out front in a police escort van. Young Alfred, Paul and Christian were also there.

'Right, let's go. I'll explain on the way.'

They sped off, lights flashing and siren blaring in an attempt to force a way through the congested streets. Gloria explained what she had discovered and showed them the photograph.

'I wonder if that's the same photo Aloysius had?' Paul said. 'If he was talking to those children and living with that man and his psycho son he probably figured out something very bad was going on and was killed for it.'

As they sped up the road she called Moses on the radio. 'How far are you now?'

'We are just at the border, we had a puncture but luckily we have that policeman from Harbel with us.'

'Which one?'

Gloria could feel her heart sinking.

'He says you know him well, Sampson Moore. He's in the front with me and Cooper. He insisted on coming.'

He would have to be in the front otherwise he would have discovered Abu in the back. Keeping her voice calm she wished them well and told them to keep the radio open.

'If we make them suspicious,' she said to the others, 'they might panic,' although it wasn't their panic she was worried about. She had a father and son killer team in a car with her nephew, a colleague's wife and their most inexperienced policeman. When Moses had said it was like the plot of a Nigerian movie he had no idea how true it was.

The radio crackled again and Moses' voice came through.

'We are through the border but we've got another puncture. It's being fixed and shouldn't take too long. I'll need a cup of coffee after this though.'

In desperation Gloria shouted down the radio that they should make sure they checked the other tyres while they were there, better safe than sorry and added.

'You're welcome to your coffee, you know I hate the stuff.'

Even through the crackly reception they could hear Moses' puzzlement but instead of a question he just said, 'Noted. We may be out of reception so don't expect to hear from us for a while.'

When she switched off, the others were looking at her as if she was mad.

'I know, I know it was pathetic but I just wanted to say something that might alert him to the fact that something's wrong.'

'Not bad actually,' said Lawrence, 'although if he works out from that that he has a killer on board he should be the next Police Director.'

Gloria had just worked out they were at least another fifteen minutes from the border with no papers to cross over when Lawrence made a sudden right turn and, heading for what looked like dense forest, hit a tiny track and kept his foot down. Christian had given a very unmanly scream but it was a second or two before Gloria had enough breath to ask what they were doing. It was made all the more difficult because she had to hang on to the handle over the window to stop being thrown around.

'If we keep on the main road it's going to take too long and we are going to have problems crossing the border. This way is much quicker.'

Lawrence had lost his usual easy-going persona and was gripping the wheel, wrenching them across the track from time to time to avoid a tree, or wild pig or anything else in their way.

'When you say 'this way' you mean you know where this track leads?'

'I mean I've heard about it, Traffic is all about roads, Gloria.'

'I thought Traffic was all about safety and if you have only 'heard' about this how sure are you?'

'We're heading in the right direction still, we should be ok.'

Exactly eight minutes of bone-jarring, terror-inducing driving through the forest and suddenly they were clear – and heading towards a river.

'Oops, that shouldn't be there,' Lawrence muttered, but made no attempt even to slow down. 'It shouldn't be too deep at this time of the year,' were his final words of comfort then they were hit by a wave as the reinforced escort vehicle plunged into the river. It didn't stall, although it slowed down and then slowed down further as the tyres hit the mud on the bottom. Lawrence was right, it wasn't too deep, well not at first anyway, but as they moved on slower and slower, the water kept rising, first over the wheels, then up the sides until it was lapping at the windows.

By this time Gloria was muttering her half forgotten Act of Contrition but only got as far as 'I am very sorry' when she felt the wheels hit firmer ground and the water started to roll back. In seconds they were across and up the bank. Lawrence, who seemed to know exactly what he was doing, pulled left and roared down the road.

'If they're through the border they'll have to come down this road. We can still be on time.'

All the panic, which had been replaced by naked fear for the last ten minutes, suddenly rolled over Gloria again. If anything had happened to Abu or the others. . . but before she could finish that thought they screeched around a corner and Lawrence jammed on the brakes which stopped them just in time from smashing into Drake's vehicle which was off the road in a ditch with the doors open and the horn blaring.

She saw the blue of Abu's Chelsea shirt before she saw the rest of him sprawled out on the road in front of the vehicle and very still, his blood mixing with the red dust. Moses was still in the driver's seat but with his head slouched forward on the wheel and the horn. Everything stood still for a second then Gloria felt the wail rise up in her and she was running wildly down the road, Lawrence and the others behind her. It was true what they said, everything flashed before her eyes, scenes from the war, her and Abu hiding together, running from the shooting, hungry and tired and her voice over and over telling him they would be alright, they would be safe, they would get through it. But he wasn't safe and nothing would ever be alright again.

She was dimly aware of the voices as she lifted Abu's head and found he was still breathing and hope began to return. As she tried to stop the blood, which was coming from a wound on the side of his head, he opened his eyes a fraction. She looked up to see Ambrose looking over at her and a small red figure she couldn't make out, by his side.

'It's alright ma'am, they're all safe.'

'Even Moses?'

'Yes even Moses, he was just knocked out for a while.'

Even as she wrapped a makeshift bandage around Abu's head Gloria began to recover her composure. Her recriminations against herself would have to wait until later. She fired question after question at Ambrose until she got the picture of what had happened. After they had crossed the border, Ambrose had seen Moses from the back of the car take out his gun and signal something to him but Sampson Moore had leaned across and smashed him on the side of the head. They had careered off the road and into a ditch and stopped with the engine still roaring. With Moses unconscious the others were ordered out the back but when Sampson slapped Hawa for not moving fast enough Abu dived at him. Sampson batted him away with his gun and then took aim at the unconscious Abu – until the large petrol canister dropped on his head from above knocking him out. Ambrose and Hawa dived at Cooper taking him down just as Gloria and Lawrence had arrived.

Gloria looked at the small figure, red from head to toe in dust.

'Pascal?'

He grinned. Of course he had heard they were coming to look for the children and he had sneaked onto the roof rack and clung on for his life all the way up the road to make sure they found Boyes.

'Eh, that road is too dusty, old ma. The government people can't put coal tar down? For why we all paying our plenty tax money now?'

The first laugh of the day was high-pitched, perhaps slightly hysterical, but such a relief. Pascal had recognised Cooper as the shadowy figure who had visited the shelter the night they had taken Boyes away. He had been waiting to use the petrol canister on him the whole journey.

Gloria was exhausted beyond belief but also relieved beyond measure. When they got back to the border checkpoint she called for back-up and also called Rufus Sarpoh. Well, he deserved first go at the story and if he ran with it there was no way it could be hushed up. They took everyone to the clinic in Bomi, which was basic but clean and efficient, to get them checked out and bandaged up. Moses and Abu were both conscious by then but disoriented and they would need to stay the night.

Hawa and Gloria were sitting on a very hard bench outside the clinic. It was getting dark and the mosquitoes were rising but they didn't move. Lawrence had gone off to look for some food for them. The CID, who were having a very busy day, had arrived for Moore and Cooper. The others had gone back to Monrovia except for Pascal who had once again overheard their plans to go and look for the children the next day and had decided to stay. As the hero of the hour, Gloria couldn't really refuse him so he had gone off with Lawrence food hunting, and, she hoped, for some clothes and soap.

Hawa's car had been waiting for her on the other side but there was no way she was going to leave Moses in that state.

'Thanks for your help Gloria but today made me realise that I did enough running during the war and every time you run you lose something else. I am not going to lose any more. If Pascal can keep on looking for his friend I think I can at least stay with my family. I will take the consequences.'

Gloria just nodded. Having almost lost Abu today she knew what Hawa was saying. Actually she'd had a very long phone call with the Chief about a number of things including Hawa's arrest warrant. With Julu, Cooper and Moore arrested, a trafficking ring broken up, Ron and the children's murderers caught, and the real cause of the plane crash likely to be uncovered, she advised him to make sure Hawa's arrest warrant was rescinded.

'Am I going to be taking orders from you from now on, Gloria?'

'No, don't worry, sir. After all this I just want to go back to running my unit again. You can take care of the murder and corruption.'

She told Hawa not to worry. She really thought things were going to work out ok.

20.

THE NEXT FEW days passed in a blur of activity. As soon as Abu was well enough to travel, Gloria sent him back to town where she knew he would enjoy a hero's welcome while she, Ambrose, Christian and Izena searched for the place the children had been taken to. It didn't take them long to find the mine. Two miles further down the road from where they had finally managed to stop Cooper and the others, a small dirt track branched off to the right first up the mountain, and then down into a valley, and there it was. A small diamond mine tucked away in the fold of these remote mountains fed by a fast flowing stream. Calling it a diamond mine gave it a respectability it certainly didn't deserve, Gloria thought. A large muddy pool fed by the stream was full of children, some as young as eight years old they would discover, standing knee or even waist deep in the water with pans, sifting though the mud for those sparkly stones. These didn't look like the conflict or blood diamonds Ron had told them about, these were slave diamonds. The children were surrounded by a few guards who stood listlessly in the hot afternoon sun.

'There's only five of them ma'am,' Christian had scanned the area immediately. 'There might be more of them in their hut,' he pointed to a ramshackle building with a corrugated iron roof. 'But I don't think so. In this heat the only way anyone will be inside is if they are sick or drunk, either way no threat to us.'

Gloria's decision about what to do next was made for her when a tiny little boy standing near the bank swayed, dropped his pan and then fell face first into the water. The guard nearest to him rushed forward and dragged him out and then started beating him viciously about the face and body with the butt of an old rifle, while the other guards shouted at the children who had stopped to stare to get back to work.

'Let's go, pick a guard and go for him.'

Christian was the first down the steep slope and in a burst of activity Gloria had never seen before launched himself at the guard who was bent over the still form of the child. It was over in a matter of minutes. With their leader taken down, two of the guards dropped their rifles and scrambled up the bank in a panic while the remaining two, mesmerised by the sudden attack, were frozen to the spot. Apart from Christian's grunts as he over-powered the guard the rest of the scenario took place in silence. With Ambrose and Izena in pursuit of the fleeing guards and the others secured, Gloria turned her attention to the children standing silently in the water. Some of them had even continued working, obviously conditioned by the brutality of the guards not to stop. The silence was only broken when the little boy Christian had rescued started retching and then sobbing, his whole body shaking. It was a scene none of them would ever forget.

The small compound next to the mine was a dusty collection of miserable mud huts surrounded by barbed wire. It was a slave labour camp with over fifty children in it. A horrible place to live and, for many of them, to die.

A few days later they were still trying to find out what had happened to all the children. Ambrose, Christian and Izena, her newest and rawest recruits, had been wonderful. They had known exactly what to do, gathering the children together to first reassure them and comfort them and then get them the medical help they needed. After that they had spent many hours playing with them and talking to them until they were trusted. Izena, naturally, had taken charge of collecting information and was building up an impressive portfolio of data which would be vital to get the children back to their families. Ambrose was now known simply to the children as 'big brother.' They trusted him, talked to him and cried with him. Perhaps her biggest surprise had been Christian who, after an initial period of awkwardness, had taken on himself the task of 'protecting' the compound. They had decided to keep the children together until they were all strong enough to leave. Christian's security arrangements, along with the football he organised in the afternoon, had done a lot to calm the children down and reassure them that no-one was going to come and take them away during the night.

It became clear that a lot of the children had run away but also that many of them had died under the harsh conditions. Sadly, two of the youngest children, including the child Christian had rescued, died before they could get them to hospital. The hard work, malnutrition and frequent beatings had all taken a toll they couldn't recover from.

Meanwhile back in town under questioning Cooper admitted that it was easier and cheaper to just bring in new children rather than improve the conditions in the camp. Even when the war ended it wasn't too difficult to arrange for groups of children to be taken 'legally' with promises of opportunities for education or work. Hundreds of poor families were desperate to give their children a chance in life. But the over-elaborate arrangements, the sense of power and control had obviously become as important to Cooper by the end as making money.

He needed to control and had come to believe he was smarter than everyone else. In fact he said as much. His need to boast and demonstrate how clever he had been made their job easier as he spilled all the details. The doctor who sat in on the interviews attached a very long name to his 'condition' but Gloria decided that Pascal's description of the 'crazy rogue' was more accurate.

Fooling Drake, a man blinded by insane prejudice, had been easy. Controlling Julu and the Police Director, who were terrified about being exposed, hadn't been much of a challenge either. But manipulating everyone so that he was even pitied for the murder of his own stepson, a murder he had arranged himself, had delighted Cooper. He had laughed about that. The actual killings, he was quick to point out, had been carried out by his son Sampson, because Aloysius was one of the few people who had seen through him and refused to be controlled by him. Aloysius had been the first to piece together what was going on – at least that there was something bad happening to all these children – and he was killed for that. Cooper had arranged the theatrical death on the beach just to confuse the police and the killings in Harbel simply to scatter more suspicion on Julu.

And that's why poor Ron had been tortured. Someone had overheard them talking about diamonds that night in Mickey's and thought Ron knew where their diamond, the one Aloysius had in his hand, was being kept. So Sampson Moore had tortured and killed Ron for something he knew nothing about.

And so the revelations went on. Underneath the surface story there was a whole spider's web of corruption, bribery and blackmail of other officials in government especially at the Ministry of Social Welfare where the Minister resigned suddenly for family reasons and went abroad. There was so much publicity that it couldn't be swept away. Rufus in particular had done a really good job. The newspapers, the radio and television were full of the story. The President had managed to turn it into positive coverage for herself by announcing sweeping reforms and demonstrating that no-one was above the law by ordering Julu's immediate trial and the detention not only of Cooper and his son but other senior officers in the army and in the police. It was certainly sweeping change but whether it was permanent remained to be seen.

It was two weeks before Gloria decided they didn't need to go to Bomi any more. Their last visit included a proper burial service for Aloysius in the little mission chapel where he had attended most Sundays.

Fr. Garman called Aloysius a child hero and told the congregation they should think of his death as a terrible crime but also as a sign of hope. As long as Liberia could produce children and young people of such quality, such loyalty, there was hope for the future. Gloria really wanted to believe that but looking at the faces in the small church still struggling with anger and grief she knew that was little consolation for them.

A real note of sadness was that they had not found Boyes in the camp that day and although some of the other children thought he might have escaped no-one had any clear idea where he might have gone. After a few days of investigating with no result Gloria sat down with Pascal. She had the sinking feeling that sitting with distressed families was something they would be doing a lot of in the coming weeks.

'We have looked everywhere Pascal. You know if Boyes was hiding in the area we would have found him by now.'

'He's not dead, old ma, don't tell me that.'

'No I am not saying that, Pascal. You know we will keep looking for him. Maybe he ran away into Sierra Leone or is in the bush somewhere. He might have gone back to his village, to his family.'

Pascal looked directly at her. 'I'm his family, you know that, auntie. You ever see his ma or pa? You ever see anyone buy him food or protect him? Village! What village? Even me I don't know what place Boyes was coming from? We lived in Monrovia, that's our village and that's where he will come back to. I know it.' He had tears in his eyes by now. 'If you want to stop looking no problem but for me I will never stop. You know, auntie, Boyes was the smart one. He didn't like talking too much but he could think, even more than me.' High praise indeed. 'So he would have worked out a plan. If I stopped these people from killing you all then Boyes would have done even more and escaped from them.'

Gloria just nodded. In her heart she didn't believe it but she wasn't going to say so. She knew Boyes was smart, she knew Pascal was resourceful, but they were still just children and this was not a Disney movie they were in. The harsh reality was that men with guns could crush even the smartest children, it was an uneven fight and she feared Boyes had lost this one. But she said none of this to Pascal who, just for a moment, allowed her to take his hand. But just for a moment.

'I am going to talk to brother Ambrose, old ma.' And he was off.

One week later and life seemed to be returning to something like normal. It was Saturday night again and Gloria, after what seemed like a lifetime, was sitting out on her porch listening to the music and the laughter from Mickey's down the road. The previous day both Abu and Pascal had been given an audience with the President who had held them up as examples of Liberia's future, at least that's what Gloria thought she had said but she had been mesmerised by Pascal's jacket which was a vivid orange and brown check. She should not have allowed Ambrose to do his shopping, and these photographs were going to be all over the newspapers tomorrow. But apart from that it had been a memorable day.

At the end of the audience the President had produced the diamond which Aloysius had been holding and which so many people had died for.

'What shall we do with this?' she asked rhetorically. 'I feel like throwing it into the sea but that would be a waste so I am announcing today the setting up of the Diamond Trust. The stone will be sold and the money will be used to help the victims of these crimes.' No-one could object to that.

Gloria was thinking of all these things as she sat relaxing on her porch. But she wasn't just relaxing on her porch. She was, she had to admit it, also hiding. It was the official celebration for Abu's birthday. After what she had put him through she felt she couldn't say no to it. She had left all the arrangements to Abu and the rest of her family. Her mother had taken control of the food preparation with an army of aunts and Abu had been involved with Leo and Morris all week deciding who to invite. When she had arrived back from the office that morning she had found her apartment decorated with old Christmas decorations and a huge birthday cake in the centre of the table. The cake was decorated in the colours of Abu's football team but Gloria was sure those shades of green and yellow contained nothing natural. By three o'clock that afternoon her apartment was full of her many relatives, several of whom were already arguing, crowds of teenagers she didn't recognise and most of her colleagues. Why on earth he had invited her whole team Gloria didn't know but she had resigned herself to a very long afternoon.

She was grateful to see Moses wave to her though, and he and Hawa came out to the porch.

'Not hiding are you Gloria?' Hawa was back to her old self, elegant, composed and relaxed.

'Of course I'm hiding and just looking for some air to breathe as well. . . oh and avoiding my family of course. My aunts will ask about the job for about ten seconds before getting onto their favourite topic of my impending marriage.'

'You're getting married!' Moses and Hawa chorused together.

'No, of course I'm not. When would I have time for that, Moses? And besides most men drive me crazy. But it will still be their main topic of conversation.'

They laughed and then after a pause Gloria asked Hawa how she was doing.

'I am fine now Gloria, thanks to you. I can hardly believe that a few weeks ago I was being smuggled out the country to go and live as a refugee again.'

'It would have been a great story for the grandchildren though, your story of escaping over the border.'

Hawa gave her a look. 'Your grandchildren maybe Gloria but not mine. I've had enough excitement for a long time. That's the thing about living in Liberia, we don't have to look for adventures, they just happen all round us every day.'

As if in response, there was a huge shout from inside the apartment. The dancing had started and her aunts were in the centre of the room shaking themselves and everything in their vicinity. Gloria's heart sank. It was going to be a very long afternoon.

—